A fragrant wind  that mingled with o and swung his long legs. The feel of the air, of sand and salt, reminded him again of the sloe-eyed Marhaba vixen. He was not one to bed every snip that lowered her lashes and raised her skirts. If he were, he'd be spending all his time ashore with his britches around his ankles. But Honifa…something about her like the scent of Eastern spices that clung to her skin, like the taste of her tongue and crush of her breasts. What evil Loki had kept him wandering the marketplace when he should have been long since aboard the *Witch's Moon* happily checking the plimsoll mark or sorting the instruments in his binnacle? And why in the name of Odin, once he'd sent the knaves packing, did he walk with her like some smitten milk-mouth? He knew why he kissed her, why he held her in his arms. Oh yes, that he knew. But he should have listened to his brain instead of his bollocks.

Praise for Maria Paoletta Gil

"The exciting tale of an obedient wife who fulfills her dreams of romance and adventure. A real page turner."

~ Judy Reene Singer, author of Horseplay

"…an unforgettable journey of bravery and passion… I loved it."

~ Linda Gould, author of The Long Way Home

"Visual storytelling at its best. A courageous heroine risks everything for one night of passion with a handsome pirate. Who could ask for more?"

~ Maria Florio, Academy Award®
winning producer, Earthworks Films

"A sexy pirate, a masked outlaw, and one courageous woman are the perfect players in this romantic saga set on the high seas and in the bazaars of Morocco. Maria Paoletta Gil paints characters and locations with vivid colors and her surprise ending will leave you wanting more."

~ Laura Liller, author of His Hollywood Blonde

Witch's Moon

by

Maria Paoletta Gil

Witch's Moon

Cover Art by *Tina Lynn Stout*

The Wild Rose Press, Inc.
PO Box 708
Adams Basin, NY 14410-0708
Visit us at www.thewildrosepress.com

Publishing History
First Edition, 2023
Trade Paperback ISBN 978-1-5092-4657-1
Digital ISBN 978-1-5092-4658-8

Published in the United States of America

Dedication

For the Ebony Prince

PART ONE

Capture

Chapter 1

Aboard the Dover Star in the month of Ab, 1852

The stench in the hold was sickening. The cabin boy pushed aside the hatch with his foot, held his nose and lowered the kettle of swill Cookie had concocted from seawater and last week's leavings. He averted his eyes from the blue-dyed hands of the man who reached up through the hatch for the soup. The old man never said thank you, although if he had, the boy wouldn't have understood him. Like all the slaves in the cargo hold, the man spoke a language full of the guttural, swishing sounds, sounds the crew made when they coughed or cleared their throats, tobacco spitting sounds. He smelled too, of foreign dirt and the yellow powder they put in their food. With relief, the boy replaced the hatch, breathed deeply to clear his lungs, and headed to the bridge with the captain's nightly tot of rum.

A warm wind blew from the African coast, pushing the *Dover Star* northwest toward open water. She was a decent ship, Captain Royce Davilow mused as he scanned the horizon; a square-rigged, two-masted brig sturdy as a Chelsea whore. Her hold, long and low-ceilinged, could carry as many as 150 slaves which, at between four and five hundred New World dollars each…Davilow grinned and rubbed his palms greedily. After a quick port in Jamaica to load a few barrels of rum, it was on to Newport for the slave auctions, greenbacks, and good times.

Mentally tallying profits, the captain tried to ignore the hum of pagan worship threading like a miasma from the slaves in the hold. The damn heathens prayed constantly to their indifferent deity. In their place, he would spit at the feet of the pantalooned mahout they worshipped. But these desert tribes, Berber, Tuareg, all of them were spineless. There was only one among the lot dangerous enough to give Davilow pause; the one they called Dark of the Moon. Concealed beneath a hooded mask, that cursed pirate plowed the watery lanes between North Africa and England in a ship with no name, attacking honest Christian slavers and liberating their cargo.

"Send Pig Eye to quiet that scum," he ordered the lad who appeared at his side with a flagon. Quaffing deeply, he turned his eyes to the endless horizon. "I know a way to keep Dark of the Moon from interfering with the *Dover Star* this night or any other night," he muttered to himself. "If that wily skimmer dares to breach my ship, I'll strike him a bargain he won't be able to resist."

****

Nador, Morocco, in the month of Aylul

Honifa woke to the screeching clamor of a dozen cats.

"*Kolhawa!*" she exclaimed, hurling a slipper at the low wall that separated the flat roof of her house from the clinic next door. "Shut up, shut up, shut up!" She

2

had been dreaming about Zalam Alqamar, Dark of the Moon, the outlaw who made war on all who violated his sanctuary high in the caves of the Rif. Honifa's mother had often told her romantic tales about him, a paragon of valor, tall and golden as the sun, a foreigner who championed the downtrodden and walked among gods. Honifa pictured him rugged and yellow-haired with powerful arms and a scarred face. As a child, she had tried to draw his likeness and searched in vain for him among the rabble on the wharves. But she was a woman grown now and ready to be married. Her father said it was time to put aside infantile imaginings and accept God's burden. And, for the most part, she had, throwing herself into her duties at her father's clinic, preparing her wedding trousseau, and honoring the dictates of her betrothed. She would be a good wife and mother, a model of propriety, the cynosure of vigilance. There was no other course.

With a sigh, Honifa swung from her bed, closed her eyes, and knelt for prayer. But when she opened them, an expletive flew from her lips.

"Ten thousand asses!"

According to the Holy Book, the first object one sees in the morning sets the tone of the day and last night, as she did every night, Honifa had placed a delicate blue and white enameled jug directly in her line of vision to guarantee a pleasant fortune. One of the cats must have overturned it during the night because it had fallen to pieces, no longer concealing what lay behind it, her ugly chamber pot. Grimly, she snatched up the odious pot and dumped its contents over the side of the roof, drenching several cats.

Fate had spoken. An unlucky day loomed.

She made her morning ablutions and dressed for work at the clinic. As usual, the waiting room was crowded; women with babies, old men, a herder or two with bleeding hands or feet, most likely from a drunken fight. Ghanim, that wily camel driver, groveled at her feet.

"Please, Missy McLeod," he whined. "Tell the honorable doctor to give me something for my pain."

Honifa poked him with her foot. "Go away, old man. You're not sick. All you want is morphia so you can sit under the date palm and dream. You waste my time. And you," she admonished another man whose hand was wrapped in a dirty, bloodstained rag. "Feed your donkey and he won't bite you. You're another waste of time."

Simon McLeod emerged through the hanging beads that separated the surgery and dispensary from the waiting room.

"Easy, lass," he scolded gently. "You mustn't chase away patients."

The men and women squatting against the walls rose in unison and rushed to him. They knew that, unlike his daughter, whose moods were as unpredictable as the currents of the Moulouya River, Simon, their beloved healer, was always dependably kind. They hovered, blessing his hands, and kissing his shoes. Honifa shooed them away.

"Go back to your places. The doctor will see each of you in turn."

Ghanim ignored her. He gripped Simon's leg and howled like a banshee.

"Good grief, man," Simon admonished. "Get hold of yourself. Come inside and let me have a look at you."

"Leave him be, Father," Honifa grumbled. "Ghanim is worthless. He drinks and beats his animals. Don't bother with him."

Simon gave his daughter a quizzical look. "No man is worthless."

****

Later, while the clinic was closed against the burning sun, Simon faced Honifa across a plate of bread and cheese in the main room of the house they shared. The shutters were pulled against the heat and a small sesame oil lamp flickered between them. Honifa's hazel eyes were troubled, and her fingers twisted the fringe of her russet braid.

"Tell your da what ails you, Honi," he said. "You're much too cynical for a girl barely eighteen."

"I'm sorry, Father," she said. "But I think someone rattled the bones against me this morning. Maybe I should cover my head and hide until midnight."

"Nonsense," Simon scoffed. "That's superstition. Besides, what enemies could you possibly have?"

Honifa thought of Ahmed Hassan's mother, her future mother-in-law, who despised her because she was a half-breed, the child of a Westerner and a Tuareg tribeswoman. But Ahmed's mother would not have thrown the bones. The insufferable Madame Hassan prided herself on being the epitome of a modern nineteenth-century woman.

"No enemies, Father," Honifa said, patting Simon's hand. "I'm being silly." She carried the plates to the washbasin. "We'd better get back."

"Here's an idea," Simon said, shrugging into the white coat he always wore at work. "Go down to the river this afternoon and get some fresh air. We need more fenugreek and bloodroot for poultices. I'll handle things here."

She threw him a grateful look, grabbed her herb basket, and fled.

****

Honifa McLeod was not dainty and retiring. She wore her height and bold features like a banner. Her reddish hair and hazel eyes announcing less than pure Arab ancestry, coupled with her sharp tongue, caused many in Nador to turn away. Were it not for her father's skills as a healer, she would most certainly have been stoned to death by a witch-hungry crowd. But irascibility and mixed blood aside, it was Honifa's medicine-making skill that caused the most consternation among superstitious gentry. If she could turn a concoction of leaves and twigs into a healing salve, then surely, she could make another, blacker sort of magic.

Honifa was dismissive of the murmuring attention she attracted. Descended from wandering Tuaregs and generations of battle-scarred Highlanders, she reasoned that her adventurous spirit was a birthright. Her mother had defied convention to marry Simon, and he had abandoned the rewards of a lucrative practice in Inverness for the thorny lowlands of Morocco. Moreover, Honifa didn't seek companionship. She enjoyed her solitary forays with a silver knife and covered basket. In the cool of the morning, while dew still misted the air, she knew with uncanny prescience which leaves and fronds to gather, which roots to wait to dig by the waning moon, and which petals closed in full sunlight sealing and protecting precious drops of fever-reducing elixir within.

She knew how to pound rosemary, vervain, and onion flower into a paste for insect bites and she could distill a sugary but effective laxative from the licorice-flavored rhizome of rock brake. Boldly, she walked everywhere: down to the riverbed and up into the Rif Mountains, across the salt marshes that hugged the sea, to the desert's edge, and along rubble-strewn alleyways where milk thistle, an antidote for mushroom poisoning, poked its wooly head through cracks in the pavement. Away from home and clinic, she was blessedly relieved of routine tasks: washing, cooking, helping her father, and especially sitting in the rose arbor behind Ahmed Hassan's house listening to his plans for their life together.

She'd known Ahmed all her life. He was her best friend and protector. When the other children teased, he put his arm around her and told her she was a wood sprite, a goddess, a budding genius among plebeians. He badgered his doting mother until she agreed to a betrothal when Honifa turned seventeen. Simon was pleased. Ahmed was a sturdy, reliable sort and clearly cherished his prickly daughter. Honifa, on the other hand, however much she cared for Ahmed, had reservations. For one thing, there was his mother, a sly termagant with the tongue of an asp. For another, the minute the betrothal ceremony was completed, Ahmed stopped calling her Honi and started addressing her by her full name. It was only proper, he claimed.

Then he told her to stop going about barefoot and to cover her head in the presence of anyone but him. These surprising prohibitions troubled Honifa but one tentacle of doubt troubled her most of all. Each night as she and Ahmed sat in the rose arbor, he took her hand in his and recited poetry. No matter how much Honifa hinted, quite outrageously sometimes, he would not hold her in his arms and kiss her. If she persisted, he bristled and sent her home. Perplexed, agitated, she would walk the path down from Nador Hill to her little cottage in the backwater, her cheeks warm, her heart beating. She'd throw herself into bed and dream of Dark of the Moon, of being crushed in his powerful arms, carried off to his Viking ship and covered head to toe with endless kisses. In the morning, the memory of arousal lingered fresh on her skin. Lately, it never seemed to leave her.

Honifa hurried across the village square, past the rug merchant's, the coffee seller, and rows of houses shuttered against the heat. She left the village behind, and skirted small fields dotted with drowsy goats. At the banks of the Moulouya River, overgrown this time of year with spider willow, she removed her boots and the hooded *djellaba* that fell to her ankles. Clad only in a sleeveless *kamis,* she roamed the riverbank cool and unencumbered. At the place where outcroppings formed a natural bench, she paused and lifted her head, expecting the sweet, welcome fragrance of yellow jessamine. Instead, she smelled something equally sweet but much less welcome, bergamot.

"Ahmed!" she called. "Where are you? I know you're following me. I can smell your hair oil."

Sheepishly, he stepped into Honifa's path and bowed formally. "*Asaalamalaikum, Habibi.* Greetings, my love."

"*Sabah elnoor,*" she answered, her response no more than a sullen, casual Good Morning. "What do you want?"

"Want?" he replied. "With a sweetheart such as you, I want for nothing. I merely longed for the sight of my betrothed."

"You see me almost every night in the rose arbor," she snapped, brushing past him. "Go away. I'm working."

He held her arm. "When we're man and wife, I won't let you work. You'll sit on a velvet throne, and I'll feed you apricots and pistachios."

"My work is holy, Ahmed," she protested. "It heals the sick."

"And I won't let you walk around like this, with your head uncovered," he continued, ignoring her remark. "Only my adoring eyes shall behold your loveliness."

Honifa sighed. The chamber pot this morning, her viper's tongue in the clinic. Today was a bad day and now she understood why. Today she must be honest with Ahmed, tell him what was truly in her heart. Tell him once and for all and damn the consequences.

"Let's sit on the big stone and wet our feet," she said.

Ahmed hesitated. "You shouldn't be barefoot in my presence," he scolded. "Not until we're married." He laughed; one scornful note. "You're not a child, Honifa. At your age, a proper young woman puts away her toys, subjugates herself to a loving man and bears his children."

She sighed. His eyes were level with hers, his cap of ebony hair sleek as an otter's pelt.

"But I'm not a bit proper. You know that. If anything, I'm the opposite. Your own mother thinks

I'm a witch."

He shook his head. "We've discussed my mother over and over. She is my responsibility. But she is also first woman of the house. As her daughter-in-law, it falls to you to care for her until the day she dies. That is the way of things."

Honifa's chest tightened. How could she tell this stubborn man of her deepest longings, of her desire for more than endless, dutiful days as a handmaiden to Madame Hassan? There was once a time when she could say anything to the man standing so stiffly beside her. She had told him she hoped to read every book in every library in every country, no matter what language it was written in, and care for sick animals and people. He hadn't laughed at her.

When she'd complained that she was tall and long-limbed where a woman should be small and round; hazel-eyed and russet-haired instead of ebony dark, Ahmed responded that she was lovely as the morning. And after her mother died, she spent her tears in his arms, so she'd be brave for her father. How could she tell Ahmed now that he wasn't enough for her? That when she heard the trill of a lark or felt the sting of salt spray on her cheeks, a great emptiness hollowed within her, and she yearned for…for what? She didn't know; only that when she searched the heavens, she saw the broad, brooding face of a man radiant as the sun.

"There are many things I want to do before I marry," Honifa began, choosing her words. She touched her breast and her stomach. "I have, I have—ah, certain feelings inside of me that I don't comprehend."

He frowned. "All will be explained once we're married."

10

"How? I have dreams, Ahmed. They're more like premonitions. Something, someone awaits me, and I am compelled—I feel I must—I don't know. It's — kismet." She trailed off. *Where are the words? Why can't I find the words?* She wanted to stamp her feet, blurt out that a life with Ahmed was the farthest thing from her mind.

Abruptly, he bowed, touching his chest, chin, and forehead. "*Ana'asef.* Forget it. You talk foolishness. Your father's been paid; the date is set. On the tenth morning of *Kamun al Thani* we're going to be married and there's nothing you can do about it."

Red with indignation, Honifa stalked down to the water and churned her scandalously bare feet, waiting for the anger in her body to cool. Instead, the white foam of the shallows began to resemble a mane of wild hair, the smooth stones a pair of pale, unreadable eyes. Transfixed, she stared at them, clear and lucid as sunrise. Were these the eyes of Zalam Alqamar, of Dark of the Moon? Was this his face staring up at her; handsome, tormenting, mesmerizing; not a fantasy at all; not a dream, but real?

Chapter 2

"Shouldn't you be on your way to meet Ahmed?" Simon asked after dinner that night.

Honifa had done the washing up, swept the floor, and trimmed the lamp wicks. She sat moodily by the open window contemplating the red moon of *Aylul*.

"I don't feel like sitting in the rose arbor tonight," she said. "It's too hot."

"That it is." Simon rose and stretched. "I think I'll pop round to Bareed's for a pint. I'll stop at the Hassan compound on my way and tell Ahmed you won't be by."

Honifa laid her cheek on the stone sill. When she squinted, the moon spun and cast off spears of fire like a flaming wheel. She sighed. Since confessing her confusion to Ahmed, a strange, contrary lethargy had overtaken her. She felt too heavy to move, yet something in her wanted to run and leap and dance like a dervish.

"As you like, Father," she murmured lazily.

He touched his daughter's forehead. "Are you ill, lass?"

"No. I'm never ill. You know that." She pulled the shutters. "Enjoy your pint. I'm going to take a bath and sleep on the roof again tonight." She dipped a bucket into the water barrel and filled the copper hip bath that had been Simon's wedding present to his wife.

"Any message for Ahmed?" he asked.

Honifa didn't answer. Simon gave her a last meditative glance and stepped into the street.

When the water was halfway up the bath, Honifa scattered a handful of lavender and a few hibiscus petals across its surface. She pulled off her *kamis* and sank into the restful fragrance. Sluicing the cool water over her shoulders, she rubbed herself gently with a *loofa*; her arms, her neck, her breasts. She watched tendrils of hair feather like tawny seaweed from the mound between her thighs and ran the *loofa* down her belly and over the tender pad of flesh. Delicately, she probed the clef of her secret place, opening it with her fingers. This is good, she thought. A relaxing bath was exactly what she needed. But she was lying.

As she touched herself, sensations anything but relaxing crept through her body. The water rippled and splashed as she squirmed in the grip of an intense, almost unendurable pressure. Breathing in rapid shallow gasps, nipples engorged, and toes curled, she rocked ever faster until the whole of her released in a paroxysm of exquisitely pleasurable pain. Drained, she submerged, trembling and unaccountably sad until her thrumming pulse subsided. Was there nothing for this compulsion that bedeviled her day and night? No end to this yearning? Feeding it as she did was somehow false, like feeding fruit shavings to a starving dog. He ate or he would die, but it wasn't what he wanted.

Honifa leaped from the bath, desolate and confused. Intrinsically, her body was telling her that survival as a woman depended on desires both visceral and emotional, of the heart as well as the flesh. Her mother, less practical than Simon, had taught her to listen to the spirit within, that inexplicable blessing at the core of her being that animated her and gave life meaning. Mother had also assured her that the stars never lied. They guided you on the path intended by God. But Honifa was also her father's child and Simon taught her that stars were chunks of frozen rocks with no power over men. Happiness resided not in mystical powers but in *her* power to choose what was right.

Wrapped in a towel, Honifa padded up and down the room. Maybe she should fly to Ahmed, drag his arms around her and his mouth down upon hers. But it would be just her luck for Madame Hassan to storm from her hidey-hole behind the acacia bush, her fists raised in outrage. Honifa supposed she must trust Ahmed's word that marriage would cure her endless shifting from color to gloom with nothing in between. She wasn't a magic lantern show and passion was no substitute for peace. As Ahmed's wife, she would have days and days of peace, no more temptations, no more dreams. Besides, he was wealthy and had promised that once he became Simon's son-in-law, he'd help ease the clinic's ever increasing financial shortfall. She would marry. It was right.

She shrugged into a fresh *kamis* and took up the lamp. Halfway to the roof, she was stopped by someone banging on the door.

"Sidi McLeod! Hurry, please!"

Honifa tossed her *djellaba* over her filmy nightshirt and opened the door on the tear-stained face of ben Abbas, their landlord. He fell to his knees.

"Fetch your father, Miss McLeod, I beg you. My child clings to its mother's womb. The midwife says she must cut it out but my wife refuses. Please ask the doctor to come quickly."

"My father isn't here, Sidi Abbas," Honifa told the distraught man. "But I'll get him. Go home to your wife. Tell her we're coming."

****

Simon constantly warned Honifa that the alleyways and dockside cafes of the Marhaba, the Waterfront District, were dangerous, full of rowdy seamen and opportunistic Europeans who bilked the trusting North Africans out of their meager *dirhams* and sold their women and children into slavery. Even her mother had considered Marhaba forbidden, an unblessed wasteland where the devil dwelt. Nevertheless, Honifa ran into the night and made for Bareed's Tavern on Yom al A'had Street in the heart of Marhaba. The cobblestones beneath her bare feet glowed ghostly white; the heat and smells of other people's dinners, of crushed cumin and roasting lamb, tobacco smoke and coronilla soap, made her dizzy.

When she reached the sea, however, the resinous astringency of paint and barnacle wash revived her. She wanted to pause and lift her face to the salty spray but dared not. Obediently, she kept her head down glancing surreptitiously at the scores of wanted posters plastered on every clay wall and shop window. A few were drawn with crude sketches of murderous-looking men who had committed offenses against the English or Spanish or Portuguese king, or Morocco's sovereign, Moulay Slimane. She paid scant attention to these but was stopped in her tracks by the largest and most prominent poster. It depicted a masked death's head, was boldly printed in Arabic and four European languages, and promised substantial payment for the capture, dead or alive, of Zalam Alqamar, the outlaw known as Dark of the Moon. Honifa's hood slipped from her head and her unbound hair tumbled wildly about her shoulders. What did he look like, she wondered, this man whose likeness could only be imagined as a murderously grinning skull.

At Bareed's Tavern, Honifa took note of two men loitering in the beaded doorway.

"Where you runnin' to, big pretty," one hissed. "Slow down so's me an' Jake can have a look atcha."

Her chest tightened. She hiked her *djellaba* and barreled through the beads, nearly tumbling into the arms of an astonished Malcolm Bareed.

"Honi! Holy Mother of God, what are you doing here?" Like Simon, Malcolm was a half-breed whose Scots mother claimed to have been ravished by a wandering Sudanese.

"My father," Honifa gasped. "Sidi Abbas' wife is in labor, and the midwife wants to use her rusty scalpel to cut the baby out."

"He's just now gone," Malcolm said. "Ben Abbas sent a houseboy to fetch him."

People were staring at the tall, wild-eyed girl.

"Cover your head," Malcolm whispered, pulling up Honifa's hood.

"I should help my father," she said, gathering the cape around her.

Before Malcolm could protest, she was gone, flying over the stones, her heart pounding. But within sight of the Mosque Al Mounia, she was caught up short by a beefy hand at her throat. Another hand gripped her buttocks and a man's foul breath singed her face.

"Lookey 'ere, Jake. The big pretty one's come back fer us."

"She's a fair piece, ain't she? Prime arse on her, too; round as a sugar bun and just as sweet, I wager."

Reeking of liquor and sweat, they caged her between them and grinned as she screamed and struggled wildly.

"Avast. Trim yer sails, wildcat," one grunted. "I'm fair to bustin' me britches."

They bound Honifa with the ends of her *djellaba* and hauled her like the Sultan's carpet to a side street. The bigger man, hairy and covered with tattoos, threw her on her stomach over a barrel and roughly pushed up her *djellaba* and *kamis,* bunching the garments above her waist. He kneaded her flesh with hands as coarse as nettle. She tried to kick but the other one held her legs.

"*Bismillahi!*" she cried. "Someone help me! *Saadni! Saadni!*"

"Heathen bitch!" the man leaning over her yelled. "Shut her up, Jake."

The other man tightened the strings at the neck of her *djellaba,* stuffed the hood into her mouth, and clamped his noxious palm over her face. She couldn't breathe. The buzzing of bees filled her head and lights swirled before her eyes. Panic gripped her, but she willed her mind elsewhere, to the icy peaks of the Atlas Mountains, to lotus blossoms floating in the lagoon at the palace of Moulay Slimane, to the spice seller at the medina in Marrakech where she had gone with her mother as a child and lost herself in the mingled fragrances of cinnamon and vanilla, candied ginger and purple thyme. Blessed darkness closed in and she felt her soul begin to depart her body. She was on a vast

17

ocean, a stormy one, with mammoth waves that boomed like thunder. The thunder became words, harsh and penetrating. They sliced through her reverie and reunited her fractured selves.

"Leave her, you mangy hounds!"

The odious hands that had vised her disappeared, and she gulped hungry breaths of air.

"Find yer own trollop," the man who had gagged Honifa spat. "This'uns ours."

But when he saw the seething tower of fury bearing down on him, he grabbed his britches and raced after his companion who was already sprinting lickety-split from the alley. Large deft fingers removed Honifa's gag and loosened her hood. She was lifted upright in steely arms and set on her feet to behold not a mortal man, but the commanding, golden magnificence of a god.

It was he, the Viking! A creature so like her dreams of Zalam Alqamar that she pinched herself to make certain she was awake. Then she sank to her knees and touched her forehead to the pavement.

"Shukraan, Munqidh." Thank you, savior.

He glared at her. "I'm not a savior, woman; just happened by at the right time. Now get off your knees and fix your clothes."

Honifa fell back on her heels and gazed up at the man, if it was a man. The alley was dark, but he seemed to glow from within; yellow hair that fell to his shoulders, eyes like winter plums. He was clad in a light shirt and fawn britches. The butt of a pistol protruded from his belt. His boots were rough, made of animal skins and fringed at the knees. He squatted down.

"What are you doing in Marhaba, girl? I see you're

not yet a woman. You can't be *jawari*."

Awed as she was, Honifa bristled and retorted sharply.

"I am not a harlot, sir."

He grunted and offered his hand. "Then get up. I'll see you as far as the mosque. You'll be safe from there."

She laid her fingers tentatively in his palm. His skin was calloused and dry, not a bit supernatural. He pulled her to her feet and walked with her a few steps. He moved like a lion, sure and predatory; rays of moonlight glinted off his lion's mane of hair. Honifa couldn't take her eyes off him. At the steps of the mosque, he nodded his leave, but she didn't move, stupidly rooted to his side. He crossed his corded forearms and appraised her. Boredom radiated from his stance. She knew she should go but his nearness stole her reason.

"I'm—I'm Honifa McLeod," she managed at last.

He said nothing, seeming oblivious to her. She made a small obeisance. "I live only a short distance at the bottom of Nador Hill, sir. If you would be so kind as to walk a little more with me."

The coldness left his face. "I'm sorry, girl. Come. I'll see you home."

Conscious of his warm hand on her shoulder, she searched for conversation. She told him she was Tuareg and Scots, that her mother was dead and her father a physician. She babbled about herbs and medicinals, her errand to Bareed's, and on and on until she realized that everything she said was being met with silence. Abashed, she spoke no more until they were in front of her house. The candles inside were lit.

"Will you come in, sir?" she asked politely.

"Sorry again, girl. I'm off on the *Witch's Moon*."

"The *Witch's Moon*?"

"She's my ship. I'm Tor Kendrick, by the by. Happy to meet you, Miss McLeod." He inclined his head. "Now, get on with you."

"Perhaps some other time?"

He shrugged. "I ride with the waves. They may carry me here in three months' time or never again."

Honifa's heart sank. In three months, she'd be married to Ahmed and walled up with his mother in a gilded cell. She bit her lip with disappointment. Tor's eyes strayed to her mouth, then to the hollow of her throat and down the length of her sheer *kamis* just visible beneath the parted cloak. She felt the heat of that gaze; her skin reddened.

"My father is inside. I'm sure he'd like to thank you for –"

"No," Tor said roughly. "I'll go now and be done with this."

She whimpered softly, perhaps made a gesture; she couldn't know what caused Tor to reach out and lift a lock of hair from her cheek. His face unreadable as granite, he closed his hand around her neck, spanning it easily. She gasped. Was he going to strangle her; choke the life from her body and toss her aside for a fool?

"Who are you?" he rasped, and bent to brush her mouth with his, lingering there.

Ham du'llah! A snake deep in the pit of Honifa's stomach slithered through her vitals, teasing each one in turn. I may die right here, right now, she thought, but I wouldn't care. She pressed herself against Tor, and his mouth grew demanding; his arms tightened, crushing her. A moan escaped her lips as suddenly, he let her go.

"This ends here," he growled, turning abruptly from her.

Startled, confused, desolate she watched him walk away and thought of Ahmed, and a string of days unraveled in her mind like knitting yarn, days and months and years in a walled compound with his mother.

Simon opened the door. "Honi? Is that you? Ben Abbas had a baby boy. How is your beloved?"

Honifa blinked. "My – my what?"

"Ahmed. I guessed when you weren't home that you decided to go to the rose arbor after all. Wonderful to be in love."

Yes and no, she thought, removing her cloak, and lighting a candle. Wonderful and terrible.

****

That night, she climbed to the roof and dragged her mattress to the edge of the low wall facing the harbor. Tomorrow morning when she awoke, the first thing she'd see would be the sea and rows of moored ships listing gently in the rising sun, one of them the *Witch's Moon.*

Chapter 3

In the days and weeks that followed, Honifa found her mind straying increasingly to Tor Kendrick. She imagined him sitting in Ahmed's place in the rose arbor, watching with interest at the clinic as she bandaged gashed limbs and brewed tincture of wild carrot and poppy seed for infection. When she wandered through the rushes with her herb basket, she felt him beside her, his warm hand on her shoulder. In her bath at night, his hands touched her, his face swayed above her, and his breath stirred the water.

Many mornings at breakfast, she asked Simon which ships were in port, not an unusual question. "I saw a handsome schooner last night," he'd say. "*Jewel of the Ocean*, she's called." Or "I think *The Dover Star* is due tomorrow, damn that slaver, Davilow." But he didn't mention the *Witch's Moon*. Someday he would, she was sure. But, as the glass was turned again and again and her wedding approached, that day became nothing more than an empty hope.

She embroidered the sleeves of her bright red wedding dress with blue irises and tiny white gillyflowers, aware that it was the last time she would wear any color but black in public. She dutifully boiled almonds in honey water seasoned with sage and coriander and tied them in little bags of gold paper to give to friends who came with wedding presents. She marked off the days until the ceremony on her calendar, ninety days, eighty-five, eighty. At night in her bed, she dreamed of flight, of freedom, and of Tor Kendrick.

She tried but failed to talk to Ahmed. He wasn't interested in her opinions, and she shied away from voicing misgivings. It didn't seem right. They sat on the bench in the rose arbor every night, he spouting poetry or complaining about his mother, she waiting impatiently for Madame Hassan to blow out the garden lantern and send her home. Once, when she suggested they postpone the wedding until some small banking matter of his was resolved, his cagey response alerted her that Ahmed was no fool.

"After we're wed," he said, his face mild, "I think I'll buy that building in the medina where the storehouse used to be. I can make it over into a clinic and Simon won't have to pay rent to ben Abbas anymore. Your father will be so happy."

What could she do? At times, she believed she was losing her mind. The Tor Kendrick she had conjured up couldn't possibly exist; and if he did, it was more and more likely that she'd never see him again. With each grain of sand, each hour obliterated, each day marked, Honifa tried to erase from her memory the rangy, smooth-muscled man with the wild mane of a lion. She truly tried, but in the end, she could not forget him. One cannot forget an occurrence so fraught that it enmeshes into the fabric of one's being and becomes part of one's life.

****

In the autumn month of *Tishran Aw'wal*, Honifa was examining a bolt of velvet at the cloth merchant's stall when a commotion caused her to look around. Like the Red Sea, the market rabble parted as Tor Kendrick strode through, head and shoulders above everyone. Haggling ceased; rowdy callers went dumb. An awed stillness pervaded the previously raucous medina. Beggars and women, true *jawari* women, gathered the nerve to accost him. But he tossed a few coins and moved on past the fortune teller, the butcher shop, the livery stables and the pie man, down toward Waterfront Street and the docks.

Honifa's heart pounded. The blood rushed from her head to her stomach and back again. He was here! The *Witch's Moon* must have just docked. In a quandary, she threw the bolt of cloth at the startled merchant and broke through the crowd of gawkers. Dare she waylay Tor with a greeting? No. She would say foolish things and look like a fool. She must think; decide what to do. She had dreamt of nothing but this serendipity, and now here he was, Captain Kendrick, not twenty paces beyond her battering heart. She closed her ears to the certain expostulations of Simon and Ahmed were they to find out, raised her hood and mounted pursuit.

She kept well behind Tor, treading carefully, buried in the folds of her robe. When he descended to Yom al A'had Street, she paused briefly, muttered an imprecation for God's merciful forbearance, and kept on, all the way to the wharf where a row of ships, their sheets reefed, swayed like a ghostly army. It was the time of day when the moon begins to swallow the sky, when the nacreous pallor of evening sends God-fearing folk home to their dinners, and people of the night rise from their beds. Tor exchanged greetings with a tall blue man posted at the base of the long boarding plank.

"It's quiet, Captain," Honifa heard the Tuareg

sentry say. "The lads are getting soused, but they'll be on board afore morning."

"Cargo battened?" Kendrick asked.

"Aye, sir."

Kendrick slapped him on the back. "Then tip a few yourself, man. I'll stand watch."

From her vantage point, Honifa looked on as Kendrick mounted the gangway. The man had saved her virtue and, quite possibly her life. It was karma, nothing more, that had brought him to the Marhaba when she'd needed his help and to the marketplace when she needed *him*. Their fates were entwined, if not in this life, then certainly in a past life and in the next. The notion gave her courage. She lifted her heavy *djellaba* above her ankles and ran to follow Tor onboard the *Witch's Moon*. But when he reached the top of the gangway, he loosened the rope and pulled it up and out of her reach. Thwarted, she watched him secure the rope and disappear.

By now, most of the wharf was in shadows. One or two streetlamps flickered weakly through reflectors caked with salt. Below Honifa, inky water swirled. Above her, the mammoth beams of the *Witch's Moon* rose like a wooden cliff, creaking gently. Fairy lanterns strung from her mizzenmast cast a pale glow, but her bow and stern were dark. Heavy hawser ropes descended from the darkness and were anchored around dockside bollards. Gingerly, Honifa touched one of the ropes. It was thick as a column. Could she traverse it without being seen? She was sure she had the strength and agility to shimmy across the thick coil using her knees to grip and her hands to pull her along. She wanted only to thank the captain, she told herself, to express her gratitude. If he sent her away, she'd leave. That's all; over and done. She would have this speck of brightness, the memory of his presence one last time before the long weeks, months, years ahead of her.

Honifa glanced right and left. A few *jawari* had emerged from their dens seeking trade, their eyes on loitering sailors, not on the shore. Mercifully, the wharf was almost empty. She tied the ends of her *djellaba* around her waist, mounted a bollard, and grabbed the rope.

****

In his cabin, Tor Kendrick studied the charts spread before him. Like the last one, there'd be booty aplenty on this voyage. He'd sail northeast through the Straits, raise the white jack, the plunder jack, and force every slave vessel between Tangier and Casablanca to strike its colors. Then he'd change course around the thirty-fifth parallel into open water and head southwest for Madagascar. He'd outrun the English Reddies, the Portuguese, even the damn Americans who were so proud of their lightweight clippers.

The *Witch's Moon,* a schooner at just over 100 tons, was swift as any colonial vessel. With a full crew, a loaded hold and twelve cannon, she could still make eleven knots in open water with no more than a cat's paw puffing her sails. Tor was proud of his ship, loved her more than any woman who'd shared his bed. In truth, there was no one, man or woman, he cared for as he did the *Witch's Moon.* He admired the outlaw woman, Yarra, for her strength and courage and had spent the last two hours ashore in her tent. She had fed him pigeons roasted in honey and played sweet melodies on her *gimbri.* But when she shed her clothes and danced for him to the sinuous Yoruba rhythms of her people, propriety restrained him from covering her nakedness with his. He'd known Yarra since she was a child and he'd left her as ever he did, with an affectionate hug and tears of longing in her dark eyes.

Tor took a deep draught of ale from his mug and stared out the cabin's mullioned bay, across the foredeck and into the night sky. The orange moon of October, fat and round as a pumpkin, promised balmy seas and he itched to be underway. He hated being in port, hated waiting while his crew gambled and squandered their shares on harlots and whiskey, hated even more when the *Witch's Moon* was hauled out for careening and he was condemned to weeks of landlubber's boredom. Puny days and nights in port were but a hyphen between the rich sentences of his life at sea. He sprung from a noble race of seafarers and was happiest high athwart ship, riding a spar, his legs braced against the roiling of the waves, his tongue tasting salt, his body alive to the wind and rain and burning sun.

Another draught and the mug was empty. Tor slammed it resoundingly on the chart table. Damn, but that wench in Marhaba had been a beauty; all innocence and guile. And her eyes, like autumn leaves they were, under the lowering sky of her dark lashes and brows smooth as raven's wings. She likely thought he was a piebald Barbary pirate with letters of marque from the Pasha to transport slaves. But he was a Norseman. The free and fearless blood of Tyr Sigurdssen and Eric the Bold flowed through his veins. In battle, he fought with the fire of ten while his focus remained cool as a Bearing floe.

But the baggage, blast her! The intriguing piece kept springing to his mind unbidden; tall as most men yet soft and yielding. What was her name? Honi, short for Honifa, she'd told him. He chuckled. That meant *Faithful One* or *Handmaid* though he doubted she'd be groveling, much less faithful to whichever man claimed her heart. He pictured her lovely face framed by the orange moon, her full lips, and skin that glowed like amber. His groin tightened when he recalled the flame that leapt to her cheeks as he'd held her. Yarra's loving wiles had left him unaffected, but when the lovely half-breed lowered her eyes, he strained his britches like a randy boy. She could have sated him to numbness, but he had turned his back and bolted like a eunuch. He shook his head at the irony of it, rolled the charts and left his cabin.

A fragrant wind blew across the land, a desert wind that mingled with ocean breezes. Tor sat on the taffrail and swung his long legs. The feel of the air, of sand and salt, reminded him again of the sloe-eyed Marhaba vixen. He was not one to bed every snip that lowered her lashes and raised her skirts. If he were, he'd be spending all his time ashore with his britches around his ankles. But Honifa…something about her like the scent of Eastern spices that clung to her skin, like the taste of her tongue and crush of her breasts. What evil Loki had kept him wandering the marketplace when he should have been long since aboard the *Witch's Moon* happily checking the plimsoll mark or sorting the instruments in his binnacle? And why, in the name of Odin, once he'd sent the Marhaba knaves packing, did he walk with her like some smitten milk-mouth? He knew why he kissed her, why he held her in his arms. Oh yes, that he knew.

But he should have listened to his brain instead of his balls.

Absently, he worried a length of the halyard, picturing the girl's smooth, bare limbs and the swell of her rump as she'd lain pinioned over the barrel. "Dammit, man!" he spat, rising to pace the deck. The moon was low to starboard. Thin clouds scudded across its surface. Three or more hours at least until the lads boarded, three or more damnable hours!

An alien noise caused him to clutch the handle of his pistol. Stealthily, he moved aft, listening. The sound, a series of huffs and grunts, was coming from the vicinity of the stern hawser. Somebody was trying to sneak aboard! Tor's dagger rested in his boot. He could slice the hawser and scuttle the thief, but he was curious to see just what kind of bilge rat had the bollocks to think he could breach the *Witch's Moon*. He crept to the rail and waited. The rhythmic panting grew closer, interspersed with little squeaking sounds, like the cries of a small animal. He grabbed the rope and shook it. Someone screamed. Not a second later, a body hit the water with a splash.

"Avast, scurvy knave. Are you drowning, I hope?" Tor shouted down.

The water below him churned. The body thrashed, gulping air, choking.

"Save me, you oaf! My cloak is dragging me down! I can't– I–oh, by the holy prophet! I'm dying!"

It sounded like the blasted Marhaba woman! He tossed the Jacob's ladder over the side and climbed down. Dimly, he discerned Honifa's form in the murky water and reached out. She was entangled in her voluminous *djellaba,* part of which belled around her like a lily pad. He grabbed a hunk of cloth and pulled. She was dead weight.

"Can you get out of it?" he cried. "Can you take it off?"

"It's tied around my waist," she gasped.

"Well untie the blasted thing!"

Honifa twisted while Tor held fast. In a moment, she kicked the sodden garment free, and it floated away like a forgotten promise. He dragged her up by her middle, slung her over his shoulder, and hauled her on deck. She stood there dripping, shivering. The thin kaftan she wore clung to her breasts and belly. She gathered her hair to wring it out, then, as if suddenly mindful of her near nakedness, crossed her arms in front of her.

"It's a little late for that, girl," he said.

Tor's jaw was tight but her eyes...her eyes compelled him and she trembled as if torn between running to him and jumping headlong back into the sea.

"Come below," he commanded curtly.

She walked behind him, her feet squelching on the boards. Inside his cabin, he tossed her a blanket.

"Dry off," he ordered.

She wrapped the blanket around her shaking with misery. "What are you going to do?" she suddenly flung at him.

"Do? Take you home and tell the man who loves you to keep you locked up." He poured a stream of ale into his mug. "Drink this. You're fair to freezing."

Mumbling to himself, he descended to the crew's quarters. This was the second time he'd saved the damned wench. It was bad enough she'd invaded his thoughts. Did she have to invade his ship as well? In the cabin boy's duffel, he found a clean pair of britches and a shirt. He'd add a few coppers to the boy's wages next month; the lad had little enough. When he returned to his cabin, he found Honifa seated at the bay, her nose in the mug. She had removed her dress and hung it over a bench. Her hair, a mass of drying tendrils, tumbled around the blanket in wavelets of tawny brown. She started at his approach.

"I'm not a stowaway, you know," she said.

His eyes locked on hers, hard as agate. What in Aesgard's Heaven was going on? The vagaries of females were a mystery. The whores craved respect and the saints begged for ravishment. Honifa was no whore, he knew that. But he'd bet she wasn't a saint either.

"Then what are you doing here?" he asked sharply.

Honifa paled at his tone. "I saw you in the medina, that's all," she began. "I wanted—I thought I might—I only meant to—" Her agitation gave way to discomfiture. "I don't know what I want," she finished miserably.

Tor frowned. The girl's eyes changed with her moods. Here in the cabin, they took on the hectic hues of a forest glade, fiery gold and rust. A few moments earlier, when she'd faced him trembling across the deck, they'd been icy green.

"Get dressed."

She held the shirt and pants on her lap but kept her eyes fixed on his.

"You don't expect me to turn around, do you?" he asked, one eyebrow raised.

Boldly, she stood and shucked the blanket. Her naked body was slender with full breasts and wide, sweet hips. Tor swallowed a groan. She was a siren come from the sea to rob him of his senses.

"What do you want of me?" he rasped.

The catch in his voice seemed to galvanize her. She bit her lip. "Tonight. Give me only tonight, nothing more."

He marked the candlelight flickering across the mounds and hollows of her flesh. His fists clenched and opened. "That's easily done. But I'm not in the business of making up for a husband's defects."

She took a deep breath and laid the boy's shirt and britches on the bench. "I have no husband. But I'm betrothed and will be married on the tenth day of *Kamun al Thani,* to Ahmed ben Hassan. I'll wear a veil and live behind a wall in my mother-in-law's house."

He could feel the heat of her body, see the tiny hairs on her lower arms, smell her scent, a musky blend of spices and wildflowers.

"What has that to do with me?" he said.

A blush began to rise from the base of her throat and she suddenly seemed flustered. Her eyes darted from side to side, and her breath fluttered. "Everything!" she blurted. "And nothing." She clasped her hands before her as if in prayer. "I've never been with a man, but before I must lay with Ahmed, I want to first to lay with you. If I don't, I'll never know what destiny lives between us." A sob escaped her throat. "I'll never know how it could have been. I'll go to my grave wondering."

The entreaty in her lovely face, the innocence and desire there, electrified him. Reason fled and he reached for her. His eyes on hers, he kissed her palms, taking first one trembling finger, then another into his mouth, sucking and releasing it. He felt her shudder.

"I'm a pirate, Honifa," he said. "Neither demon nor god, just a man like all the others."

"No, you're not," she cried. "When I saw you in the medina, a djinn walked up the bones of my spine and whispered in my ear. He said if I didn't run to you, I'd regret it for the rest of my life. Don't send me away, Captain Kendrick." The plea sounded like a command. "Make me yours if only for one night."

The fire that was coursing through him erupted. He swept her in a savage embrace and cast her down on the bed. She buried her face in his neck as he ran his hands over her body. He hungered to take her swiftly, roughly, uncaringly. But he held himself in check. Slowly, touching, stroking, tasting with his fingers her erect nipples and the moist cleft between her thighs, then with his mouth, he gentled and aroused her. When her moans shrilled, he lifted her against him and clasped her buttocks, entering slowly, probing the wet tightness of her, holding himself back lest he hurt her. When he thrust, she writhed and cried out in pain.

"Easy, Honifa," he murmured, his mouth pressed to her ear. "Keep fast to me, ride with me."

Thighs grasping, fingers digging, she released to him with a feral cry, biting his shoulder like a wild animal. Only then, with the deepening of her breathing, did he seek his pleasure, plunging deeply, emptying himself and flooding her with all the pent-up passion she had stirred. A roar of fulfillment gathered in his gut and he threw back his head and bellowed, laughing, hugging Honifa, swaying with her from side to side until she too laughed with delight.

They were still for no more than a moment, each savoring the wonder of what had transpired. Then, she sought his mouth with hers and they loved again, over and over the urgency of their need undiminished.

As the October moon traversed the sky and night waned, he loved her as often as she wanted, beneath him, astride him, her body a saintly offering, a godless jezebel, and a galloping Diana, hands in her hair, mouth open in a scream of liberation. Keen as an acolyte, she followed the ways of his passion, claiming him as no other had before. She gave of herself and demanded of him.

The hourglass drained and Tor finally found sleep in the cradle of Honifa's arms.

****

She gazed down at the man beside her. In repose, the planes and hard angles of his face softened. The corded muscles of his arms and chest, the veins that bunched like blue serpents beneath his rough skin, the scars that covered his body were no longer threatening. She rubbed her cheek across the stubble of his chin and his wonderful lion's eyes opened.

"Honifa," he said, and kissed her.

Her body ached. There was not one centimeter of her that wasn't bruised and tender, but her spirit had soared as she'd known it would. He had claimed her, mastered her, loved her, and then shown her how to do the same to him.

The ship's clock struck. "It's nearly dawn," Tor said. "My men."

She nodded. In silence, their backs to each other, they dressed.

"The quartermaster will see you safely home," he said. "I wish it were not so."

"I know," she replied. "But it is."

She opened her palm and showed him an oddly shaped object she'd found on his table. It looked like an ancient talisman crudely carved with the phases of the moon, full, gibbous, three-quarter, half and crescent. The back was inscribed in a script she didn't recognize. He took it from her and studied it a moment. Then with a sudden motion, he snapped it in two, wrapped one half with the thin strip of rawhide, and tied it around her neck.

"Thank you," she said. "It's beautiful. What is it? What does it say?"

He shrugged. "I don't know. It was given to me in Persia as a good luck charm. It helped me through—" He paused. "It helped me through something I thought I'd never be free of." He stepped away from her and smiled. "I don't know what's on the back, a magical sign maybe, an incantation. I don't care to know. It's better that way."

She pressed the coin to her throat. "I'll never take it off. Will you wear the other half?"

He said nothing.

"To show our entwined destinies," she explained and watched his jaw harden.

"Best we go now, Honifa. I hear my crew returning."

She put her hand on his chest "When next you come this way, I'll be a married woman."

"The esteemed Madame Hassan," he said flatly.

"No. That's my mother-in-law. I'll just be Honifa, *only* Honifa."

"First wife to Ahmed," he added in a choked voice.

She put a finger to his mouth, the fierce, gentle mouth that had explored the length of her body and made it sing. "Our fate is in the hands of Haiwa, the mother of the Earth, who watches over us."

His gaze was intense. "Do you pray, Honifa?"

"To Allah, every day, many times."

"I haven't prayed in years, but I shall call upon Freya to protect you since I cannot."

She nodded sadly. "Different lutes play in our ears, but all can hear the music of the sky."

He delivered her into the hands of a trusted mate and did not return to his cabin that night but lay under the stars, sleepless.

Chapter 4

The *Dover Star* luffed lazily in a cat's paw breeze.
Captain Davilow paced the bridge. From time to time,
he strained his eyes through the foul mist for the
shadowy shape of a wherry. He listened for the
betraying squeak of an oarlock or the clang of an
anchor chain; even for the rattle of his nemesis, Zalam
Alqamar's pagan talisman, a pendant depicting the
moon in all its phases. As much as his hooded mask and
midnight raids, the pendant had given Dark of the
Moon his name.

Davilow watched and listened but there was no
sign of the cursed privateer; no sound, no lantern light,
nothing. He had arranged, as always, to meet him at
midnight, but midnight had come and gone, and soon
his crew would awaken and stumble to their chores,
unsteady with last night's rum and carousing.

Davilow checked the position of the stars. Where
was the blasted pirate? This week alone, riding his
phantom, nameless ship, Alqamar had sunk the *Reyna
Dorado* off the Spanish coast and the American trawler,
the *Ivory Eagle*, lightening their loads of two hundred
and sixteen healthy tribesmen from the Kidal and
transporting the lucky bastards back to their homes.
How he knew which ships to maraud, which crews to
maroon, and which slaver captains' severed heads to
mount on pikestaffs was a mystery to all but Davilow.

Only he had possessed the cunning and wisdom to strike a bargain with the hooded outlaw. In exchange for the *Dover Star's* safe passage, Davilow had divulged the routes of every schooner, galleon, and barkentine sailing from the Cape and points north with a hold low to the line and bursting with slaves. You could say he was Dark of the Moon's partner in crime, the crime of freedom that is. How ironic; how lucrative.

"Attack every slave ship," he had posited to the outlaw. "Tear open their cargo hatches and free every damn slave inside. Spare only the *Dover Star*. What's one piddling ship carrying a piddling bunch of slaves when I'll give you the means to free ten times that number?"

Alqamar had taken the bait and the resultant scarcity of available slaves had caused Davilow's prices to soar. He was the richest human trader in the Algarve.

Impatient, eager to be on his way for his hold was packed to the rafters with cargo bound for the Malabar Coast, two hundred and sixty Dahomeyan savages, coffered, beaten, and stacked like logs, Davilow descended to the quarterdeck and leaned into the night. Damn and blast! It was impossible to see anything in this muck! He yanked the ship's bell and shouted for his crew. Minutes later, Lookie slid from the crow's nest.

"There's a sloop, sir, just cresting the horizon; nothing below the bowsprit, no name anywhere. I'm sure it's him."

At last. "What are her colors?"

"The skull and crossbones, Captain. She's coming about and heading straight for us. Shall I post the gunwales?"

Davilow frowned. He expected Alqamar in a wherry alone, not with the blue-skinned Tuareg first mate who rarely left his side and certainly not with his damned crew. The blasted freebooter wouldn't dare; he knew better than to go back to guessing where and when to strike when Davilow did everything but give him a map.

"Let her come," he ordered Lookie. "We've nothing to fear."

The nameless ship plowed forward and Davilow, banking on his protected status, didn't react until it was too late. A flame cut through the murk as Alqamar's ship fired broadsides. Caught off guard, Davilow shouted his sleepy men to the starboard gunwales seconds before the Tuareg, leading a cohort of bloodthirsty raiders, muskets at the ready, scrambled over the portside rail.

"Greetings, Captain."

Davilow spun. Under cover of fire, Alqamar had snuck onto the *Dover Star*. He could barely make out the godless swine, swathed as always in black from head to foot. The man even covered his eyes with a thin strip of black gauze. What can you tell of a man when you can't see his eyes?

Davilow gathered his wits and touched his forehead with the tip of his knife. "Salaam, my friend. Welcome aboard."

Alqamar said nothing but stiffened when Davilow took a step forward. Davilow retreated. The man was a colossus.

"You have information for me," said the colossus.

"Call off your men first. You were to come alone; you always come alone."

"I would have but after what you did to the Dahomeyans." Alqamar paused. "You've decimated their village. Only the aged and infirm remain."

"Unavoidable, my friend. They resisted but I can hand over ships carrying twice that puny stock."

Alqamar listened grimly as Davilow named names and outlined routes. "That's three separate cargoes for you, man," Davilow said. "Raid the hell out of them but keep to our agreement; leave my ship alone. Now, on your way," he added genially, wanting to be rid of the scourge. He had suffered Alqamar's wrath once before. The beast had destroyed everything, and it had taken all Davilow's energy to build, crew, and provision a second ship; not to mention reset his broken limbs.

Alqamar lifted his chin, an infinitesimal movement but enough to summon the Tuareg who, quick as a bolt of lightning, snatched Davilow's knife. To a man, the crew cowered. Pig Eye blubbered and Lookie near pissed his boots.

Alqamar grabbed Davilow's stock and lifted him to his toes, choking him. "Perhaps you shouldn't have trusted the word of a felon," he taunted.

"Unhand me!" Davilow cried.

"Or what?"

"Or–or—," Davilow blustered.

The Tuareg chuckled. Alqamar's men stood braced, their eyes everywhere.

"Or I'll ruin you. I'll tell the world who you are. You'll be hunted down like a dog."

Alqamar hoisted Davilow clear off his feet. "And who am I, scum?" he snarled.

Davilow kicked his legs and flailed his arms. With a swipe, he ripped the mask from Alqamar's face.

"You're Tor Kendrick!" he shouted. "The mighty Dark of the Moon, scourge of slavers, is none other than a bloody turncoat, a traitor to the brotherhood of the sea."

He got no further. Alqamar slammed him down on the deck and drew his musket.

****

Three days before her marriage, Honifa bathed in the Haman, the traditional sauna. She accepted gifts of food from her father's patients and a sequined purse from Madame Hassan into which Ahmed had stuffed gold coins, most of which his mother had removed without his knowledge. On the day of the ceremony, the Hennaya drew designs on Honifa's hands and feet, and she and Ahmed were carried around the wedding hall to much music, dancing, and feasting.

Four months later, two veiled women swathed in long, black *haiks*, one tall, the other squat, entered Simon McLeod's free clinic in Nador. Their body servant remained outside with his arms folded. The clinic was closed for the noon meal, and Simon was busy boiling instruments and arranging salves and bandages, tasks his daughter used to attend to. He looked up as the women entered.

"Honi!" he cried, embracing Honifa. "How wonderful to see you!"

He salaamed to Madame Hassan and bid her to sit in his chair. She looked askance at the rump sprung cushions and remained standing.

"Ahmed told me you were pregnant," Simon said to his daughter. "Why haven't you come sooner?" He placed his hand on Honifa's stomach and frowned.

Madame Hassan knit her thick brows and fixed

him with a disapproving glare. "Examine her," she barked in Arabic; she neither spoke nor understood English.

"I'm watched every second, Father," Honifa said. "I can't move; I can barely speak. She only let me come today because I pleaded with Ahmed and, for once, he went against her." Honifa lowered her eyes. They were red-rimmed.

"What is it, lass?" Simon asked. "I'm troubled."

"She thinks I've cast a spell on her son. She tells me my belly's too big. She accuses me of debauchery. When I tell her Ahmed can divorce me if he wants, she says she'll have me killed for bringing shame upon the house of Hassan."

"Ahmed would never let her hurt you, Honi. He loves you."

Honifa sighed. "He's very good to me, but I—" She swallowed and turned away.

"Tell me," Simon urged tenderly.

Honifa surveyed the small surgery. The herb jars were half full. Dust caked the shelves and she was certain the dispensary cabinet was bare. Simon's tobacco tin stood open and empty, and his white coat was dirty and frayed at the sleeves. Ahmed's boast to relocate the clinic to larger quarters had come to naught. Madame Hassan controlled the purse strings as well as her son.

"Don't worry about me, Honi," Simon soothed, following her gaze. "It's not as bad as it looks. Besides, I'm going to give up the house and live in the surgery, and I'll ask the patients to pay in cash from now on instead of duck eggs and pickled quince. I hate quinces anyway."

Honifa smiled fondly. "I miss you so much," she said.

Madame Hassan shot her a glance. Simon stepped protectively in front of his daughter.

"It's all right," Honifa said. "The old bat doesn't scare me."

"Lay back, lass," he said. "Let me see what's happening with my little girl."

He unpinned her veil, uncovering his daughter's anguished face. Madame Hassan waved her hands and bore down, screeching in outraged Arabic. Simon told her sternly that he was Honifa's father as well as a physician and to kindly control herself or leave. He removed his daughter's *haik*, pushed up the hem of her heavy black *saya,* and undid the straps of her leather sandals.

"Your feet and ankles are swollen," he said. "So are your legs."

His expression neutral, his eyes focused inward, Simon probed Honifa's abdomen. He looked into her mouth and pressed his ear to her chest. Madame Hassan sucked her teeth and grumbled.

"Do you know you're six, close to seven months gone, lass?" he questioned gently.

"Yes," she replied.

He covered her. "It's nothing to be ashamed of. You and Ahmed were betrothed for ages and now you're married. It's understandable if you and he—"

Honifa stopped him with a gesture. "Not Ahmed," she said, resting both hands on her protruding stomach. "This child isn't Ahmed's."

"Were you taken by force?" Simon asked, his eyes wide.

"No, no. Nothing like that," she reassured him.

He studied her sharply for several moments. "I see. Come into the house, please. I need to sit down."

In Simon's kitchen, Madame Hassan glowered at the crusted dishes on the sideboard. She furrowed her finger through the dust on the back of the chair he offered her and, grunting with disapproval, once again indicated that she preferred to stand. Simon and Honifa faced each other across the table as they had countless times before. He offered her water and a plate of figs. There was obviously nothing else to eat.

"There was a man," Honifa began. "A few months before the wedding." She took a sip of water. "I pursued him."

Slowly, she confessed her enthrallment, her unexplainable obsession to seize one night of passion with a lover as irresistible to her as breath, before condemning herself to surrender of another sort.

"I shouldn't have done it, Father," she said. "But I couldn't stop myself. I was as one possessed, and if I wasn't under lock and key at Madame Hassan's these many months, I'd fly to him again."

Simon studied her for a moment and then, surprisingly, he nodded. "I understand, Honi. It was that way with your mother and me. We fought everything and everyone to be together."

"But you and *Umma* loved each other," Honifa exclaimed. "I know nothing about this man beyond what I feel." She slid her eyes away. "The servants on Nador Hill gossip that he's a pirate and a rogue and—" She hesitated. "A slaver."

Simon grew suddenly still. "A slaver? Who is he, Honi?"

"Tor Kendrick," she replied, relishing the taste of the hard syllables of his name on her lips.

"I've heard of him," Simon said gravely. "He's from the north, a huge man with yellow hair. They say he's in league with the devil. Even Dark of the Moon fears him."

She buried her face in her hand. "Oh, Father, what am I to do?" she wailed.

Madame Hassan snorted.

"Does Kendrick know you carry his child?" Simon asked.

"We had that one night," Honifa sniffed. "Nothing since, nothing more."

Simon rubbed his chin. "Much depends on the appearance of the infant. I doubt it will resemble Ahmed, Captain Kendrick being fair and you—well, your skin is dark enough, but your hair and eyes—Oh, my dear child."

Honifa dried her eyes with the edge of her veil. "I might be able to convince Ahmed the baby is his if it has even the slightest look of him. But not his mother. She hates me. She goads Ahmed every day in my presence, quotes the Holy Qu'ran, the verse about killing depraved infidels and walling up unfaithful women until they die. I can protect myself, but if the baby is born with skin like a peach and—" She touched her stomach and bit her lower lip.

At the mention of the Qu'ran, Madame Hassan raised her head abruptly and spoke to Honifa with guttural emphasis on each word. "Your naked face is offensive to me. I shall tell my son how you disrespected me." She spat on the floor. "I wish to leave this house."

Honifa rose. "I'd better go. I'll try to come again, but it's difficult."

She veiled herself and followed Madame Hassan to the door. Simon clutched her arm.

"Don't despair, lass," he said. "I know someone who may be able to get you away from Nador Hill and hide you."

"Who, Father?"

"It's better you don't know. This is dangerous business and your mother-in-law is a powerful woman."

Honifa hesitated. "I can't risk your safety, Father. Perhaps there's another way."

Madame Hassan smacked the back of Honifa's head. "*Yahdim!*" she snarled, calling her daughter-in-law a piece of garbage.

Simon planted himself between her and Honifa. "There is no other way." He sighed. "Are you willing?"

Honifa straightened her veil and glared at her mother-in-law. "All right. Anything to rid me of this snake."

Simon put a finger to his lips. "Then leave it to me. Can you steal into the rose arbor at night after everyone has gone to bed?"

"Yes. I sleep alone. But the walls of the arbor are steep as any dungeon. No one may enter from the outside, or escape."

"I'll send word, a note concealed in a packet of medicinal powders. When you receive it, wait in the garden at the third hour. Don't fail me."

"I won't, Father, but—"

Madame Hassan made a growling sound and tapped her foot. Simon ushered his daughter into the street. He put three fingers to his lips as if blowing a kiss. "Remember, Honi, the third hour. Be ready."

****

Royce Davilow awoke to the sound of his name. His bones ached and his mouth tasted of blood. For a moment he thought he was on the *Dover Star*, but then he felt the drag of irons on his wrists and ankles. He was manacled! He moaned and remembered that instead of leaving him to die, Dark of the Moon had thrown him to the deck and trussed him like a spitted pig. His yellow-bellied crew had hung back like petrified ninepins while Tor and the blue man hustled him aboard Alqamar's so-called nameless vessel that was nothing more than Tor Kendrick's *Witch's Moon* stripped of her pennants and jackstaff, her bowsprit letters covered. And now he was the blasted buccaneer's prisoner shackled like a slave aboard a counterfeit slave ship.

He sat up and looked around. He was in a cave. The walls were hung with blankets, the floor beneath his bare feet was covered in sand, and a fire blazed in a circle of stones. And he was not alone. A small woman dressed like a boy in leather leggings and a vest was staring at him. She was black as the Nubian night with a wooly thatch of African hair and wide, pink African lips. Her teeth glowed viciously as she pointed a pistol dead between his eyes.

"Eat, slaver."

Someone had placed a clay tagine on the sand beside him. He sneered at the woman. A coal tar bitch giving him orders! At least she spoke English.

"Where's your master?" he demanded.

Her mouth curled in a mocking smile. "Yarra has no master."

The slave who called herself Yarra was diminutive in stature and endowed with swelling hips and buttocks. Davilow looked her up and down. Comely enough, but he disliked the smell of these blackamoors.

Davilow smiled. He would bide his time, be a model prisoner, eat and drink what they gave him and wait. He lifted his manacled wrists. "How do you expect me to eat like this?" he whined.

She laughed and, in the firelight, her throat glistened like polished ebony. To Davilow's surprise, she barked an order and another woman, Bedouin by the look of her, emerged from the shadows, removed his bonds, and melted away. Yarra thrust out her chin.

"Now eat," she ordered.

Davilow lifted the cover of the tagine. The scent of lamb and spices rose to his nostrils. Moroccan food, meat and syrup and nutty sultanas that stuck in the holes of his teeth and made him wince. He tore off a piece of flatbread and dipped it into the sauce.

"Will you join me?" he said, offering the bread to Yarra. "There's plenty here."

She sneered above the pistol. "I don't eat with vermin who traffic in human flesh."

Davilow's jaw tightened. He longed to slit the vixen's neck, watch the blood run down her belly, and soak into the sand. He bit into the bread. The flavor was pleasing, and he set to devouring every morsel in spite of the pain in his gums. When he looked up, Yarra was gone.

He emptied his bladder into the tagine. Through a gap in the folds of the hanging blankets, Davilow saw a sliver of night sky. Unmolested, he walked outside and found himself in a clearing surrounded by the smoky hillocks of the Rif Mountains. People, freed slaves, no doubt, sat around small fires, horses whinnied softly, and an earthy smell of livestock filled the air. He was in a place concealed from good Christian notice and crawling with two-legged scum who should be in chains. Clearly, this was the camp of Dark of the Moon. He studied the horizon for breaks in the hills, a path of escape, and chuckled. The unarmed slaves paid him no attention and he could liberate the pistol from the dusky, meaty-haunched Zulu baggage in the blink of an eye. He bent casually to pick up a sharp rock.

"Captain Davilow."

His eyes fell on the hem of a familiar blue robe and rose up the column of cloth to the turbaned head and muffled face of the blue man, Alqamar's first mate.

"Put down that rock and come with me. Dark of the Moon is ready to see you."

Chapter 5

Honifa was doomed. Weeks had passed and her
father hadn't come for her. She was sure he had tried to
save her, but what could a foreigner do in Nador, even
one as beloved as Simon? He had no money, his
patients were poor, and his friends, ben Abbas and
Bareed, were also his landlord and a barman. There was
no reason for them to risk their livelihood and
reputations for his sake.

The babe inside of her had ceased to kick quite so
mightily as before. It was *Huzairan*, the end of her
eighth month, and her time was almost upon her.
Dispiritedly, she sat in her room and read the Holy
Book. It was the only book her mother-in-law allowed.
Honifa knew the *surahs* from memory, but her eyes,
nevertheless, followed the delicately twining script. *In
the name of God, the beneficent and merciful,* she
mouthed softly. Madame Hassan was asleep in the next
room and no one dared make a disturbing noise.

The corpulent Mistress of Nador Hill slept often;
morning naps, after dinner lie-downs, a quick snooze on
her divan before bedtime. Yet, she still managed to
close her eyes in the evening and not open them again
until the *muezzin's* morning call to prayers. Honifa
begrudged every snore and snuffle. Bored and restless,
she lay rigid in her bed at night, eyes locked open,
staring through her gated window into the courtyard.

The courtyard floor was inlaid with blue lapis, the tinkling fountain tiled with carnelian butterflies, the trellised dome twined with asphodel, pipe vine, and Osiris lilies. She longed to rise from her bed and sit there, cool the feverish thoughts that stole her sleep. But her mother-in-law had forbidden such folly, out of pure meanness, Honifa was sure.

Ahmed usually came into her room after his bath, his hair slicked back and smelling of bergamot. He'd slide beside her and kiss her lips, sometimes like a hummingbird, sometimes like a limpet. He'd part her thighs and pound his slender shaft into her, twice, thrice, maybe even four times, then collapse with a groan upon her distended middle. She felt only annoyance and an uncomfortable shortness of breath. Lately, she had begun to complain that his attentions disturbed the baby, and he'd obligingly left her alone, joining her only for a game of chess and then retiring to his room. He was a considerate husband but weak in the face of his mother's vehemence. A man and the only son, Ahmed was supposed to control the family's fortune. But he was in the habit of taking whatever money he needed for himself and allowing Madame Hassan free access to the rest. She held on to her purse with a dead-man's grip, doling out *dirhams* as if each coin was a part of her anatomy. There was never enough for Simon's clinic. Honifa had asked Ahmed to make good his promise, but Madame Hassan only groused, "Order that lazy wife of yours to mind her tongue or I shall cut it out." Honifa had tried to sneak a few mutton chops or a sack of okra to Simon via one of the maids, but the stubborn Scot always sent them back.

Glumly, she leafed through the Holy Book and

paused at the Ninety-third *Surah*, the *Surah* of the Early Hours.

I swear by the early hours, when the day is covered in darkness, that God has not forsaken me nor become displeased, for surely what comes after shall be better than what has come before.

"Let it be so," she prayed. "Let this torment end."

****

"Daughter-in-law!" Madame Hassan's strident call cut through Honifa like a honed cutlass. "Do you hear me? Come scrape my feet. These clumsy girls have the hands of cactus melons."

Honifa made her way to Madame Hassan's room. The Mistress lay on her divan, bare feet sticking out beneath her skirt like engorged leeches. Honifa bowed salaam and pulled up a low stool. She selected the correct pumice stone and applied it lightly to the horny protrusions on the woman's heels. Madame Hassan kicked

"Too rough!"

Honifa ducked. She had learned to deftly dodge the woman's many pokes and slaps, a feat that earned her even more rebuke.

"Your calluses are thick, madame," Honifa said mildly.

"Your head is thick!"

She set the stone aside and massaged her mother-in-law's feet with carob butter.

"Bring me that dish of stuffed dates," the insufferable woman ordered.

"You know they make you flatulent, Esteemed Mistress," Honifa warned.

"Stupid girl! I know no such thing. My insides are

sweet as yarrow. Bring me the dates and feed them to me one at a time."

Honifa obeyed. It was simpler, and she truly didn't care if Madame Hassan's guts heaved like a volcano. In time, the sated woman dozed and Honifa slipped back to her room. She opened her sewing box and began to affix tiny silver beads to Ahmed's *babouches*. He disliked walking barefoot at home and demanded that his slippers be always at the ready and in excellent repair. He owned several *babouches*, braided, sequined, with toes that were tipped in gold or pointed like the royal slippers of Sultan Moulay Idris.

In the brief months of their marriage, Honifa had discovered that her husband was fastidious about his person. His *keffiyehs* must hug his head at exactly the correct angle, and his vests must be fortified with buckram to conceal the softness of his middle. He washed his hands frequently and his entire body vigorously after morning *salat* and again before sleep. Yet he seldom broke a sweat, spending his days as he did in the medina, drinking coffee and smoking with friends. At night, after leaving Honifa's bed, he usually sat with his mother.

A servant came in to light the lamps. Honifa put aside the *babouches* to make ready for dinner. She jumped slightly as the babe tumbled in her womb. Would this child Tor had seeded be ruddy gold like its father or brown-skinned? She had dipped her hands in rosewater and tapped her right foot three times, hoping for a sign. But the only vision that swam before her closed eyes was of a shining-haired giant with the face of an idol and a body as hard as stone. In the months since she'd lain with Tor, her memory of his caresses, his voice, the scars that marred his powerful hands, was as vivid as the feel of the child within her. She'd never forget him, but that brief, plangent interlude in her life was over. If deliverance never came, she must get on with the business of bearing her baby and keeping it safe.

"The master bids you come to table," the servant said.

Honifa groaned. She would have liked grapes and tea with ginger, but she'd be forced to swallow endless courses of Madame Hassan's favorites: fatty lamb swimming in oil of mint, spiced doves baked in sugar crust, and thick coffee sweetened with geranium honey.

She covered her head and made her way as gracefully as she could to the small salon where the family took its meals. Surely, she mused, as she kept her eyes humbly averted and her body close to the wall, even if the babe was dark as a Maghribi twilight, even if she could excuse the slightest mark of foreign blood with the fact of her own mixed heritage, surely it would be obvious to anyone with sense that the child, born scant months after her wedding, was full-term. Then, according to Sharia law, she must be lowered into the stoning pit with her baby strapped to her back. If they survived stoning, their battered bodies would be sealed up in a wall without food or water, nevermore to see God's light.

Honifa entered the dining canopy and sank awkwardly onto an ottoman.

"You look tired, wife," Ahmed said. "Do you sleep at night?"

"She honks like a flock of geese," Madame Hassan complained. "I can scarcely close my eyes for the noise."

"Perhaps you should eat more," Ahmed suggested, eying Honifa's barely touched plate.

"That baby must be wide as the caliph's pantaloons," Madame Hassan grumbled, then narrowed her eyes. "Though I can't imagine, at mere weeks married that—"

"Please allow me to speak to my wife," Ahmed interrupted the screed he knew was sure to come. His mother told him over and over again that Honifa's child was planted by another, but Ahmed had not yielded to suspicion. Fixing his wife with a concerned stare, he said gently, "You are three or four months with child, correct?"

Madame Hassan harrumphed. "Don't bother to ask. Beat her and seal her and her bastard alive in a tomb." She bared her teeth, small gold and white pincers. "Mother will find you a biddable wife, Ahmed, my angel. Wouldn't you like that?"

"Excuse me," Honifa said, bile flooding her mouth. "I don't feel well." She rose and lumbered from the room.

Madame Hassan shrieked imprecations to her son to remain where he was. They grated on his ears like sand in the teeth. He knew he should comfort his wife, but it was easier to heed his mother when vitriol struck her. He would go to Honifa later, with the ivory and sandalwood chess box and a small glass of licorice water. They would play quietly, and he would try not to pester her with questions. She always answered them equivocally, anyway. It seemed to Ahmed that when he asked about the babe, when he repeated his mother's assertions, denying them even as the words fell from his lips, he believed he saw the truth leap into Honifa's eyes and then die there, unspoken. As her belly grew, it had become hard for him to ignore the curl of fear and uncertainty that lodged in his gut, swelling with each passing day like the neck of a cobra with a rat stuck in its throat.

****

Back in her room, Honifa gazed pensively at the slowly darkening garden. She must not lose hope, but daily it receded, its promise a desert mirage wavering falsely in the mind's eye, then gone. In any case, her fate had already been inscribed in the golden book. All she could do was pray that her child be born with dusky skin, her husband remain steadfast, and Madame Hassan perish under the hooves of a galloping camel.

A servant slipped into the room. "This medicine came for you," he said, holding out a small envelope. "Madame Hassan says it is useless chickweed and you may have it."

The envelope's seal had already been slit. Honifa discarded the packet of powders and extracted a folded slip of paper upon which Simon had written:

For ease of delivery. Take at the third hour and it will be quickly done.

The message was coded to foil Madame Hassan and her spies. Her father was telling her he would free her at the third hour, the third hour tonight! Her skin flushed; her heart raced. Apprehensively, she looked about. There were no locks on her door, but she pushed it shut, nonetheless, and pressed her back against it, breathing rapidly. Tonight, she and her child would be free. She had no idea what Simon had planned, only that whatever it was, it would release her from this house of Hell, from Madame Hassan's hatred and her husband's gathering doubts.

She packed a small *tassoufra* bag that could be easily concealed underneath her *haik*. She had no true possessions, only a tiny miniature of her mother and father and her half of the broken talisman Tor had given her. She took it from the bag and ran her thumb across its crude engraving that could have been ancient writing or marks of celestial navigation. Engulfed in memories, she didn't notice when Ahmed pushed open her door.

"A game of chess, wife?" he asked.

She closed her fist around the talisman and whirled to face him. "Husband," she blurted.

He set down the chess box. "What is it you have in your hand?"

Heart thrumming, she presented her open palm. "A trinket that caught my fancy at the medina; nothing more."

"Let me see."

He turned it over, frowned, and bit the edge with his teeth. "When did you purchase this?"

"Oh, eons ago; long before we were wed."

"I thought I knew every piece of jewelry you owned. I've never seen this."

She concealed her hands in her sleeves so he would not see them trembling. "It's not jewelry, Ahmed. Just a good luck charm, an amulet to ward off the pains of childbirth." Too late, she realized her mistake.

"You bought a birthing charm before we were married?" His jaw was tight, his tone caustic.

Her brain buzzed like a thousand cicadas. The *tassoufra* lay on her divan. She picked it up. "Girls do that all the time; girls as young as ten. We purchase magic potions to make us fertile and ask the wise *earafa* if our husband will be handsome." With effort, she curved her mouth into a smile. "Now put the silly thing back in my pouch or throw it away. I'm already with child and my husband is handsome as a Lord."

Ahmed pouted but he threw the token onto the table. "You vex me, Honifa. There is no peace in my house. A wife's duty—"

Honifa's breathing calmed. She set out the chessmen as he launched into his familiar litany: bow under the yoke, respect your betters, blah, blah, blah. He kept it up through two games then relented.

"You are tired, wife, and I need my bubble pipe." He cast a contemptuous glance at the pouch on the table. "A woman brings forth her children in pain. My mother reminds me often of the agony she suffered for my sake. You will, too, no matter the soothsayer's skills."

After he'd gone, Honifa tied the talisman around her neck and sat at the window, waiting for the third hour.

****

She marked every chime of the clock. When it struck three, she sped from the window, tied the *tassoufra* around her middle, and donned her *haik*. Carrying her sandals, she tiptoed into the rose arbor, ears and eyes alert. A high, white moon, shiny as a knuckle of bone, lit up the sky. Seeking concealment, she sat in the shadow of the date palm on the bench where Ahmed used to court her. Nervously, she scanned the windows that looked onto the courtyard: the sitting room window, the summer kitchen, and the salon she had left precipitously only hours before. All were dark. It seemed so long ago that she and Ahmed advanced from childhood playmates to sweethearts. Gradually, her affection had turned to despair as he'd sunk deeper under the influence of his mother. If only he were not so weak. If only she could trust him again. If only she hadn't met Tor. She clutched the moon pendant around her neck, the keepsake of their union. How perfect was life's irony? She'd been a silly snip yearning for adventure and here it was. Apt the poet Omar's rhyme: *In and out, around, above, below, life is a magic shadow show around which we puppets come and go.*

A light blazed in the summer kitchen. Honifa shrunk back. It wouldn't be Ahmed or his mother. The kitchen was for servants. But what if one of the maids were to dip a cup of water and wander into the garden to enjoy it? She might be able to explain her presence, even ask they not tattle to their Mistress. But how to explain the presence of another, however, of her father should he suddenly appear? An unbidden sob escaped her lips, the horrifying sound echoing in the empty garden. Her eyes darted nervously. Would she ever see Simon again? Would she ever be able to return home to the clinic, to her herb basket and wild walks among the pipe vines and honeysuckle? No. Once she fled, Madame Hassan would declare a *jihad* and hunt her down as an infidel. Oh, where was her savior? Let him be swift and silent as smoke. Let him hide her so well she'd never be found. The light went out. Honifa swallowed and tried to still the fluttering of her pulse. The third hour was approaching. Would this night never end?

Something thwacked off the trunk of the date palm

high above her. She looked up. It was a rope with a kind of grappling hook on its end. It swung and thwacked again, digging this time into the bark, and holding. Someone on the other side of the wall pulled the rope taut and then slackened it, testing its strength. A dark form in the shape of a man appeared at the top of the wall. He flattened himself and reached a hand down to her. He was too far away. She stood on the bench, arching her toes, straining upward but unable to reach him. Suddenly, the garden brightened as a long, steady beam swept the courtyard swaying like a metronome. Several windows leapt with light. She was discovered!

"Oh Holy Jesus, I'm discovered!" she cried out, panicking. "Merciful Allah, save me!"

The hand grabbed her wrist. "Quiet, Miss!"

Quaking with fright, kicking her legs, Honifa felt herself pulled to the top of the wall. She collapsed against her rescuer and clung to the heavy folds of his robe. It was indigo blue. He was Tuareg, a blue man.

"*Shukraan*," she panted, thanking him.

He put a finger to his lips then pointed below where a donkey waited, hitched to a cart. Wordlessly, the man twined his leg and one arm around the rope and, with the other arm, lifted Honifa onto his hip. They descended to the street.

"Who's there?" a rough male voice called out from the other side of the wall. "Show yourself or die."

Honifa tensed. One of Madame Hassan's henchmen! The blue man cut the rope with a long-bladed knife. He shoved Honifa into the cart and covered her with a blanket. She huddled there miserably, praying as she never had before. After what seemed like hours of bumping and swerving, the blue man reached back and removed the blanket. The scent of laurel and cypress engulfed her. She knew it well. They were in the Rif.

Chapter 6

At the Hassan compound, screams rent the air. Ahmed followed the sound to Honifa's room where he found the servants searching in corners and his mother on her knees, tearing at her hair.

"*Umma*," he cried. "What is it?"

"That woman, that wretched woman!" she wailed. "Your unfaithful wife has taken her devil seed and gone; deserted and disgraced you and this noble house a thousand-fold."

"Calm yourself, please," Ahmed begged. "I'm sure she's gone to see Simon."

Madame Hassan glared at her son. "Stupid, stupid boy. She's gone, I tell you, gone to her lover." She rocked back and forth. "Oh, how can I face anyone ever again! What cruel fate, what evil destiny! You should have listened to me when I warned you against her. Impure slut! Dirt under my feet!" She rose clumsily. "What's missing?" she hissed, her eyes darting. "What has the harlot stolen?"

"Nothing, madame," the servant reported. "Everything is here but her sandals and *haik*."

"That's my *haik!*" Madame Hassan cried triumphantly. "I want it back." She raised her fists to Ahmed. "Find her! Find her so I can kill her!"

Ahmed's face creased. "Honifa knows better than to disrespect me, *Umma*." He glanced at the servant,

"Ah, Esteemed Mother. I can't believe she would do such a thing."

Madame Hassan dug her nails into his arm. "Believe it! She came to you with her womb despoiled. She lied to you, made a fool of you. All your friends in the coffeehouse, all our relatives know it and laugh at us. Ooh, I cannot bear the shame of it. I won't!"

Ahmed delivered his mother into the hands of the servant. "Please go to your room and lie down, Esteemed Mother. I'll look into this and see what must be done."

"There is only one thing to be done, you idiot," Madame Hassan hissed. "Send men to search every corner of Nador and beyond, to the very ends of the desert if you must. Spare no expense. Find her no matter how long it takes. Find her and the bastard she harbors and slay them both." She clutched at him, shook him, slapped his cheeks. "Wake up! You are a Hassan. See what is before you and heed your loving mother."

With a final kick, she sent him off.

****

After tumbling all night in the wooden donkey cart, Honifa was deposited in a cave that was dark and dank despite a lantern and several woven hangings. She held her stomach and moaned, trying not to be sick. Had her Tuareg brother freed her from one prison only to leave her in another?

But the cave became her home where she gave herself over to the cosseting of two Bedouin matrons and into the charge of a Yoruba woman called Yarra, whose gruff manner softened whenever she blew the melodies of the African savannah into her flute. Honifa was nourished on cool, foamy goat's milk and sugared kumquats. She slept as though drugged, dreaming of nothing, no heated visions of a towering sea captain with skin like polished bronze or nightmares of a harpy-headed virago pecking at her eyes.

She discovered that her cave was one of several in the outlaw camp of Zalam Alqamar, the rebel Dark of the Moon. It was warmed by a beehive stove where the women boiled tea and cooked guinea hen on skewers. They perfumed the earthen floor with rushes of pine and rosemary and gave her rosewater to wash in. As the weeks passed and her baby stilled, readying itself for birth, she felt strong enough to explore what lay beyond, to leave her snug sanctuary and walk the land, a terrain of smudged, brown hills and silver sky. She asked Yarra if it was permitted.

"You're not a prisoner," Yarra said. "Go wherever you like, but stay within sight of camp. Alqamar has charged me to keep you safe."

Honifa had yet to meet her host and she wondered how Simon had come to make the acquaintance of such a notorious brigand.

"Is Zalam Alqamar here?" she asked.

"He comes and goes," Yarra said with a slow, dreamy smile. "When he's ready, he'll send for you."

"You're very fond of him, aren't you?" Honifa teased.

Yarra's face grew serious. "Fond is the wrong word," she said. "I worship him. All of us here do. He gave us our lives and restored our liberty. He has the strength of ten men, the beauty of a prince, and a heart as fierce as a mountain lion."

"I see," Honifa said. She couldn't wait to make the

acquaintance of this paragon.

"He's like a giant tree, and I'm an insignificant vine twining around him," Yarra went on almost prayerfully. Each day, I dig my roots deeper, and soon, I shall mesh so tightly with him that only an ax can cut me away."

"I see," Honifa said again, at a loss for words in the face of Yarra's determined adoration. She had sacrificed everything for one night with Tor, but would she die for him? Honifa didn't think so. She believed in life.

"So," Yarra said, clapping her hands together, breaking her trance. "Go! Walk around. Smell the air."

"I have no clothing," Honifa said. "Only this nightshirt I came in. My *haik* is gone."

"Those ugly things," Yarra said disgustedly. "Women here disdain such garments. We dress as we please. Only Alqamar goes about with his face covered and that's by necessity."

Yarra herself, Honifa noticed, wore short leather pants and a tooled vest. Her arms and legs were bare.

"I'll bring you something loose and comfortable," she said. "Since you're so fat."

Honifa thanked her, a little halfheartedly. She supposed she was as fat as a Nile hippopotamus and much less attractive; nevertheless, she hoped Yarra would return with something pretty as well as comfortable.

As Ahmed's wife, she'd felt stifled, compelled to sacrifice whatever charm and beauty she may have possessed to his sense of propriety. After they were married, he no longer gazed at her with burning eyes, winked at her behind his mother's back, or reached under the table to stroke her knee. When he thrust himself into her at night, he squeezed his eyes shut and flattened his lips. Honifa wondered if his expression was one of passion or pain. There were mirrors all around Madame Hassan's house, but Honifa had stopped looking into them, afraid of her drawn, pale face, and ballooning form. At Alqamar's camp, however, she'd begun to feel womanly again, and not only because Tor's child stirred within her. She sensed that she was secure in this hidden outpost and she wondered what adventures awaited her beyond the cave.

"Put these on," Yarra said, tossing Honifa a brocaded shirt and a pair of voluminous, knee-length *sulwar* trousers with a wide, drawstring waistband.

The filmy pants were the delicate coral of ripe mangoes and the emerald green shirt covered her stomach but left her throat and slender arms exposed. Honifa plaited her hair, pulled on her sandals, and ventured out to meet a new world.

****

Alqamar's headquarters were set in a declivity ringed by hills beyond which the peaks of the Rif Mountains rose against a storm-gray sky. Honifa strolled past small campfires where women roasted coffee or suckled infants. She spotted a few older children seated together sharing their morning meal, and several men talking quietly. Stately Ibo tribesmen mingled with the fine-boned people of Amhara; powerful Samburu in loincloths bent their heads in conversation with robed Somlais, and fair-skinned Berbers bowed cordially to blue-black Afar.

Honifa saw men limping on bandaged limbs, their

backs scarred by whip lashings, and women whose necks bore the scarlet brand of iron chokes. All, she was told, had been rescued by Alqamar from slave ships and hidden here until they could make their way home. Too bad she never would do the same. She had broken the law, betrayed her husband and sullied his family name. If she returned to Nador, she'd be placing herself, her child, and Simon in mortal danger. Madame Hassan would not rest until she was dead.

Honifa moved among the freedmen and campfires and rued her lack of courage. Instead of trimming her mother-in-law's horned nails, she should have lopped each of the hag's ugly sausage toes from her ugly feet.

An elderly woman smiled and pointed to Honifa's stomach. "Why the angry face? God has blessed you."

"*Sabah elnoor, Jeddah.*" Honifa bowed respectfully, calling her grandmother.

"You must be happy for you are in a holy place."

Honifa nodded and moved on. That woman could indeed be my grandmother, she mused. If I had a grandmother. Simon always said he and Honifa were two alone against the world, unwanted by relatives, Scots and African alike, and good riddance to the lot of them. But she remembered that he had once opened an envelope and lovingly withdrawn a nosegay of purple flowers tied with ribbon.

"Heather," he'd whispered reverently wafting the dried petals under her nose. "You can still smell the gloaming on it."

Another time, he accepted delivery of pastries, crushed and beginning to mold.

"Dundee cakes," he grinned, biting into one, oblivious to the green parts.

"Where did it come from?" Honifa asked. "Who sent it?"

"Scotland," Simon replied, and, "No one."

After *Umma* died, her father had become bitter. He told Honifa he'd known for months that her mother, pregnant with their second child, was in precarious health. He'd begged his father in Scotland for passage to a hospital in Inverness but his pleas had been rejected. Ben Abbas took *Umma*'s body and the stillborn boy called Maliq to his own crypt in the Mellah, and Simon had eventually found peace ministering to the impoverished and sick of all races and tribes. In his quiet way, Honifa ruminated, her father was as much a champion of the oppressed as the noble Zalam Alqamar.

She stopped by a waterfall to watch a group of chattering laundresses slap and scrub in a sparkling pool. Behind them, several horses grazed in a bramble enclosure. Behind them, however, there was nothing, and she realized the camp was not in a valley as she had first believed, but in the midst of a cordillera with the high ridges of the Rif above her and endless, cloud-obscured slopes below. The desert was leagues away, the desert and her enemies. Her father was leagues away too, and the man she loved, whose ship might be bobbing like a speck on the distant ocean, was invisible and forever lost.

The baby moved and Honifa rested her hands atop her distended belly. "Hello, Little One. Enjoying our walk?"

"Talking to yourself again?" Yarra quipped, coming up beside her.

"Again?"

"You mutter in English all the time," Yarra said. "The Bedouins don't understand but I do. Who's the pirate?"

Honifa felt herself color. "No one."

"Your child's father?" Yarra persisted. "Your husband?"

"Yes," Honifa whispered. "No."

"Ah." Yarra nodded, taking Honifa's arm. "You've wandered far. Let's go back and you can tell me all about it."

****

In his foul cave, Davilow spat. How long did that heathen swine Alqamar intend to keep him here? He wasn't shackled, but his freedom was only an illusion, a cruel joke. Outside the blue man or some coal-skinned African beast stood watch day and night. Davilow could see the hills and smell the horses, but how to reach them! His tongue probing inflamed gums, his mind raced while he paced.

The little baggage, Yarra, appeared to be in charge. She rapped orders to the guards in a firm voice, accompanied the woman who brought his food, and watched him speculatively as he ate it. Davilow had to admit she was a fair slag. He rubbed himself at the thought of her lush contours tightly encased in leather, almost the same color as her skin. When he held his head just so, her body appeared naked in the firelight, brown flesh and brown leather in tasty fusion. He could throw her down, stuff her mouth with her vest, and bite her small, high breasts that were sure to taste like chocolate. Then he'd unlace the front of her britches and plow her like a cutter plowed the waves. There were no true men in this godforsaken encampment, only slaves without masters, oily Arabs, and godless Blackamoors who swung from trees. Davilow licked his lips. All he had to do was point his sturdy British staff at the hungry little mouth between Yarra's legs and the monkey bitch was his.

****

"Tell me about the man," Yarra urged. Honifa knew it was only an excuse for Yarra, in turn, to talk about Dark of the Moon. But she obliged. She lay against her pillows to ease the constant ache in her back that had sharpened since the beginning of summer.

"He's a sea captain," she said briefly. "We had one night and parted."

"Then he doesn't know? About the child you carry?"

Honifa shrugged. "It doesn't matter. I'll never see him again." She sat up. "But I'd like to see my father. I can't go back to Nador, but do you think Alqamar would bring my father here?"

"Perhaps," Yarra said. "I'll ask him. He likes to please me."

"He loves you?"

Yarra's face took on the mazed, dreamy expression it wore whenever she spoke of Alqamar. "Not yet. His heart is filled with anguish at the world's brutality. But he allows me to love him from afar. When I play the *gimbri* and sing my songs, the torment in his face disappears and, for now, that's enough."

Honifa shifted position. She wanted to tell Yarra everything about Tor Kendrick except the slaver part. She wanted to relive their brief, fierce encounter on the *Witch's Moon* with someone gripped in her own powerful love. But she was so tired. She, who had trekked everywhere with her herb basket, had been laid low by a simple morning's walk. Her chin dropped to her chest. Yarra took up her flute and in seconds, Honifa was asleep.

She opened her eyes to a grinding pressure in the pit of her stomach but before she was fully awake, it had gone. She waited but the sensation didn't return. The cave was empty and Honifa wondered how long before the Bedouin woman arrived to cook dinner. She ate a slice of persimmon and looked outside. The light was muted, the air filled with smoke from small pit fires dotting the encampment like glowworms. Honifa smelled roasting meat. Her mouth watered and she washed her hands in anticipation of supper.

In time, the Bedouin arrived with a basket of spiced lamb and a *djerba* of goat's milk. She stoked the beehive oven to life, threaded the meat onto skewers, and arranged them neatly on the coals.

"You're well?" she asked, running her palms over Honifa's stomach.

Honifa nodded.

"How long since you felt it move?"

"Not for a while."

The woman grunted. "Your time is near. Tonight, tomorrow, no more than a day. I'll bring my things and stay with you."

"What about Yarra?"

The woman grinned. "None of us will be seeing her now. Alqamar is in camp."

After they had eaten, the woman left to fetch clean bedding. Honifa undressed and pulled on a freshly laundered nightshirt that smelled of sunshine and mountain air. She tried to sleep but couldn't. She dug into the pillows for her *tassoufra*, pulled out the miniature of her parents, and gazed at their dear faces. "You're going to have a grandchild," she told them. Her fingers closed around the talisman Tor had given her. "Where are you?" she wondered aloud. "Would it please you to have a son?"

She replaced the treasured objects in the bag and looped the strings over her neck so they would be near her, against her skin and heart, when the baby was born. She curled on her side, but sleep continued to elude. Sighing, she rose, pulled a light blanket over her shoulders, and wandered outside.

Chapter 7

Honifa walked her usual route, past the embers of dying campfires, to the edge of the clearing and the little waterfall that spilled into the pool where the women washed clothes. The pool was inky black and glistened like polished obsidian. She waded in. Heaviness gripped her, a heaviness that built to pressure and then to stabbing pain. She knew what was happening; she had assisted her father at countless births and strove to remain calm and alert.

When the pain subsided, she retraced her steps to the cave where the Bedouin woman would be waiting, following the path she believed wound away from the pool. Instead, she came upon the banks of a small stream she had never seen before. No more than a rillet, it bubbled and frothed down into a tangle of dense underbrush. She traced its course in the opposite direction, upwards and away from the brush, reasoning that the rillet must be runoff from the pool and would eventually lead her back to camp. But she wasn't far along when another pain overtook her, longer and sharper than the first. She grasped a branch and held tightly, breathing rhythmically, pulling along the trail that seemed to be narrowing and ascending into blackness. Merciful Heaven, where was she?

The night engulfed her, dark as pitch. An owl hooted, tiny, invisible claws scratched yet she plowed on, each step more tortuous than the one before, her body clenching and relaxing with increasing frequency. Was she going to have her baby here in the woods, in the dark, alone? With a groan, she heaved herself to the top of a small rise and gaped in awe. She had landed on a peak that jutted into a domed sky, blue as a sapphire and flecked with stars. The fires of camp twinkled weakly far below as she lay beside the widened stream, now almost a river, and gave herself over to waves of grinding spasms.

Her screams rent her ears then faded as she drifted in and out of consciousness. She gripped the *tassoufra* and, with great effort, rolled to her side. Water gushed noisily at her ear. She scooped it onto her chest and face hoping the cool droplets would clear her head and focus her on the task before her, birthing the child. As pain engulfed her, she imagined a man watching her, broad and tall and close. The scent of wood smoke clung to his robes.

"Tor?" she whispered.

"Easy, woman," the man rasped. His voice was no more than a croak that issued from the back of his throat, harsh and low.

He jumped easily over the water and crouched on a rock beside her. Her arm was across her face but she could see that he was covered, head to foot, in black. Even his eyes were shrouded.

He laid his hands upon her. "You're with child."

"Not for long," Honifa gasped as a fresh spasm washed over her. "Can you help me to the camp, please?"

"It's a steep drop," he said. "We'll never make it down in the dark." He pulled her to him so her back rested against his chest. "You haven't much time."

Firmly held in the man's arms, leaning against his chest that was hard as the rock upon which he sat, Honifa felt comforted.

"The hour has come," she said. "But I can have this baby easily enough now you're here. My father's a physician and I've helped him many times. My name's Honifa. Who are you?"

He made no answer at first, only fingered the *tassoufra* at her neck for a moment, then drew her closer, close enough for Honifa to feel the pounding of his heart. Finally, he lifted her into his arms.

"I'm Zalam Alqamar. My cave is nearby. You can have the babe there."

****

Throughout the night, Honifa lay on a blanket in Alqamar's cave, alternately writhing and dozing. In quiet moments he read to her the poetry of Omar and Castelaigne, and humorous passages from the diary of a man called Samuel Pepys that made her giggle through her discomfort. Alqamar's dark, rasping voice and masked visage focused her attention, but sometimes her eyes strayed to her surroundings, to the Spartan cave, so far from the ocean, that would be the birthplace of Tor's child.

"My mother-in-law wants to kill me. A blue man rescued me from her garden and brought me to your camp," Honifa said. "My father arranged it but I don't know how."

"The Tuareg is my second in command," Alqamar said. "Ben Abbas is one of us. He conceals freed slaves in his cellar until we can take them out. Now rest."

"Dear ben Abbas," Honifa murmured drowsily.

She slept briefly. When she awoke, he held a bowl to her lips and she sipped a cool, mild brew that tasted like spiced ale. The drink blunted her pain and loosened her tongue. She told Alqamar about Tor and, delicately, about her single night of soaring pleasure. "It was nearly *Duhl Hija* before I knew for certain that the captain of the *Witch's Moon* had planted his seed in me," she recounted softly. "My husband was already astride his donkey, on his way to the wedding banquet. There was no time to find Tor, no way to know if he even cared."

"You think men so heartless?" Alqamar asked.

"You aren't heartless," Honifa replied and grasped his hands as a fresh paroxysm seared through her. He raised her nightshirt and held her thighs apart, touching her gently.

"Not yet, Honifa, but soon. Tell me about Nador and your life there."

And she did. She spoke of her mother and little brother gone to heaven, and of her love for Ahmed, a love of friendship and fealty now soured. She told how Simon had introduced her to the pharmacy of nature and tried to explain the depths of joy she felt walking the banks of the Moulouya gathering herbs, her steps light with the song of morning larks and sweet breezes.

"I understand," Alqamar said. "There is nothing so fine as freedom, as the wind and the rain and the burning sun on your back, the smell of good meat roasting, laughter and love, and endless, open days to live as you please."

"Yes," Honifa breathed. "Oh, yes!" This man who hid his face from her possessed a kindred spirit. "I didn't know that my child's father was a slave trader," she confessed, biting her lip. "I hate what he does, stealing young men and women with small children from their homes and subjecting them to the most heinous cruelty before selling them like fettered chickens. The Holy Book tells us that animals are soulless, but even they are not so wicked as that. And yet,"—she covered her head with her hands— "if I were to see Tor Kendrick again, I would run to him and entreat him to love me as he did aboard his ship." She beat her breast in anguish. "Oh, I'm hateful; no better than he!"

A stabbing pain seized her and she gathered herself to meet it. Alqamar knelt and held open her thighs.

"Hush, now. Don't waste strength on recriminations. I too abhor slavery. I'm unfamiliar with this Captain Kendrick but God has fashioned each of us as we are and we do what we must. Now push!"

Honifa bore down with all her strength, grunting and panting more times than she could count until the baby gushed from her slick as an eel.

"You have a son," Alqamar said.

His voice caught and his hands trembled as he looked down at the tiny boy in a kind of dazed rapture, clasping it to him until Honifa held out her arms. Her child was golden as a sheaf of wheat and heavy as a bear cub. Alqamar shook off his stupor and took away the afterbirth, washed mother and babe, and then wrapped them warmly in his robe.

"Thank you," she said in a haze of joy and fatigue.

Alqamar loomed above her, imposing as a monument, covered in black from his turbaned head to his heavy boots. The hood of his robe had fallen to his shoulders and Honifa strained to see his eyes through the gauze mask. But he turned abruptly and ducked from the cave into the night.

Chapter 8

Honifa's son, Maliq, named for her brother that never saw day, was nearly six months old. He kicked his chubby legs and smiled with Tor's mouth and her speckled eyes. The Bedouin woman had returned to her desert homeland, but before she left, she gifted Honifa with a sturdy camel-skin sling with which to carry Maliq on her back or against her chest while her hands remained free for gathering herbs. Alqamar visited often, bringing presents; a silver rattle for Maliq, a silken dress for her in shades of turquoise and rust to match the colors of her eyes. It seemed to her that when he held Maliq, he was about to let his mask slip, the actual as well as the internal one. But he never did. Dark of the Moon remained an enigmatic outlaw.

One day, he brought someone along with him, the old woman Honifa had met on her first day out of her cave. She asked Honifa to call her Jeddah, and said she was the camp's medicine woman. Grinning toothlessly, she deposited a sack of her belongings beside the fire.

"My aged bones are weak. I'm too old to dig rhizomes or climb for the youngest shoots. Alqamar tells me you have medicine-making skills. Let's join together and learn from one another."

Honifa and Jeddah established a modest dispensary and their days fell into a pleasant rhythm. Honifa hadn't seen or heard from her father since her escape though she'd sent word to Simon via the blue man that he was grandfather to a healthy boy.

"I keep asking Alqamar to bring my father here," she complained to Jeddah one day as they gathered feather fern on the rise above the washing pool. "But he doesn't answer me. Do you think I should tell Yarra? Maybe he'll listen to her."

"Don't depend on Yarra, especially when she's with Alqamar." Jeddah chuckled. "She loses track of things."

Honifa shifted Maliq, heavily asleep against her breast. Her eyes followed the bank of the rillet that became a stream high above the camp near Alqamar's hidden cave.

"I suppose I'll have to ask him myself," she said. She handed Jeddah her basket. "Can you take Maliq while I climb up?"

"I don't believe Alqamar welcomes uninvited callers," Jeddah warned.

"He's been very generous. And, anyway, he visits *us* whenever he likes."

The old woman bared her pink gums. "Zalam Alqamar can do what he wants. He commands and we obey."

But Honifa's mind was made up. "The man's a liberator, not a demagogue," Honifa responded heatedly. "He claims to believe in a person's right to be happy, and my father will make me happy." She untied her sling and strapped Maliq onto Jeddah's back. "I'm going up there right this minute. Can you manage?"

Jeddah's eyes moved from Honifa's determined face up to the mountain peak. "I can manage," she said slyly. "The question is, can you?"

****

Honifa climbed the path with broad, resolute steps, Jeddah's words prickling her like thistle burrs. *Alqamar commands and we obey*. Well, the great Dark of the Moon may have everyone else in camp under a spell, but he was only a man, a wonderful man to be sure, despite his vigilant reserve that colored their conversation with circumspection, and his words with calculation. If she knew nothing of the leonine slaver she had surrendered to beyond the pleasure of his body and the horror of his calling, she knew even less of Zalam Alqamar. He could be Copt or Egyptian, Tunisian, or possibly Libyan. He read books in English, Spanish and French as well as Arabic, and he was by turns tender and fierce, suspicious, welcoming, and above all intriguing. He stirred in Honifa a longing to know him better, as well as a longing of another sort, one she believed that, after Tor, she would never experience again.

A mixture of excitement and intransigence propelled Honifa up the path. If Alqamar refused to bring Simon to her, she would appeal to logic and demand he take her to him. Simon had arranged her rescue after all; he had a right to see for himself that his daughter and grandchild were well.

At the top of the rise, a gray void of sky enveloped her, studded not with stars like the last time she had been in this place, but with jackdaws and a lone, circling hawk. A screen of mist obscured the camp below and Honifa felt momentarily disoriented, as though suspended in midair. Across a rubble-strewn clearing, she saw a thin ribbon of smoke threading from a cleft in the rock; Alqamar's cave.

She moved toward it, then paused. Her *sulwar* trousers were torn and dirty and now that her stomach had shrunken, they drooped over her ankles. She hiked them up and wrapped the drawstring around the several layers of extraneous cloth that bunched at her waist. By contrast, the leather vest she'd borrowed from Yarra was too small and barely concealed her breasts. Her hands and feet were filthy, and leaves and twigs stuck in her hair. Maybe she was being hasty. Maybe she should go back down, have a bath, scrape the mud from her nails, and cover her wild curls with a scarf. She was having second thoughts about her mission when she heard angry words emanating from Alqamar's cave.

"Damn and blast you for a wily traitor!" a man shouted. "You can't keep me here against my will. Give me back my ship."

Honifa slunk into the bushes and listened.

"We had an agreement," the man continued. His voice was curiously high-pitched and imbued with a kind of desperate bravado. "Release me and I won't let it be known what a scurvy turncoat, what a lying, treacherous—"

Suddenly, the man gasped as if he'd been struck. Honifa watched as the blue man, called Tamajaq, emerged from the cave dragging a manacled, red-faced prisoner. The prisoner had limp, black hair, and a trimmed, mud-colored beard. He wasn't tall but solidly built with a neck like a bull's and spindly, bowed legs. He tried to shake off his jailer but the blue man propelled him forcibly across the clearing toward Honifa.

"Good Morning, sister," Tamajaq said pleasantly, pausing directly in front of where she was hiding.

"What are you doing here?"

Honifa poked her head out of the brush and took a step forward. She shook leaves from her clothing and pushed back her hair.

"*Sabah elnoor, Akh,*" she said, greeting the Tuareg in their native dialect and calling him brother. "I wish to speak to Alqamar."

The corners of Tamajaq's eyes crinkled with mirth. "Go home, Miss. When he wants you, he will summon you."

Honifa bristled. "If he's in there, I insist he see me now!" She lifted her foot, to stamp it or to push past Tamajaq, she wasn't sure, but before she was able to set it down again, the blue man appeared to change his mind.

"Stay where you are," he cautioned, pulling a length of chain from his robe and securing the prisoner to a tree with a heavy padlock. "I'll have a word with Dark of the Moon." He plucked a pinecone from Honifa's vest, obviously discomfited by her intention to appear in the emperor's presence looking like a drudge. Muttering, she tightened the drawstring on her *sulwar*.

Tamajaq's grin returned. "That's a good start. See to your hair as well." He jerked his chin at the prisoner. "And keep away from this fancy-pants."

Honifa raked her fingers through her hair and shook the worst of the underbrush from her clothing. The chained man leered at her, his mouth a gaping hole of blackened stumps.

"What's a tasty tart like you want with the likes of an outlaw, darlin'?" he said. "I'm worth ten of that jackanapes. I had a chest full of gold on the *Dover Star* and I can get more." He lunged the length of his chain, expelling fetid breaths into the air. "Though once you have a taste o' Royce Davilow's battering ram, I'll wager it won't be me money you'll want."

Honifa recoiled. The prisoner, though dirty, was dressed more like a nobleman than a felon, in a frock coat with brass buttons and fine-spun though torn hose. There were silver buckles on his shoes and his soiled stock was ruffled and, quite possibly silk. He didn't look like a rescued slave; more like some sort of miscreant who'd offended Alqamar. Then she remembered. The man called Royce Davilow was a slaver and his ship, the *Dover Star,* carried slaves, as did the *Witch's Moon.* A spark flared in Honifa, then quickly died.

She wanted no discourse with Davilow unless he knew something of Tor. But what did that matter? If some astounding quirk of fate planted Tor at her side at this very moment, he'd surely scorn her, a married, disheveled runaway. He was a creature of the open sea, a vagabond, and a slaver. He wouldn't want her and she didn't want him either. Whatever destiny they shared was not for this turn of the Wheel. She might dream of ravishment in Tor's arms, but she'd never expose Maliq to his father's profession.

Honifa turned expectantly as the Tuareg emerged from Alqamar's cave. Behind him, a sudden shaft of sunlight sliced through the waning mist like a blade, obscuring rather than illuminating what lay beyond it.

"Dark of the Moon will see you," Tamajaq said. "Go to him."

Honifa hesitated, tugging again at her vest, and rubbing her mud-caked sandals back and forth on the ground.

"Are you going in or not?" the blue man said. He unwound the prisoner's chain.

Davilow winked at her. "Stay here with me, girlie."

Giving the odious slaver wide berth, she walked, shoulders high, to the mouth of Alqamar's cave. Unfortunately, the opening was low and she had to stoop to enter, destroying the imperious impression she'd hoped to convey.

"*Ahlanwasahlan,*" Alqamar welcomed Honifa as she blinked in the sudden dimness.

He stood by the glowing embers of the pit fire, tall and broad as an ebony obelisk, hooded and masked, hands low on his hips, looking anything but welcoming. Honifa's breath caught and apprehension gnawed at her stomach. She bowed her head.

"God's peace, good fortune, heavenly mercy, and a host of blessings," she pronounced with required formality.

She thought she heard Alqamar chuckle but when she looked up, he was as motionless and silent as before. She cleared her throat.

"Many thanks for all you have done for me," she began.

Alqamar made no response, but, as always, he watched her with a kind of fierce, unnerving absorption.

"I dare to ask another favor of Dark of the Moon and hope you'll forgive me for my boldness," she announced, but not as forcefully as she'd planned.

Something dangerously predatory in Alqamar's stillness always made her wary. She'd been alone with the man only once before, the day he'd helped deliver Maliq. Yet now, in the same, spare cave, without Jeddah or her son or anyone else to diffuse his potent magnetism, Honifa proceeded with caution, her former bluster notwithstanding.

"I have no right but only you can help me," she continued, hating the hesitancy in her tone. She took a step forward and felt rather than saw his muscles tighten. "I'm aware that I can't leave this encampment but I'd like to see my father. Please, can you bring him to me?"

Alqamar said nothing. What she could see of his eyes behind the gauze mask were hard and colorless as diamonds.

"Why don't you answer?" she entreated. "The favor I ask is small, especially for one such as you." She attempted a small shrug. "I thought we were friends."

He shook his head. "An outlaw has no friends."

"That's not true. What of the blue man?"

"Tamajaq is my brother."

She scoffed. "The Tuareg are more brothers to me than to you. I can tell by your accent that you're Mauritanian or perhaps from some province close to Spain." She smiled a little when she saw his shoulders relax. "I'm grateful that you helped me bring Maliq into this world. I can never repay you." She cleared her throat and rubbed the back of her neck.

"Are you in pain, Honifa?" he asked, concern smoothing his scratchy voice.

Now she started to relax. This was Zalam Alqamar, not some crude villain. He had held her newborn in his arms and shared her joy at his birth.

"It's only that you are so tall and I have to tilt my head way back to see you. It hurts my neck."

He grunted what could have been a quick laugh

and sank onto the pine rushes. Honifa sat opposite and prayed to find the words that would melt his heart. But before she could speak again, he posed a question.

"What makes you think you can never repay me, Honifa?" He bent forward and placed a hand heavy as a brand on her bare calf,.

She narrowed her gaze. Surely the great Alqamar was a better man than the foul Davilow with his silver buckles and stinking teeth. "I have nothing to give in exchange," she answered, opening her empty palms. "Your kindness shelters and feeds me." She pointedly picked a dead leaf from her baggy pantaloons. "Even the clothes I wear are from you."

This time his laugh rang loud and true. "I shall raid my stores for elegant jewels and patterned lengths of satin from Italy. Would that please you?"

She glanced at the hand that easily spanned her leg. "It would please me to see my father. If Tamajaq whisked me from Madame Hassan's garden, can he not whisk my father from his clinic under cover of darkness and—"

Alqamar withdrew his hand. "That would be foolhardy. And it will put Simon in grave danger. Have you forgotten that it was he who initiated your rescue? Ben Abbas will also come under suspicion and I can't risk losing a man who's crucial to my operation."

Honifa sighed.

"Madame Hassan's henchmen watch the clinic day and night hoping Simon will lead them to you," Alqamar continued. "They lurk outside ben Abbas' house and Bareed's Tavern. Your mother-in-law is bent on retribution. Don't underestimate her hatred."

Honifa beat her fists on the ground. "Oh, how I

wish she were dead!"

"A futile wish," Alqamar said mildly. "Better to kill Ahmed. His inheritance passes to an uncle who, I'm told, will banish his hated sister-in-law to impoverished relatives deep in the western desert. Without money, she is powerless to harm you or anyone else. You'll be a widow, free to come and go as you please."

"A widow?" Honifa's voice quivered. "Then Ahmed hasn't divorced me?"

"Not yet, though he forgets you with a second wife, a gift from his mother."

Honifa shifted uncomfortably.

"Madame Hassan can do to you what she pleases without fear of reprisal. You're still her daughter-in-law," Alqamar explained maddeningly. "Only Ahmed's death can release you. Shall I kill him for you? Such a favor I won't hesitate to grant."

Honifa pictured Ahmed as she had first seen him, a little boy bawling in the street the day his father was being buried. How could she do him harm no matter what kind of man he had become? She clasped her hands in prayer.

"Leave Ahmed alone, please," she said. "Don't hurt him, I beg of you."

Alqamar's manner had gone from imperious to teasing to formal. But now, something menacing crept into his tone.

"How prettily you plead for his life, this husband from whom I helped you escape. Is it possible that you love him still?"

"No," she hastened to explain. "I never loved him as a wife. If I did, I wouldn't be in this predicament. I would have never lain with a slaver and my son would be a true Hassan."

"Yet you can't bear to see him harmed. You ask a great deal of me, Honifa; your safety, the company of your father, and assurances that your husband not be killed." He crossed his arms. "The man himself is of no consequence to me. But I will do nothing to jeopardize the safety of my camp."

Honifa listened to the hiss and crackle of the fire. She had failed. She'd meant to be brave and clever, demand her due, or, at the very least, soften Alqamar's heart. But she had plunged headlong as always, acted without thinking, and lost. She huddled on the floor, dispirited, knowing she should leave. Then, from above, as soft and warm as the sirocco, Alqamar whispered an invitation.

"Come to me tonight."

He was standing above her, hooded and inscrutable as ever. Yet something subtle had changed in the air between them. He offered his hand and helped her stand.

"When the camp sleeps, take your lantern and go to the washing pool. Wait for me there."

"Tonight?"

"If you dare."

She drew herself up. "And if I refuse?"

He leaned back against the table, his long legs crossed at the ankles, a picture of unconcern. "No one refuses me."

Chapter 9

Twilight descended upon the camp of Zalam Alqamar. In her cave, Honifa prepared the evening meal while Jeddah tickled Maliq with a pigeon feather. His round belly shook and his pudgy legs pumped the air.

"Stop that," Honifa shot. "Or he won't sleep."

"You're full of thorns tonight," Jeddah observed. "Have you been moving your bowels?"

"Give him to me," Honifa demanded crossly, taking her son into her arms. "Serve yourself. Food's ready."

"It's Alqamar, isn't it?" Jeddah said, spooning porridge of wheat berries and root vegetables into her bowl. "His refusal to dance to your tune has killed your appetite."

It was true. Honifa's stomach had turned to water. Alqamar's invitation was keeping her on edge. She mashed a bit of sweet potato between her fingers and fed it to Maliq. He swallowed and opened his mouth for more. "Greedy little bear," she said, giving the child her breast. In time, his eyelids fluttered, and his rosy lips went slack. She smoothed his fuzz of butterscotch hair and laid him gently in his cradle. Jeddah, too, dozed. Honifa set a basin of water to simmer and stripped off her clothes. It had been a tiring, disappointing day. A bath would calm her.

She scrubbed the grime from her skin and sluiced water over her neck and across her breasts, down her belly, and between her legs. There was no hip bath in Alqamar's camp, but a cloth dipped in water sweetened with tincture of mint and ambergris and run over the sensitive places on her body, her nipples, and the bud of Athta where the soul of the goddess of Venus resided, reminded her that the sensations Tor aroused had returned to her body a thousand-fold. She longed for his hands and mouth upon her, for his commanding staff to open and inhabit her, to fill and claim her until they were one. Exasperated, she wrung out the cloth and emptied the basin. Jeddah lifted her feet and grumbled.

"You trying to drown me, child?"

Honifa wiped the floor, wound her damp hair into plaits, and massaged her skin with almond lotion. She put on one of the dresses Alqamar had given her, a long, red *abaya,* whose neckline, and side slits were embroidered with sunflowers and examined her reflection in the tall glass. She was slender again, though her breasts were still large and heavy with milk. Her skin, which had paled during her entombment at Madame Hassan's, shone like oiled sandalwood, and the roundness of her face had given way to her former, well-defined cheekbones. Above them, her eyes slanted sharply upwards; below them, her mouth was full and lushly curved. Honifa smiled. She was no beauty, no pale Queen Zubeydah, or blue-eyed lassie of Glen Garioch. But she had her own appeal and tonight, it pleased her.

"You look like the cat that knocked over the cream pitcher," Jeddah called from her pile of bedding. "You've dressed up and used all the drinking water for your bath."

"I'm going back to visit Alqamar."

Honifa had decided to meet Alqamar but not let him touch her. His massive body and dark magnetism played havoc with her nerves. She'd keep her distance, behave rationally, and remind him that she spent her days in service of his camp. Her poultices and potions made it possible for the slaves to heal quickly and return home, and for this service, she deserved a simple favor, the presence of her father in whatever way he deemed best. She would not argue the method. If she could, she'd plug her ears against the rasp in his voice that vibrated over her flesh like Yarra's *gimbri*.

"I thought Dark of the Moon sent you packing," Jeddah chuckled. She sat up and hugged her knees. "Did I ever tell you how I came to meet him?" she asked mildly.

"Yes," Honifa said. "You've told me. Many times."

"The slavers raided my village and stole my daughter and her husband," Jeddah began, ignoring Honifa's forbearing sigh. "They returned a year later for my grandson. I can still hear his pitiful cries and see his little legs disappear into the sack as they carried him off. I had no one left and I vowed to bring the boy back." Jeddah spat into the fire and sparks sizzled. "I found him in Nador, beaten and starved, the last in a coffle and ready to be loaded on the *Dover Star*. I pleaded with Captain Davilow. He laughed, took all my money, and kicked me to the ground. That night, I sought out Zalam Alqamar. My troubles moved his great heart and before the moon rose that very night, he raided the *Dover Star* and dragged her captain and crew ashore in chains. My grandson is safe in his village now, with a family who can teach him to be a man."

"It's a wonderful story, Jeddah," Honifa said. "I know it by heart."

"Yes, but not the last part. I never told you what Alqamar did to the men of the *Dover Star*. I never told you all of it." Jeddah poked the fire with a stick and seemed to read appalling images in the flames. "He beat them bloody with his fists, every last one of them, all by himself until he was exhausted and could barely raise his arms. Their screams were wrenching. I had to cover my grandson's ears. Then he set the ship adrift, torched her sails, and let her burn to cinders. "Jeddah blinked and the firelight shone on her tears. "Alqamar saved my grandson but he's a tortured man; some might say brutal. His heart is full of vengeance, too full for tenderness."

Honifa shuddered. The inhumanity of slavery had hardened Alqamar and yet his voice softened when he spoke of his mountains and the wildness of the forest. Dark of the Moon treasured freedom and lived his life in service of it. Surely, he would let her go.

****

The air was cool and damp as Honifa stepped carefully around dying pit fires. Most of the camp's inhabitants were in their caves, but a few men slept on the ground, curled under their robes. A light breeze stirred the pines and tickled the nape of her neck. Honifa shivered, partly from the cold but also, she knew, from fear. When she reached the washing pool, she raised her candle and looked around her. It was quiet; mist obscured the top of the waterfall and she shivered as drops splashed her face. She should have worn her cape, she thought, setting the candle on a stone, and rubbing her arms. She was foolish to have come in a delicate *abaya*, perhaps foolish to have come at all. There was no telling what mood Alqamar would be in. He might listen to her reasonably, even converse with her, or he might send her packing. The idea was reprehensible. She wouldn't allow that to happen, nor would she succumb to seduction.

Her low candle illuminated a small circle on the ground, and Honifa's eyes widened as a pair of boots stepped into it. Alqamar moved through the light, soundless as a panther, until he stood beside her.

"I've been waiting for you," he said in his deep, gravelly voice.

"Jeddah waits for me, too," she said nervously. "I told her where I was going and that I'd be back faster than it takes for a cloud to swallow the moon."

He took up her candle and began to walk around the edge of the pool toward the copse. "You'll be longer than that. Follow me."

She kept her eyes on the glimmering beam of the candle, ignoring the thrumming of her heart and mentally rearranging the words of her plea to best advantage. Just past the waterfall, Alqamar shone the candle on an opening in the rock no taller than a sheep. He bent nearly double and ducked inside, then reached out his hand to Honifa.

"It's a short way from here," he said, leading her sideways through a narrow passage. "Keep your head down."

They crept through a tunnel cut into the rock behind the waterfall. Honifa heard it gushing what seemed like a handbreadth away. In due course,

Alqamar raised the candle above his head. They were in a cavern. Water-darkened cliffs vaulted above them and bats swooped and screeched. Honifa put an arm over her head. Without a word, Alqamar started down another passageway, this one tall and narrow. The sleeves of Honifa's dress brushed against moist stones as she plowed after him, on and on, her eyes glued to the dimly lighted path, wondering if they were bound for the hellish depths of *Gahenna.*

Their journey was fraught with turns and switchbacks, steep inclines, and careening descents. Conversation was impossible. When she paused for a moment to catch her breath, she saw that the passage behind her was shrouded in darkness. She would never be able to find her way back but she trudged on gamely, fighting panic by thinking of Maliq asleep in his cradle, his pink mouth pursed like a delicate bud, his pale lashes fluttering on his cheeks.

"Here," Alqamar said, halting so suddenly she nearly fell into him. "Hold the light while I move the stone."

He splayed his huge hands against a boulder the size of a man, rolled it away, and pulled her into a widened cavity. For a moment, he stood before her, solid and unknowable as the godforsaken place he'd brought her to. Then he pinched the candle and all light died. The dark was heavy and thick as blood; Honifa held her hand before her face and saw nothing. The air smelled of pine and wood smoke and her own sweat mingled with almond lotion.

"Are you afraid?" Alqamar said.

Her pulse threaded and she knew an unaccountable shiver of desire.

"I don't know."

He stirred and she heard the rustling of cloth and felt his warm breath as he drew close. She reached up to touch his face but he grasped her wrists and pressed his lips against her palms. His mouth was soft and warm, his chin clean-shaven. For a moment, she held his face like a chalice. She had held Tor's face in just such a manner, caressing its rough planes and angles. How she had wanted him! And now she wanted Alqamar.

He slid his hands down her breasts, clasped her waist, and lifted her off her feet. His heart beating against hers, he tasted the hollow of her throat and neck. When he claimed her mouth, Honifa moaned and clung to him, every nerve in her body attuned to his hardness and strength and the crushing dominance of his kiss.

Her brain reeled from one turbulent notion to another. *What am I doing! I meant only to talk to him. My legs are like water. My flesh burns. Oh heavenly torment! I must stop him.*

Alqamar's arms were vises. He sank with her to the ground, his mouth biting and sucking, his tongue teasingly insistent. Honifa was surprised when she was laid, not on rubble but upon a lush carpet of fur, thick and wooly, like the coat of a lamb. She lay back and gripped the carpet as he undid her sandals, kissed her insteps, and ran his hands up her legs, pushing the hem of her *abaya* to her knees, her thighs, her hips. He rubbed his hands across her belly and smoothed the pad of flesh between her legs, parting the soft skin with his thumbs and teasing the tender inner flesh. Honifa tensed as waves of pleasure coursed through her. She dug her fingers into the fur and raised herself to him.

Damn freedom, she thought wildly. It had been too long.

"Please," she groaned. "Oh, please."

She lifted her arms and he pulled off her dress. He raked his hands down her back, cupped her buttocks, and stroked her breasts, all the while probing every curve and crevice of her body. Wherever he touched, she burned, and in the darkness, there was only him, his rough hands and smooth mouth, his breathing and heated murmurings, his fingers dipping inside of her, his tongue. Honifa abandoned herself to exquisite sensations of arousal and release, abandoned herself to Alqamar as she had to Tor, and fires she'd thought dead blazed anew.

Senses alive, her body trembled as she felt his naked skin against hers, and her heart leapt with joy. She feathered the silken hairs, soft as meadow grass, on the iron of his chest, and explored the knotted muscles of his arms and broad, deeply scarred back.

"You've been whipped," she breathed.

"Hush," he said, covering her mouth with his.

He entered her and Honifa's being was reduced to raw ecstasy, to the pounding thrusts of the man above her and the ferocity of her response. When he spent himself, he cried out her name, a cry that echoed in the depths of their subterranean cavern like the roar of a lion.

****

Honifa thought she may have slept, or traveled in her mind for a brief spate of time to another place, perhaps to the captain's cabin on the *Witch's Moon*. The rapture she had just experienced with Alqamar had been as intense and prolonged as the exaltation of her few hours with Tor Kendrick. Again and again, Alqamar had driven her to violent surrender, riding her like a stallion, then guiding her hips with masterful hands as she rode him. She turned in his arms and warmed herself against his body.

"Is it morning?" she asked dreamily.

"Almost," he answered, his breath sweet and pleasant on her face.

"It's so dark in here, yet the air is fresh."

Alqamar stroked her cheek. "This is a magic place, Honifa, known only to me, and now to you."

She smiled. "I'll never be able to find it without you."

"I'll bring you here as often as you like," he said.

"Tomorrow?"

Alqamar laughed and rolled away from her.

"I have business in Nador tomorrow," he said. "Important business."

"What's so important as this?" she purred, sitting up and wrapping herself in the lambskin.

Without Alqamar's arms around her, she was cold. She heard him pulling on his clothes. Can he see in the dark, she wondered, like a jungle cat.

He lit the candle. "I'll send for you when I return," he said flatly. He was Dark of the Moon again, distant, unknowable.

"Let me see your face," she entreated.

"It's best you don't. I'm a wanted man. From the Cape to the Pillars of Hercules, north across the ocean and east to the Black Sea, there's a price on my head."

"I know; I've seen the posters. But I would never betray you."

He touched her cheek and trailed his knuckles

down her throat. She let the sheepskin fall, and he stroked her breast.

"I don't believe you would," he said. "But it's safer for you this way. I protect what's mine."

"Am I yours, Alqamar?" Honifa asked. She had meant to sound coquettish but her voice choked with wonder.

"If you want to be, Honifa," he replied gravely. "Think on it. Think long and hard. I'm not a man to be toyed with. Pledge yourself to me and only death can break the bond." He rose abruptly and ducked through the low doorway that had been sealed with a stone. "Dress yourself," he ordered.

Stung by her lover's retreat, Honifa dragged her *abaya* over her head, strapped on her sandals, and joined Alqamar by the heavy stone. She had not asked about her father, and the word "freedom" had never entered her mind until now.

"Take that passage," he said, handing her the lantern and pointing to the way they had come. "Turn always to the left and you'll find the waterfall and the pool."

"Aren't you coming?" she asked.

"I'll watch until your light disappears."

"But—" She took a step toward him. What had just happened in the tiny cave had been miraculous. The moment deserved something more, a parting kiss, words of love. *If* he loved her. Did she love him? All she knew was that not since Tor had she felt such contentment, such a blissful sense of balance and rightness. "Must we part so abruptly?" was all she managed to say.

He touched her hair with his gloved hand. "Think

about what I said, Honifa. It might be that we'll never need to part again." He kissed her lightly, his breath soft through his scarf. "Or it might be otherwise."

He walked away from her out of the lantern light and into blackness.

****

The sun was cresting the horizon when Honifa emerged at the waterfall. For only the second time in life, she knew a passion transcending reason. Her body ached from Alqamar's commanding touch; she had felt the weight of him and the glide of his skin under her fingers, so smooth but for the welts on his back that were so like Tor's.

"You're up early."

Honifa turned to the familiar voice. Yarra was squatting on her heels outside her cave, angrily whittling a block of wood.

"Greetings, Yarra," Honifa said. "I couldn't sleep. You're up early, too."

"I haven't been to bed," Yarra grunted. "I was awake all night waiting for Alqamar, but he never came."

Honifa swallowed. "Perhaps he had important business."

Yarra jabbed the blade of her knife into the block with such force the handle vibrated like the string of a zither. "It had better not be with a woman."

Chapter 10

The handbills were everywhere, in every souk, along the waterfront, up and down Yom al A'had Street, even on the walls of the mosque where a sign was posted forbidding signs. You couldn't walk a step in Nador without being confronted by the crude drawings of a woman with the word *Reward* scrawled across her face. Three months ago, two of Hassan's spies had nailed one to the date palm outside Simon's door, and ever since, they'd been camping underneath it, watching his every move.

Reward for the Death or Capture of Honifa, first wife to Ahmed ben Hassan, Wanted for Crimes Against God and Nature.

He'd torn up the first bill and thrown it away, but he couldn't tear up all of them and there must have been hundreds.

"Why does Ahmed do this?" Simon complained to Malcolm Bareed, thrusting a crumpled poster across the bar.

"It's not the boy but his mother," Malcolm replied. "She leads him around by the nose; always has." He pulled a pint of lager and slid it to Simon. "Have you spoken to him?"

Simon took a long swallow. "I tried, but Madame Hassan won't open her door to me."

"What about ben Abbas?" Malcolm asked. "He has

influence. Maybe he can do something."

Simon sighed. "He's done enough already. He arranged for Honi's escape on condition that I never question him about it. Besides," Simon added, draining his glass, "I owe him two months' rent."

Malcolm nodded in bleak commiseration. "It's a sad business," he said. "But at least you know Honi is safe for now, and the babe."

At the mention of his grandson, Simon smiled weakly. "A little boy named Maliq after my own son that died. I'm chuffed, I am. I long to see them both."

Malcolm pulled another pint. "Go to ben Abbas," he urged. "The man has a good heart. He'll want to help."

Simon finished the second pint and wiped his mouth. "I may do that." He pushed a coin to Malcolm who pushed it back. "My money's no good at your clinic, man. What makes you think yours is good here? Come for supper tonight," Malcolm added. "Fawzia's making haggis. She does it with cumin but it's not too bad."

Closely shadowed by one of Madame Hassan's spies, Simon left Marhaba and walked uphill toward the home of ben Abbas. Most of the stalls and souks in the medina were closed for the evening but the ungodly wanted posters still glared at him as he made his way home. He passed a café where several young men in white *djubbhas* were smoking and playing dominoes. One of them was Ahmed. Simon greeted him but Ahmed kept his eyes on the tiles.

"Have you a moment?" Simon asked politely in English.

Ahmed slapped down a tile. "Go away, old man,"

he said in Arabic.

His companions snickered.

"How can you do this to Honi?" Simon persisted. "Have some compassion. She's your friend and I've been like a father to you."

Ahmed raised his head and stared at Simon with bloodshot eyes. "Honifa is no longer my friend," he muttered. "She's my wife and she has disgraced me. And my father is dead."

He sucked hungrily at the bubble pipe and expelled an ammoniated miasma of oily smoke. Simon leaned on the table and the young man shrunk away as if he were diseased.

"Please, Ahmed," Simon begged. "You cloud your judgment with opium and you let yourself be led by your mother's hatred of my daughter. Be a man and act honorably."

Ahmed scraped back his chair and stood unsteadily. "How dare you!" he cried, parting the folds of his *djubbha* to expose the pistol he carried. "If you were a man, you'd tell me where Honifa is." He fell into his chair as suddenly as he had arisen. "Go away," he slurred, this time in English. "Tell my wife to come home. Tell her by the Prophet's Holy Law she must do her duty to her husband. Tell her—" His head lolled. "Tell her—"

Shaking his head, Simon climbed toward the street where he and ben Abbas lived. All around, women squatted at braziers in their gardens, on rooftops, or in little kitchens, preparing supper. It had grown late and although he knew he'd be greeted warmly and invited to eat with the family, he didn't want to interrupt ben Abbas at table. He decided to go home, boil the two duck eggs a patient had given him, and root around the crumbs in the biscuit tin for pudding. But standing in the middle of his kitchen was a tall man in fawn britches and buckskin boots. His yellow hair was tied in a queue that fell to his shoulders and his massive arms were bare. A crude pendant hung from his neck.

"Excuse me, sir," Simon said. "How did you get in here? The clinic is closed."

The man turned and flashed a brilliant smile. "Dr. McLeod," he boomed, extending his hand. "I'm Tor Kendrick."

Simon shrunk back. This was the slaver who'd ravished Honi. "I should slit your throat," he spat.

Kendrick draped his arm around Simon's shoulders and hissed into his ear. "I'm not your enemy, man. I bring news of your daughter." He released Simon and bellowed loud enough for Madame Hassan's brace of spies to look up from their bread and beer. "I seek your services, my good doctor, as I'm told you're the best medicine man in the Algarve. My crew is down with the shivering shits and my ship smells like an old man's fart. Can you give me something to dry up the poor bastards?" He dangled a purse of coins and winked. "You won't regret it."

"Keep your voice down," Simon muttered, intrigued despite himself. If the man knew where Honi was…

He slammed the door shut and pressed his back against it. "What's this all about?"

Kendrick made certain the shutters were tightly closed before speaking. "Honifa wants to see you," he said.

His daughter's name in this vagabond's mouth

irritated Simon. "Why should I trust you?" he demanded hotly. "You deal in human traffic."

"So it is said," Kendrick replied coolly. "Believe what you will, but I have seen Honifa and she longs for the sight of her father. If you have courage, I can grant her wish."

"And what of the bairn? I'll not risk his safety," Simon said.

"Maliq is my son," Kendrick answered. "I protect what's mine."

"And my daughter whose life you ruined? Would you protect her as well?"

"You weary me, old man." Kendrick sighed. "Time is short. If you do exactly as I say, I'll bring you to her before sunup and have you back here day after that."

"How?" Simon asked.

Kendrick outlined a daring plan. He would make a big show of leaving the clinic with a sack of medicine for his crew. Then, he'd return later that night, loudly proclaiming that his men had been cured in only a matter of hours and that he wanted to show Simon his gratitude at the tavern with a fat bird and all the wine he could drink. They'd leave together with the spies, naturally, in pursuit. Once inside the tavern, however, Simon would board a donkey cart waiting in the alley and be on his way to Honifa. Kendrick would return to the clinic near dawn with one of his men slung over his shoulder, a red-haired Scot like Simon and pretending to be drunk. The next day, the man would open the clinic to admit the first patient, the real Simon returned from his visit with Honifa with his identity concealed under a hooded robe.

"No one will be the wiser, man," Kendrick said.

"Are you up for it?"

Simon studied the strapping man whose overpowering presence seemed to fill the small kitchen. He had the eyes of a lynx, direct, disarming eyes that belied his villainy. Could he be trusted? Kendrick drummed his fingers. Simon wasted no more time, picked up the breadknife and slipped it into his waistband.

"Lead on, MacDuff."

****

It was morning but still dark when Simon, whisked from amidst the unruly throng of patrons at Bareed's and loaded into a donkey cart, finally arrived at his destination. The Tuareg driver waved him down from the cart, jerked his thumb upward and ordered him to climb. Simon regarded the rocky path, steep as a ladder, that was cut into the side of a bluff.

"Is that where Honifa is?" he asked.

The blue man began to climb hand over hand and Simon, with no other choice, followed.

"If my daughter is up here," he wheezed, "the lass must have turned into a mountain goat."

"She's a sure-footed one," the Tuareg said, hauling Simon over the last rise to a clearing ringed on three sides by dark underbrush and stately pines.

The gray and pink and purple sky spread above them like a roof, and below the jagged precipice upon which they stood, verdant ledges descended to a panorama of distant woodlands, meandering watercourses, and golden plains. Simon gazed in awe. This is how God must feel, he thought, when he looks down from heaven.

"Go into that cave," the Tuareg directed, indicating

an opening in the cliff face. A soft circle of light shone from the cave's mouth.

"You sure she's in there?" Simon asked. He'd been forced to place his faith in Kendrick, grudging though it was, but he wasn't quite ready to trust this taciturn blue man.

"There's food and drink inside," the Tuareg said. "Help yourself and I'll bring Honifa to you. Do not leave under any circumstances."

The man's English was flawless; his tone was solemn and his dark eyes held no menace.

"Dinna fash yourself, laddie," Simon joked nervously. "It's not like I can tramp through a bit o' bracken and gorse and find me way to the wee kirk o' the glen, now, is it?"

Surprisingly, the Tuareg laughed, and Simon wondered exactly what kind of man he was dealing with who lived in surroundings suited to falcons and bats yet understood the language of Robert Burns. He duck-walked into the cave and was amazed when he stood erect, how like a home it was. A small pit fire burned and resin-scented smoke rose to a cleft in the rock roof high above him. A low table off to one side was set with crockery, utensils, and three clay *tagines*. Pillows, woven blankets, and animal skins covered the floor, and books and scrolls were neatly arranged on a ledge under an oil lamp. A bottle of wine cooled in a bucket. Was it for him? A glass of Rhenish would certainly calm his nerves.

"Honi!" he called. "Are you here? Did you make all this for me?"

No one answered but Simon was hungry, having never gotten around to boiling the two duck eggs.

Gingerly, he lifted the cover from the first *tagine*. It contained warm triangles of unleavened bread brushed with oil and sprinkled with coarse grains of salt. He stuffed one into his mouth. The second *tagine* held a stew of meat and yams, and the third, a round of soft cheese melting into a creamy sauce. Simon glanced around.

"Honi? Where are you?" he asked in a wavering voice.

Again, silence. He waited a few moments then heaped a plate, poured the wine, and began to eat. When he had finished, he lay back against the pillows and, without meaning to, fell asleep.

Chapter 11

Honifa had risen early to collect the delicate mugwort plant before its buds opened and the juices, so useful to repel insects, dried. Mugwort could also be brewed into a mildly soporific tea that stimulated blood flow and she hoped she could gather enough to ease the labor pains of the frightened young Ibo woman who was about to give birth to her first child.

She fed Maliq, strapped him onto her back, and with her basket and an ivory-handled knife, set out for the stream. She skirted the washing pool and tried to find the low opening that led to the hollow where, just two nights ago, Alqamar had made love to her. There were many caves strung in the hills behind the waterfall, some false and some large enough to fit a herd of camels, but none was low and narrow as the cave she sought. After a while, the horizon lightened. Streaks of purple fanned from the hills, muted to gray, and dissipated. Honifa hurried to the stream with Maliq giggling and bouncing on her back, his chubby feet gleefully pummeling.

She knew that Alqamar was in Nador. Nevertheless, she slept fitfully waiting for his summons, straining to hear his footfall outside the beads that hung at the mouth of her cave. She avoided Yarra, not a difficult undertaking since, when Yarra wasn't occupied running the camp, she'd taken to sulking in her quarters, no doubt waiting for the same footfall. The Yoruba had been kind in an offhanded way and protective, still ignorant of Honifa's feelings for the same man.

Memories of the rugged outlaw haunted Honifa. His breath on her naked skin, the length of him inside of her, the passion they had shared in that fierce darkness rekindled sensations she'd striven to suppress. She still dreamed of the captain of the *Witch's Moon*, the handsome giant in buckskin striding the gleaming decks of his tall ship, hair frosted with rime, skin weathered with spray, eyes like sunlight on a field of grain. But for Tor Kendrick, she would have bowed to the moving finger that wrote her destiny. But for Tor Kendrick, she might have come to enjoy Ahmed's lukewarm caresses, learned to withstand her mother-in-law's rages, and bided her time until the old woman died. Her son would have been Ahmed's son, and honorable motherhood might have led her to triumph in the house of Hassan.

Sighing, she added valerian to her basket and quantities of trailing willowhite, wondering just where among the hills and green valleys of camp hid the cave where Dark of the Moon had held her in his arms. Maliq started to fret and she sat on a bed of moss to nurse him until he dozed, heavy on her chest, his tiny fingers gripping the moon talisman. Gently, she took it from him and held it in her palm like an offering, to whom she didn't know, some almighty deity indifferent to her quandary. Despite his calling, she loved the man who'd tied the broken stone around her neck, and despite herself, she loved his sworn enemy.

The chariot of the sun raced toward dawn; one by

one, the stars twinkled off. Honifa mused on the bittersweet nectar fate had decreed she drink. The man she dreamed of transported men and women like sweepings in a waste pile, and the man who covered his face lived a life of secrecy and flight, distant from those who worshipped him, closed to any woman who would claim him. True love was whole, open, and unashamed. It was best she forget them both.

The sun rose white and opaque as a pearl. The rays were pleasant on her skin. She took a long, refreshing swallow of sage-mint tea and settled more comfortably, one arm around Maliq, the other pillowing her head. She watched a flock of far-off black birds, tiny as peppercorns against the feathery clouds, and was just about to close her eyes when she caught sight of the swirling hem of a blue robe. Rising, she greeted the blue man.

"Tamajaq, my brother. *Asalamu alaykum.*"

"*Wa Alaikum Salaam,*" he replied. "Come with me."

Honifa wrapped the sling around Maliq and settled him on her back.

"Is something wrong?" she questioned.

Tamajaq's mouth twitched in a half-smile. "Something is right. Please."

He bowed and bid her follow him through a thicket of myrtle to the place behind the washing pool where the stream narrowed and began to climb.

"This is the way to Alqamar's cave," she said.

"Yes," he replied. "Can you make it up the path with Maliq? I'll take your basket to Jeddah and fetch you this evening."

"This evening?" she said, handing over her basket.

She was elated at the prospect of being once again in the company of Dark of the Moon, but also confused at the manner of his invitation. It was daytime. Was he ready to reveal himself to her?

"Does Alqamar expect us to stay with him all day?" she asked Tamajaq.

"Do as you're told," he answered without answering and prodded her toward the cave with a warning not to leave it until he came for her at dusk.

"I don't understand," she said, but the blue man was done with words.

Curious, Honifa began her ascent, deep in speculation. Alqamar's cave was his refuge, a place that only the blue man dared visit uninvited. Even Yarra had never been inside. Was Honifa to be the new favorite, installed at Alqamar's command to cook and clean and wait upon his pleasure, primed and panting like a harem girl? The idea was at odds with her newly conceived notion of independence and also with her hunger to see him. Almost at the top of the path, she set her jaw and turned to climb down, jostling Maliq who let out a yelp. When she reached behind her to steady him, she felt a warm wetness in his wrappings, a heavy, malodorous wetness.

"Damn! Jeddah's been feeding you Muscat grapes again," she muttered and continued the few remaining steps to Alqamar's cave. Stooping, she peered inside. A glimmering lamp, a plate with a rind of cheese, and an empty wine glass told her he had just eaten. But where was he? She ducked through the opening and immediately noticed a pair of legs in scuffed shoes and badly mended hose sticking out from the far side of the table. They looked familiar. She inched closer. They looked…looked…

Simon opened his eyes and flung out his arms. "Honi! My sweet child. Oh, Thank God you're safe. I've worried so."

Tears ran down his cheeks. He embraced his daughter and grandson, reluctant to let them go. "Are you well, lass?" he said, his voice shaking. "And the bonny bairn?"

She unstrapped Maliq and carefully placed him in Simon's arms. Grandfather and grandson studied each other solemnly and broke into smiles at the same instant.

"His nose is just like *Umma*'s." Simon handed Maliq back to Honifa. "But he smells."

Honifa laughed. She laid Maliq on a blanket and cleaned him up, all the while grinning, talking with Simon, asking, and answering many questions. She told him about Jeddah and the clinic she had tried to model after his, and he glowed with pride. He said he was well enough and busy, that Malcolm Bareed invited him often for strange dinners of ginger neeps and curried souse. He dandled Maliq on his knee, sang him all the verses of *Rumble-Bumble,* and fed him pieces of salt bread. The day was spent in sweet reminiscence and fond silences. As shadows lengthened, Maliq slept and Honifa spoke of her longing to go home.

"Nador's no place for you now, lass. Best to stay here."

"But where is here?" she wailed. "I'm in the middle of the sky."

"You can't want a better champion than Dark of the Moon. And by the by, Tor Kendrick's not the *bamysot* I thought he was. It was he who organized this visit."

Simon recounted the ruse he and Kendrick had perpetrated on Madame Hassan's spies. "He did it for you and the bairn."

"Then he knows about Maliq," Honifa said, wide-eyed.

"Aye. But it's hard to tell how he feels. The man's a mystery."

Color began to suffuse Honifa's face. "Sometimes I imagine Tor lifting Maliq and swinging him over his head," she said wistfully. "They're laughing and so am I. He lifts me too and we're light as dandelions in his arms. Then the three of us mount a winged horse and ride over the moon to—" She stopped and regarded Simon through lowered lashes. "It's a stupid fantasy. I know Tor will never come here. Alqamar is his enemy."

She tried to turn up the lamp but her hand shook so badly Simon had to complete the task for her. Still trembling, she turned away from his searching gaze, and began to rock Maliq vigorously, and unnecessarily as the child was fast asleep.

"Easy, lass. You'll wake him," Simon said, gently taking the boy. "What ails you?"

"I never want to hear Tor Kendrick's name, not ever again," she cried. "Nor any man's name!"

Simon laid Maliq on the blanket. "Tell me."

"I'm a fool, Father," she admitted miserably. "I dream about Tor day and night. I look at Maliq and see his face, and yet I crave to see the face of the one who keeps me here in his camp."

Simon nodded. "This place is well-hidden, Honi. Do you know where you are?"

"Far away from where I long to be," she replied glumly.

"Well, you can't go home," he said. He told her about the posters calling for her death that hung side by side with Alqamar's.

"I can't believe Ahmed hates me enough to have me killed," she said.

"His mother does. I'm not sure what drives the boy."

"Then all hope is lost, isn't it?"

"Not forever, Honi. I'll talk to Kendrick when I return. There's a chance he can take us to London. England's far away, too far even for Madame Hassan."

"Leave home?" she replied glumly.

"We'll make a new home."

Honifa nodded thoughtfully. "Then why not to Scotland where you were born?"

"I'm not wanted there, Honi, and I'd never subject you to the cruelty your mother suffered when we were in Inverness." He stared into the flickering lamp flame a moment, then brightened. "I could open a clinic in the Cotswolds. Farmers are poor the world over but patients can always settle accounts with good meat and vegetables, just like here."

"Then let's do it," Honifa said warming. "Let's escape to England. I'll work alongside you."

The sky turned from gray to lavender and the cave filled with shadows. The blue man crept quietly inside.

"It's time to leave," he told Simon. "You'll be escorted down the mountain and driven back to Nador."

Simon held his daughter and grandchild close. When he released them, his face was tear-stained. "Guard yourself, lass. You can be impulsive, even reckless. I couldn't bear to see you harmed."

"You'll not forget about sailing to England, will you, Father? Although not on the *Witch's Moon*. Some other ship, perhaps.

Simon stroked Honifa's cheek and followed the blue man out.

****

Yarra had worn a gully deep as the Suguta Valley at the mouth of her cave. She paced and muttered, stopping occasionally to fire her knife into a pile of logs and wrench it out again. Alqamar had been home and not come to her, not once. He had listened thoughtfully to her report on the state of the camp, but when she'd invited him to share her evening meal, he gazed at her with sadness in his golden eyes and said, "No, Yarra. Save your *gimbri* for another tonight."

Four kinds of a jackass, she was! Alqamar was a lusty man spending long months at sea or astride the white mare Shabanou or her son, the magnificent stallion Sultan, leading caravans of freed slaves across the desert. Many women loved him but they were women of the voyage, transient and easily forgotten. Yarra was a trusted comrade who sang away her beloved's cares and soothed his weariness.

Yarra in Yoruba meant child. She was the last of twelve and her father had run out of names. When the marauders invaded, Alqamar had saved her although she'd been terrified of his mask and black robes and believed him Sango, the merciless god of thunder and lightning. He gave her a home in the Rif among others like herself, Yorubas and Mahi, Baribas, San and Fulani, Tarqui and Mandinka, all freed captives in awe of and indebted to Dark of the Moon. She learned to hunt with a bow, ride astride, and read and write at the hands of an Egyptian who traced his ancestry to Pharaoh Amenhotep. Many times, Yarra could have joined a convoy south to her homeland but elected to remain with Alqamar.

Five years passed before she confessed to loving him as a man. He'd smiled and said that someday a husband would steal her heart, and continued to reject her charms which only increased her longing. She'd begged philters and potions from shamans but nothing melted him.

Cursing her fate, Yarra jammed her knife into her boot. Evening's duties beckoned: securing the camp's perimeter; making certain all its inhabitants were accounted for, and standing guard over the English prisoner while he ate his supper. She would have preferred to slit his throat, but Alqamar claimed that Davilow had his uses.

In a foul temper, she strode to the Englishman's cave, took the basket of provisions from the Kikuyu posted outside the entrance, and set it down with a thump.

"Easy, sweetheart," Davilow said, picking up a round of bread from the floor and dusting it off. "I don't know what you savages eat, but I don't like dirt in me vittles."

"Hurry and be done," she snarled. "I've work to do."

He bit off a hunk of dried sausage and winced. Yarra noticed a swelling in his jaw and smiled at the pain his teeth must be causing him.

"So," Davilow said, swigging from the waterskin. "Is your man in camp or not?"

Yarra kept her face impassive.

"The tall one over there with the scars on his face," Davilow continued conversationally, referring to the Kikuyu guard. "Whenever he's on duty, his wives visit him, can't leave the poor fellow alone. He must be quite the cocksman."

Yarra stood mute, her arms folded.

"Anyway," Davilow went on in a friendly tone. "They gossip like magpies. Seems your beau, the sainted Alqamar, is somewhat of a cocksman himself, only he likes to plow one furrow at a time and, right now, yours is fallow."

He belched loudly and shoved the basket away. "Too bad a fine woman like you, queen of the camp and all, is forced to yield to another. Bet you don't know who she is, do you, darlin'." He picked something from his tooth and spat it into the fire. "I do."

Yarra stomped to the mouth of the cave where the Kikuyu was consuming his own meal.

"Tell your wives to stay away while you're on watch and to keep their tongues from flapping around in their mouths," she hissed at him. "Or Alqamar will hear of your indiscretion."

"That's the ticket, girlie," Davilow shouted. "But don't hurry off. I have more to tell you."

"I don't listen to scum," she spat.

"Aw, now don't be so hasty, princess." Davilow rose and approached her. Yarra gripped the handle of her knife. "You and me," he wheedled, "we could work together against the real scum, a man with the bad grace to betray the woman that's dedicated her life to him. Now, what do you say, hmm? I'll tell you the name of your rival and mayhap you'll do a piddling favor for me."

Yarra whirled to face the Kikuyu. "Chain him!" she commanded. "And if he utters one more word, beat him."

She marched from the English prisoner's cave and thundered around camp, checking the stables, the storehouses, and the sentries deployed at all four compass points. She prodded people into their beds and brooked no excuses from laggards. When all was quiet, she headed for the washing pool to cool her raging ire. She felt no appetite for supper, only gnawing hollowness, more like a pain, in the pit of her stomach. Almost without thinking, she made her way through the copse toward the path that led to Alqamar's private aerie. She knew the place was forbidden, but she had to know why he would not lay with her, why he had told her, with such sorrow in his beautiful face, to sing her songs to another.

Halfway up the climb, Yarra paused to sniff the air. Donkey. She studied fresh droppings and wheel marks and heard the distant creaking and clopping of a cart. Someone had just left. Ever alert to danger, she parted the bushes and gazed at the pallid shimmer of lamplight spilling through the mouth of her beloved's home. Then smoothly as a snake, she climbed to the cave's roof and peered down through the air vent. Smoldering embers provided a dim view of emptiness, but she felt that something was amiss and begged Olorun, the mother and father of all creation, to give her a sign. No sooner had she uttered the last words of her prayer than the Yoruba *Orissa* answered. Plaintive notes of a lullaby threaded up through the smoky opening. A woman was singing, a woman whose voice was deep and throaty and, to Yarra's keen ear, slightly off-pitch. She knew the melody and the words.

A flogged camel won't rise; water begged doesn't quench. Walk alone my little one. Seek knowledge and you will prevail.

Suddenly, Tamajaq's tall form appeared and Yarra lay like a stone as the Tuareg and Honifa hurried out of the cave and into the clearing. Moonlight shone on Honifa's wild profusion of red-brown curls as she carried her babe from a place no one was permitted to enter. Were it not for the blue man, Yarra would have pounced on the half-breed witch and slashed her treacherous, duplicitous throat.

Chapter 12

Breaking from his usual habit of stealing quietly into camp at night, Alqamar arrived back from his latest freedom caravan in full sunlight, guiding Shabanou straight to the center of the busy camp. Tamajaq and a retinue of aides followed close behind as he laughed and joked with the horde that rushed to greet him and receive their gifts, a trinket or toy, a length of cloth or a carved pipe. Everyone got something; nobody was left out. Yarra had not emerged from her cave and he called her name. She approached with a bullish expression.

"Look what I've brought you, Yarra," Alqamar said.

Though he was veiled as always, there was an evident pleasure in his gravelly voice. He handed her a delicately curved golden harp no bigger than a lotus bud on a silver rope. Its strings were silken as gossamer and two intricately carved leaping stags formed grips that allowed the player to strum with either hand. Those nearest to Yarra exclaimed at its beauty. She said nothing.

"Don't you like it?"Alqamar asked, noting her silence. "It's Celtic and older than the Druids."

She muttered a few words of thanks and held the harp to her breast but forbore to look at it. Instead, her eyes followed Alqamar as he moved on to Honifa and Jeddah.

"That's Malabar tobacco," he proclaimed proudly to Jeddah, presenting her with a large sack. "The finest available and enough to last months. And for the boy," he added, "this wooden horse, a replica of the one at Troy." The horse was painted white, just like Shabanou, and caparisoned with red and silver fringed cloth. Its hooves ended in rollers and it rattled when Alqamar shook it. Maliq squealed and wriggled in his mother's arms.

"*Shukraan*, Alqamar," Honifa said. "Thank you."

The heat in his eyes shone through the gauze and she reddened at the memory of their nights in the cave. He didn't gift her with a Nubian unguent jar or a mortar and pestle from the quarries of Carrara. Instead, he bent low in the saddle and whispered into her ear. Her color deepened and onlookers grinned as Alqamar and his cohort rode off to the stables. The crowd dispersed; all except Jeddah, who sucked her teeth and scowled, and Yarra, who stomped off, the little harp's silver rope clenched in her fist.

****

Honifa didn't take a bath that night. She was too conscious of Jeddah's evil eye and intimidated by the old woman's ill-tempered grumbling.

"If you have something to tell me, do so and be done with it," she finally snapped.

"And why should I talk to a stubborn girl who only ignores my warnings?" Jeddah responded. "A person is born with just so much breath. I'd rather not waste what precious little I have left on you."

Honifa sighed. "It's not your concern, Jeddah."

"It's everyone's concern. You've set things in motion best left at rest."

"I don't know what you mean."

Jeddah filled her pipe with a generous pinch of Malabar tobacco. "Then you're stupider than I thought," she snorted, declining to explain.

Honifa had to agree. When her lover was away, she vowed to turn her back on him, take control and not allow the man to lead her around like a pig with a ring in its snout. But Alqamar was here and he'd whispered so tenderly in her ear that her vows meant nothing. She ate a little soup and rather than engage in the charade of pretending to be busy while she waited for Jeddah and Maliq to fall asleep, she pulled on a clean pair of cotton *sulwar* and a sleeveless vest that fastened with tiny buttons made of polished calcite, lit a candle and slipped out through the beads.

The night was warm, the moon almost transparent, like a globe of glass. She hastened to the washing pool hoping Alqamar would already be there. She didn't want to chance meeting anyone but him, aware their trysts wouldn't long be kept secret in a place as insular as the camp, especially now the great Dark of the Moon had publicly made her blush. Yarra was sure to find out and Yarra, Honifa knew, was a formidable enemy.

At the pool, Honifa raised her candle. The air was still and fragrant with oleander and night-blooming jasmine and just as she had the first time, she set her candle on the stones and waited for a pair of black boots to step into its ring of light. Instead, Alqamar came up behind her, wrapped her in the folds of his cloak and pulled her against his chest. She pressed her back to him, felt the power of his arms, the hardness of his body.

"Let's go," he said.

He swept her up and, bending slightly so she could retrieve the candle, carried her to the ridge of caves. His step was sure and swift; he knew exactly where he was going, past many openings in the rock until he found a narrow domed cavity in the cliff face, tall as a minaret.

"This is a different place," Honifa observed.

He entered the cave sideways but the entrance opened to a wide passage that like before, twisted and turned, rose and fell. She tried to pay attention but Alqamar's hands against her thigh and breast made it difficult to concentrate. The journey seemed endless, and after a while, she rested her head on his shoulder. He tightened his grip and brushed his covered cheek across the top of her head.

"Are we nearly there?" she asked.

"Lift the candle," was his answer.

They were inside the tiny cave. The air held the same sweet freshness as before and the curly lambskin rug covered the floor.

"What happened to the stone?" Honifa whispered.

Alqamar set her down and laughed softly. "Many roads lead to the same destination."

He smoothed his hand across her breasts to the bare skin at her waist. Her flesh burned at his touch, but she shivered. She pulled his head down to hers, and through the thin scarf that covered his lips, breathed her desire into his mouth.

"I know, Honifa," he groaned. "I know."

It was she this time who doused the candle, threw it to the ground, crushed the flame with the heel of her sandal, and tore at Alqamar's robe and mask. She wanted to feel his tongue in her mouth and the rough skin of his cheek. Hungrily, she dragged at his shirt and he in turn ripped open her vest. Calcite buttons flew everywhere. He untied the strings of her *sulwar* with expert fingers and, grasping her buttocks, lifted her. She gripped him as he plunged fiercely, the essence of each of them reduced to throbbing pressure and wild, exquisite release.

Lying naked on the lambskin amidst tumbled boots, sandals, trousers and shirts, the violent heat of their first coupling banked to warmth, Honifa and Alqamar explored one another in darkness as enveloping as a shroud.

"I'm taking a caravan south in a few days," he said. "Come with me, you and Maliq."

Honifa thought about tramping across the desert with the daring outlaw, pausing to share a meal at a sparkling oasis and sheltering in his tent at night. The idea was appealing.

"Will we be long?" she asked.

"It depends on what we meet."

She snuggled against him, rubbing her palm along the iron of his stomach and the thatch of curling hair at his groin.

"I'd like to travel north," she said. "Not to the desert, but to the sea."

"The sea is a treacherous place," he replied. "And no harbor is safe for you right now."

"I won't be afraid if you're with me," she purred, shifting her weight, and straddling him.

"We'll see, Honifa; perhaps someday." He grasped her hips and entered her. All talk ended.

They made love slowly, lingeringly, exploring the limits of desire and fulfillment. At last, Honifa slept, sated and secure, her leg around Alqamar's like a vine coiled against the trunk of a giant pine. She awoke to candlelight, and to Alqamar crouched beside her in full regalia.

"Already?" she said.

She wanted him again. Though he was draped in folds of black from head to foot, she saw, with the eyes of her heart, the ridges of his bare chest, the smooth, hard muscles of his arms, his powerful thighs and the heavy shaft between them.

"Yes," he said. "It's time."

Reluctantly, she pulled on her *sulwar* and crawled around gathering up the knots of calcite that used to be her buttons.

"I'd like to join you in the desert, Alqamar," she said. "But there's much to do at my clinic." She fastened the two buttons still attached to her vest, thinking how best to rephrase her request for safe passage out of the camp to a distant land where no one knew her. He was unmoved by subtlety; she decided to be direct.

"When you return, will you take me for a ride across the ocean aboard your ship that has no name?"

Alqamar chuckled, a response that disconcerted Honifa.

"You find me humorous?" she asked, stung.

"I find you enchanting," he said. "The beauty of your form is matched only by the brightness of your mind." Then his voice grew serious. "But say what you mean, Honifa. You're asking more of me than a chance to feel sea breezes in your hair."

"It's not that I want to go away," she began after a moment's silence.

Alqamar put a finger to her lips. "Not now, Honifa.

126

Let's talk tomorrow night, and the night after, and every night before I leave camp again." He added slyly, "if we have time for talking," He drew a length of gold chain from his pocket. "For the broken amulet you always wear. Your lovely neck deserves better than a frayed strip of raffia."

Honifa lowered her head to receive the chain. The graceful links gleamed in the soft candlelight.

"It's beautiful," she breathed.

"No more than you." He took her hand. "Shall I carry you out?"

"Let's walk together," she answered. "Side by side."

"All right," Alqamar agreed. "Side by side."

****

Alqamar remained in camp for many weeks. Each night, Honifa met him by the waterfall and he carried her to the same small cave, always by a different route, and loved her there with bold ferocity in total darkness. Honifa gave up asking to see his face, but not her hope to escape confinement. With little time remaining before he departed south with another convoy of freed slaves, Honifa again posed her request.

"Alqamar," she murmured one night as she lay atop him, enveloped in the lambskin blanket, the length of her pressed against him, from breast to belly to thigh.

"Mmm?" he grunted softly.

She had been dozing. She did that often, closed her eyes and drifted off, replete with his love. He'd awaken her with a kiss or with his insistent mouth on her breast or between her legs.

"When will you set me free?"

Alqamar wrapped the blanket tighter around her.

"You're free here," he said.

"That's what you say, but I'm only as free as the limits of the camp," she replied. "I'm a prisoner just as much as the English captain. I want to see my father. I want a home and a life without boundaries."

His fingers smoothed her hair. "I can't protect you in Nador," he said. This was always the answer, her safety.

She rolled off him and sat hugging her knees, shivering in the cool air. "I know. But how long before Ahmed's people seize my father, torture him for information or hold him hostage to reach me? He told me there are reward posters all along the Barbary Coast and as far west as Tiris. The blue man found a poster at Insalah and there are more, deep in the Sahara, in Ghat and Madombey. Who knows? You might come across my likeness on a temple wall in Greece. Madame Hassan's vengeance knows no bounds."

He didn't reply at first, and Honifa sensed there was something more than reluctance in his silence. It was as if the ponderous darkness of their little cave had entered his soul.

Finally, his voice soft and sad, he said, "You would leave me, Honifa?"

"Not happily, but for my son, for my freedom, yes," she answered flatly, without hesitation.

Alqamar covered her trembling shoulders with the blanket and held her close. "Are you still determined to go to sea?"

"Yes. Abroad to England. My father says it's a good place."

His chest rose and fell. The scent of their passion filled the air. Honifa buried her head in her hands. How warm and secure she was in Alqamar's embrace. How could she part from him? And yet…

"I ride out at dawn tomorrow," he said. "I'll think on it and when I return, you'll have my answer."

****

As was her custom, Yarra saw the convoy off as the first weak rays of sunlight nudged the rim of night; Alqamar, Tamajaq, and fifty freed men, women, and children on their way to their homelands. She checked the stores and bindings, wished the blue man *Bissalama* and offered Alqamar a ceremonial cup of spiced ale.

"Take care of things while I'm gone," he said.

"Don't I always?" she responded tartly.

He stared off into the horizon for a moment. The morning was chilly. The camels stomped and snorted. Their breath hovered like cloudlets and their harness bells jingled.

"Things can't always be as we wish," he said, handing her the empty cup. "I told you that long ago, Yarra, and I've never lied to you."

His fingers touched hers and she yanked her hand back as if stung. "May God ride with you," she said formally.

"And may he watch over you as well, my very dear friend."

Instead of saluting Alqamar as he disappeared over the rise and into the trees, Yarra turned and walked away. She resisted the impulse to wave or worse, to run after him, her arms outstretched and pleading. His will was irrevocable and he had chosen Honifa over her. But the choice hadn't truly been his. The half-breed had bewitched him, drugged him with her potions and elixirs. Yarra had seen the sorceress at work in her dispensary, measuring, mixing, stirring bits of this into pinches of that and swirling the mess in a cauldron until it bubbled like the waters of Styx. She had watched Honifa decant clear and cloudy liquids into clay jars and listened to her devilish incantations as she marked the jars with a soot stick: *For Wasp Sting; For Scaborous Rash; For Toothworm.* But who knew what each jar contained? Who could tell if the liquid labeled *Toothworm* would rout the voracious little beast or cast a lover's spell upon an unsuspecting and true-hearted man?

Her thoughts awhirl, Yarra dove into her cave. She tossed Alqamar's ceremonial ale cup into a corner alongside her *gimbri* and golden Druid's harp and squatted before the fire. Her beloved's face rose with the flames, his shining tiger's eyes and yellow hair, the hard line of his jaw and wide mouth. How she loved him! But he was gone on safari until three demi-moons had risen and set, gone and beyond Honifa's predations until the hot season was full upon the Rif and the streams dried to trickles and the sky dulled from blue to a gray pall as sulphurous as her soul.

Yarra poked a stick into the fire to dispel Alqamar's image. She would use his absence to think clearly, rationally. With her knife, she began to carve notches into the firestick until it resembled a row of teeth. She ran her thumb across the sharp points, pondering her handiwork. Suddenly Eshu, the clever god of chance, entered her soul and sowed there, like the tiny teeth, the seeds of an idea. The sun outside her cave rolled from east to west and still, Yarra sat, fingering the sharp points of the firestick, shaping her idea into a scheme, a brilliant scheme that would send her straight into the arms of her beloved and Honifa to her doom.

Chapter 13

Davilow writhed on his dirty blanket. He clutched his head and moaned. His body burned with fever and the swelling in his cheek had given birth to an obscene litter of other swellings, hard knots of tormenting agony that throbbed in the pit of his arm and in his groin. His skin was dry and blotchy, his sweat foul, his wrists and ankles raw from the shackles he'd worn since the monkey bitch had ordered him chained. He smelled meat roasting and his gorge rose. Soon, the Kikuyu would shove a bowl of sops and watery gruel under his nose, the only food he was able to stomach. Bara, Yarra, whatever her barbarous name was, no longer came to guard him at mealtimes, her prisoner having been rendered impotent by iron manacles and a short length of chain. Davilow would have cursed his rotten fate, but he was too weak for rage. He rolled himself into a ball and mewed like a kitten.

"Greetings, scum."

Davilow fixed bleary eyes upon his visitor. Surprisingly, it was the coal-skinned whore, no doubt come to gloat.

"Do you know why you're here, Englishman?" she asked, arms folded, legs planted wide. Just like a man, he thought.

"Go away and let me die in peace," he whined.

"You're not going to die," she said. "I'm going to

send the tooth puller to you and save your miserable life."

Davilow's barber had pulled out almost a score of his teeth. It had hurt like piss on puss but his pain had eventually lessened or disappeared altogether. In time, his gums had stopped aching and he'd been able to eat everything from hardtack to sticky buns. Why not be rid of the few teeth he had left?

Yarra had captured his attention. "A tooth puller? When?" he asked.

"When you do what I want."

Davilow studied the mud-bellied rat snake. What was she up to?

"Your man," he began. "Oh, excuse me," he added with a spark of his old spirit, "your *former* man wants me to feed him information about the movement of slave cargo along the Barbary Coast but my lips are sealed tighter than a nun's hole until the thieving turncoat returns my ship and crew to me."

In an instant, Yarra had him around the throat, her knife pointed just below his chin. His breath caught and stars swam before his eyes.

"Shall I kill you now?" she hissed.

Davilow tried to swallow. Every nerve in his body screamed. "If you wanted me dead, you would have stuck me like a pig on a pikestaff long ago." He gasped. "What do you truly want?"

She sheathed her knife and regarded him sourly. "I'm here to set you free."

He barked a hollow laugh. "Why? So I can perish in the desert, lost and alone?" He lifted his chin and grinned. "If it's all the same to you, girlie, I'd rather not die slow while scorpions swarm over me shriveling skin. Slay me now and be done with it."

She sat on her haunches and glared. "I'll give you a camel, a map out of here and enough provisions to see you safely to where the *Dover Star* is dry-docked. Your crew is gone but there are always other cutthroats crawling the waterfront looking for shares."

Now it was Davilow's turn to glare. "Why? What do you get in return?"

"Take the tooth puller with you. When you reach the desert, leave her there and ride away."

"Her?" he guffawed. "If it's the tooth puller's life you want, why not just do the deed yourself?"

"She mustn't have a mark on her. It must look as if you and she were in league and the two of you simply lost yourselves in the desert."

He narrowed his eyes. "I see. And when I turn up later aboard the *Dover Star*?"

Yarra twitched with hatred. "Tell everyone you and she were separated in a sandstorm. Say you searched for her everywhere but ultimately had to save yourself. Make a show of mourning your dear friend and partner."

"What makes you think I won't betray you?" he said.

"You can try but once Honifa is gone from Alqamar's life, her spell will be broken. He won't believe anything you say. He'll turn to me."

"Ahh, the tooth puller is the bountiful Honifa who stole Dark of the Moon from under your nose."

Yarra fingered the hilt of her knife.

"There, there, my ebony friend," Davilow murmured sitting up, his pain magically forgotten in a rush of enthusiasm. "Your secret is safe with me. The half-breed is nothing. One bitch or another, you're all the same."

"Then we're in accord?"Yarra said.

Davilow rattled his chains. "What options do I have?"

"Well," Yarra replied mildly, "you can die in agony while tooth worms gnaw away your innards or you can live to sail another day."

"My hold chock-a-block with slaves?" he said, managing to rub his palms together.

Yarra winked, acknowledging their unholy alliance.

****

Honifa entered Davilow's cave late at night. She preferred to work in full sunlight, especially when examining the inside of a patient's mouth, but Yarra had come for her after supper and Yarra was in charge.

Honifa raised her lantern. The English captain lay by the fire, still and pale as a corpse. Only his eyes, red-rimmed and glaring, told her he was alive. She shrank back.

"He's chained," Yarra called from the doorway where she stood guard. "He can't hurt you."

Yarra gave her a little push. Honifa crept slowly inside, knelt beside Davilow and opened a lacquered box. She removed several instruments, the loosening and extracting forceps, a scraper to remove carious tissue, tweezers, and a curved, slender needle. She placed all of these in the hot coals, using the tweezers to position the needle precisely. She took three stoppered bottles from her medicine bag, speaking softly to her patient as she did.

"This is vinegar distilled from apples to cleanse the

135

affected area; this, astringent oil of cloves; and this, tincture of poppy seed to dull the pain." She set two small bowls beside the line of bottles, some folded cloths and a length of shiny thread. "See how fine the thread is?" she said. "It's made from the intestines of a fox and very strong. I'll use it to suture the cavity after the tooth is extracted."

"Get on with it," he growled.

Honifa told him to tilt his head back and open his mouth. She saw that two of Davilow's teeth would have to be removed and most of his few remaining ones were in poor condition.

"You must rinse your mouth daily with fresh water and a paste of lollium, salt and pine turpentine," she instructed. "I'll bring you some in the morning, and a *siwak*, a chewing stick to scrub your teeth."

Davilow looked intently over Honifa's shoulder toward the door where Yarra stood but he said nothing. Honifa set to work. Her movements were efficient and exact. She spoke little, short phrases like, "open wider," "bite on this," "spit," sensing that Davilow, unlike most of her patients, scoffed at soothing talk. He was stoic, grunting briefly when she pulled the teeth but otherwise silent. She would have called him a good patient but for the meanness in his cold eyes. Relieved to be finished, she began to gather up her things.

"What's yer hurry, girlie?" Davilow mumbled wincing.

He was on his feet, somewhat unsteadily but on his feet, nonetheless. He took a step in Honifa's direction, then another. She started; he was unchained! She spun around to summon Yarra but there was no one in the doorway. Davilow lunged and grabbed her wrist.

"Yer comin' with me, sweetheart. Were goin' fer a little ride."

She screamed and struck him with the water bowl. It shattered. Davilow jammed the soaking cloth into her mouth twisting her arm and pulling her against him. She tasted his blood and sweat on the cloth mingled with the sharpness of vinegar. She struggled but he threw her on her stomach, trussed her arms to her body like a game bird and hobbled her ankles. He snapped an iron slave collar around her neck and warned he'd slit her throat if she made a sound. He yanked her up and dragged her outside by a leash attached to the metal choker. Wildly, frantically, she looked around for Yarra, for anyone, but the camp was deserted. The crisp air and a thin layer of frost on the ground had driven the occupants inside to sleep, their bodies muffled in blankets. Davilow's buckled shoes crunched rhythmically as he skirted the main clearing with sure steps and headed into the woods, Honifa stumbling behind. Her thoughts were in turmoil. Where was he taking her? How had he gotten loose? Had he been chained at all?

She saw a figure perched on an outcropping far in the distance. It was a smear of shadow in the brake but something about its stance, bold yet wary, solid yet slender as a whip, turned her blood to ice. It was Yarra. She must have discovered the trysts with Alqamar and arranged this travesty to exact revenge.

****

Davilow pulled Honifa along, hour after hour, through a narrow col canopied with spruce branches in some places, open to the sky in others. By the high, bright moon, she could see that they were leaving the

forested ridge and descending through the timberline to
a savannah of low scrub and grassy plains. As the sky
lightened, the terrain underfoot grew sandy and a light
wind whispered in the brush. The air was no longer thin
but dry and slightly warm. A scent like decay overlaid
with heavy perfume filled her nostrils. Moments later, a
field of tall pínnata flowers waved their poisonous
yellow plumes and Honifa knew they were nearing the
desert.

"We'll rest here," Davilow said, and unlaced the
front of his britches to urinate. Honifa looked away.
Soon it would be morning and if her captor intended to
lead her into the desert, they would reach it just about
midday, the sultry hour when air clogged the lungs like
wool batting and nothing moved, not even sand grains.
She thought of Maliq awake, crying for breakfast,
waiting for his *Umma*'s arms to lift him from the cradle
and hold him to her breast. She made a strangled noise
deep in her throat.

"Whazzat?" Davilow said. "Oh yeah." With a
smirk, he removed Honifa's gag. "You can scream all
you want now. Ain't a soul around to hear."

"Untie me," she said, and then, seeing the hard
glint in his eyes. "Please."

He obliged cheerfully and appeared recovered from
his ordeal. His color was good, and his eyes were no
longer glassy with fever and pain. He kept her hobbled
and left the collar in place though he let the leash
dangle to her waist. Apart from these restraints, she was
free to move about as best she could.

"You're a good tooth puller, girlie, a heap better
than my barber, the old sot. What's your name, Honifa,
right? Remember me? I'm Royce Davilow. You can

call me Captain."

He was expansive, elated. Honifa eyed him closely. Her father had told her about euphoria, a feeling of joyful invincibility that imbued patients recovering from long bouts of suffering. Euphoria didn't last and usually ended with prostration. She would wait for that moment and, please God, free herself. She knew the desert the way this Englishman didn't. She would prevail.

"Where are we going?" she asked.

He put a finger to his lips. "That's for me to know, pretty girlie."

"We have no provisions for crossing the desert," she pointed out. "No water or food. Our clothing is wrong. We need to consult a map or join a caravan. Perhaps you should let me go and head for the sea."

He eyed her up and down. "You're a handsome piece, and clever. You could be of use to a man like me." He yawned elaborately, unrolled a bark scroll, and held it up to the rays of the morning sun. "According to this, it's not far now."

Honifa thought she had been discrete and Alqamar was a man of few words, yet they had both underestimated Yarra. Envy had driven her to betray the camp's location and all who believed they were safe there. That was why Davilow hadn't faltered once but marched from mountains to plains to the desert's rim without pause. He had a map! Honifa wondered what else Yarra was prepared to do for retribution.

Davilow soldiered on, through another patch of spiky pínnata shimmering in the morning sun, and across a desolate tract of sand and rubble littered with the discarded shells of thousands of chitin beetles.

Honifa's sandals crushed brittle carapaces, large and round as frog's eggs, releasing puffs of acrid-smelling dust.

"Phew!" Davilow fanned the air. "They stink!"

No worse than you, Honifa thought, but kept her venom to herself. She planned to feign docility until she knew his plans for her. She hoped they were not the same as Yarra's which were surely homicidal. She peeked at the map over Davilow's shoulder and saw that it depicted the eastern coastline of Morocco, the Rif Mountains and a section of the Sahara. A line snaked south from the Rif camp and skirted along the edge of the desert through a series of small towns before turning northeast toward the sea. A large X was drawn over the city of Al Hoceima.

There was also a curious second line, this one a dotted string of arrowheads that originated at camp, vectored into the desert, and ended at a crudely sketched butte from which a single, heavily drawn arrow pointed directly into the desert's broiling heart. Honifa pondered the twin lines, one to Al Hoceima and the other a cortege to certain death. She knew which one was meant for her.

The sun rose inexorably higher and waves of searing heat transformed the space around them into a kiln. At a curious mesa-like dune, Davilow cried, "Thar she blows!" and broke into a run. He plowed into it and climbed to the top signaling Honifa to follow. Impeded by her hobbled ankles she stumbled awkwardly up. The dune was as massive as a butte and she reached his side swaying with exhaustion. Around them, the endless desert spread, white and featureless as a winding sheet; the pale horizon of sky and sand a nearly indistinguishable blur.

"The Sahara," she whispered in awe. "We can't possibly cross it."

Davilow looked at her with the small, transfixing eyes of an adder. "We won't have to, dearie."

He lugged her along the edge and down the other side of the butte to a point where its base became friable.

"It's here! It's here!" he crowed. "The jungle bitch kept her word!"

A saddled camel placidly working its furred jaws was tethered to a lone palm tree. Beside the beast was a pull-cart with long handles, the kind poor peasants used to lug their belongings. It was laden with mounds of cloth, a basket of bread and dried fruit, and a water canteen. Davilow scrambled onto the wagon, motioning Honifa to hurry. He tore the top from the canteen and drank deeply, passing it to her. She wiped its mouth discreetly before taking several sips.

"My bones are like water," Davilow said, slurring his words. "I need sleep."

He secured Honifa's chain to a wagon wheel and dove into the pile of cloth.

"May I have some bread?" she asked.

He toed the basket of bread and fruit closer to the side of the wagon where she could reach it.

"Eat all you want." He yawned. "This might be your last meal."

His euphoria was passing as she knew it would. Exhaustion and certain collapse would follow. Her freedom was near.

Honifa filled a round of flat bread with a handful of figs. She had no appetite but sustenance was crucial, sustenance and rest. She crawled underneath the wagon and tried to get comfortable. Yarra had planned well. Alqamar and Tamajaq were away from camp. Jeddah would notice she was missing but she was an old woman and nobody listened to her. Besides, it was widely known that Honifa wandered far afield with her herb basket and if she chanced to be with Alqamar, she'd not return until he did.

She finished her meal and looked around. The butte rose like a monolith between the flat plain on one side and the rolling desert on the other. Was this the point where Davilow would abandon her and ride to Al Hoceima and the coast?

Honifa listened to her captor's snores. The camel's stomach rumbled wetly. Its hump was as plump as an udder and its great, splayed hooves stomped at dung flies. It was well-equipped to carry Davilow across the vast, unyielding Sahara. The cart, on the other hand, was puny, its wheels thin as barrel stays. If she tried to drag it across the sand, it would sink to its spokes and move no more, stranding her.

Such was malevolent Yarra's plan.

Chapter 14

Davilow woke in a surly mood. It was dusk. He had slept all day. A swig of water did nothing to assuage the thirst and dryness that coated his vitals from the inside of his mouth to his bowels; he needed rum. He rolled over and looked down at his prisoner sleeping on the ground beside the pull-cart. She had wrapped her cloak around her but her feet and part of her shapely calves remained uncovered. Christ, but she was a juicy piece, honey-skinned and curved like a fine violin. He wagered she made sweet music, too, with her knees pressed against her shoulders and her ankles clasped around a man's back. He hadn't had a woman in months, he thought, rising to unlace his trousers, but right now, the pity of it was he needed a piss more than a piece.

He relieved himself against a rock, admiring his girth. Captivity had done nothing to reduce his manliness, he acknowledged proudly. Soon, he'd be tumbling wenches up and down the Barbary, barking to his crew and relishing the heft of a bullwhip in his fist as he lashed the backs of slaves, turning their arrogance to surrender. Too bad he had to kill Honifa first, but a woman on a ship was trouble, especially a handsome one.

He climbed back onto the wagon and studied his map, tracing a finger along the lines and arrows Yarra had drawn. She'd instructed him to head the camel into the desert in the morning cool, taking Honifa and just enough water and food for one day. When the sun was directly overhead, he was supposed to untie Honifa and head back the way he'd come, leaving her behind. If all went well, he'd arrive at the butte before nightfall where he could load the camel with whatever he wanted from the cart and make for Al Hoceima. There, he'd trade the camel for a horse and ride all night to a hidden cove in the bay and the *Dover Star*.

But Davilow had wasted the day in sleep and now the night stretched before him, his task not yet begun. He licked his lips and glanced again at the map. There must be a friendly tavern in Al Hoceima or at the very least, a merchant who might have a cask or two aging in his cellar. He could abandon his captive tomorrow. Right now he needed a drink.

He hopped from the wagon and kicked Honifa awake. "On yer feet, dearie."

She blinked and he saw the expression of desolation, briefly absent in sleep, return to her face as swiftly as the solstice night.

"Hoist the cart. Let's go."

"Where?" He backed Honifa into the wagon like a dray horse and curled her fingers around the handles. "Surely not into the desert? Not now. It's night."

"Quit yer moaning and follow me."

He spat into his hands, rubbed them together, and prepared to mount the camel, pulling at its reins to get the animal to lower itself. The cursed varmint refused. Davilow yanked the straps roughly several times but the beast stayed put.

"Ya stinking pile o' shit!" he cursed. "Get ye

down!"

The camel turned its head and spat at him. Enraged, Davilow roared a string of curses and kicked it viciously. The camel began to trot forward and Davilow, still holding on to the reins, was lifted off his feet and dragged for several yards before letting go. Honifa set the cart down and watched as he righted himself, angrily wiping sand and gobs of camel spittle from his clothes.

"What're you smiling at?" he shouted at her.

Honifa stopped grinning. "Camels are stubborn," she said. "You have to talk to them in a certain way."

"Talk to them. Bloody hell. I'd sooner gut the rotten animal and feed its entrails to the jackals." He unsheathed his knife.

Honifa quickly shouted a few words in a strange language and made a loud, clucking sound. The camel turned toward her, looking for all the world as if waiting for instructions.

"Make it come back and sit," Davilow ordered.

Instead, she walked to the camel and stroked its neck, talking gently. Presently, it lowered to its front knees, then to its back ones, and finally, it folded its legs and rested low to the ground.

"You can ride it now," she said. "But don't make any loud noises, and don't kick it."

"Don't kick it? Bloody hell."

****

Their little caravan made its way into the rapidly approaching night, Davilow swaying atop the camel, clutching the pommel with one hand and Honifa's chain with the other, and Honifa dragging the pull-cart. The sky covered them like a blue-black rug rent with tiny pinholes through which starlight glittered. The air was warm and fragrant with orange blossoms and soon, as small pastures ringed by fences began to appear, the flowery sweetness gave way to the musky scent of livestock, and, still later, to aromas of smoke and lamb *kefta* rising from chimneys.

"We must be coming to Al Hoceima," Davilow said.

The village of Al Hoceima was built around a dusty square, brightly torch lit and circled with shops. Most of them were closed but the café appeared to be thriving. Through its domed doorway hung with ragged curtains, men in skullcaps and flowing white *dirra* emerged carrying drinking cups and smoking fat cigarettes.

"Glory be!" exclaimed Davilow, attempting to spur the camel on with a few smart snaps of its reins. The animal stopped dead in its tracks. Davilow slid forward and got himself wedged in the hollow between the great beast's neck and hump.

"Help me down, woman!" he cried, yanking Honifa's chain. But she resisted him, transfixed by something that had captured her attention.

"Damn and blast!" Davilow bellowed, brandishing his knife. "Get me off before I scuttle this stinking dromedary and keelhaul it for sharks!"

Honifa coaxed the camel to the ground. Davilow dismounted.

"You two beasts of burden stay put," he ordered, tying the camel to a fence post and securing Honifa's chain with a padlock. "I'm off to wet me whistle."

She sank to the ground, numb with exhaustion and fear, and tore the object of her fixation from the fence.

Reward for the Death or Capture of Honifa, the poster read. *First wife to Ahmed ben Hassan, Wanted for Crimes Against God and Nature.*

****

Alqamar halted the freedmen's caravan at the base of Mt. Tidiqin just above Imazz Ouzane. He rode through the snaking line to the rear of the convoy where the blue man waited, his dark eyes questioning.

"Take the lead, Tamajaq," Alqamar said. "I'm going back to camp."

Tamajaq nodded but reached out to stay Alqamar's departure. "Is anything wrong, Captain?"

"I'm not sure," Alqamar said. "My mind's not at ease."

"I'll see this lot safely home," the blue man assured him. "*Inshallah*, my brother.

They grasped one another's wrists briefly and, in seconds, Alqamar was flying over hard-packed sand toward the crevasses and spiky peaks of the Rif. He picked through the col and arrived at his camp in the glare of noon immediately noticing that Davilow's cave was unguarded. Yarra must be with him while the Kikuyu had his meal, he thought. But something nagged his consciousness and he dismounted and looked inside. The English prisoner's cave was deserted.

"Yarra!" he called, walking Sultan to the center of the common.

The afternoon was frigid and the area was empty but for a few hearty men who looked at him and then looked away. Yarra's cave was deserted as well, though her fire glowed brightly. Burning to ash at its center were her Celtic harp with the leaping stags and the broken pieces of her *gimbri*. He stood quietly for a moment, then went to Honifa's dwelling. Jeddah, holding Maliq swaddled in blankets, ran out to meet him, her eyes wet with tears.

"Oh, thank God you're here," she cried with relief. "Honifa went out last night and never came back. Is she with you?"

Alqamar took Maliq from her. "Have you seen Yarra?" he asked.

"Yarra? Who cares about Yarra! Honifa went to pull the English prisoner's tooth last night and never returned home. Please tell me she spent the night with you. I've looked all over camp and can't find her."

Alqamar smoothed Maliq's pale head and handed him back. "Watch over him carefully, Jeddah," he said. "Never let him out of your sight. If anything happens, bring him to the Church of the Holy Rood. You know the place I mean. Do you understand?"

She took the child, her face crumbling. "Yes, I understand. But where's Honifa?"

He pressed her arm in brief reassurance. "I don't know yet, but I'll find out, I promise you."

He strode across the compound to the washing pool and searched the stables and along the rillet up the path to his cave. Finding it as he had left it, dark and cold, he retraced his steps and headed to a copse of felled pine logs, their bark brindled with lichen and green-gray moss. On fine days, when Yarra was a small child, he took her there to watch speckled parulas build their nests. She admired the industry of the little birds and their high-pitched, musical warble and Alqamar enjoyed her delighted smile.

He found her there, as he thought he might, sitting

on the ground, elbows on her knees, her chin in her hands. She turned at his approach. The expression on her face fleeted from pleasure to defiance to fear.

"Captain," she said. "I thought you'd be halfway to Tendrara by now."

He threw off his hood and tossed back his long, yellow hair. His gauze mask fell away and he stared down at her with hard, feral eyes.

"Where's Honifa?"

"Honifa? How should I know? She's none of my business."

He crouched before her. "Davilow is missing."

"That can't be. I kept him chained. Unless—"

"Unless what?"

She blinked, swallowed, and slid her eyes away then back to him. "Well, if Honifa and the Englishman are both gone, perhaps they fled together, perhaps—"

He rose and drew back his hand, palm open, ready to strike. Yarra flinched. She knew what he was capable of.

"No, please!" she cried.

He loomed over her. His shadow draped her like a curse. His eyes glittered. "Don't play me for a fool. What do you know of this?"

"Nothing! I know nothing! I swear!"

"This better not be your doing. I've killed for less."

She swallowed and inched tentatively toward him. "Let me help you find them. Perhaps they left a trail."

"What makes you think they're together?"

"Oh, small things," she replied lightly though her lips trembled. "Honifa was always begging to bring the Englishman something to ease his suffering. She's very compassionate. Just yesterday, she pulled a tooth for him and sat by his side until he slept, or at least that's what she told me she did."

"Weren't you with her?"

"She made me leave. She had given him laudanum and in any case, he was shackled. I had my many duties to attend to, the watchpoints, securing the perimeter –" Her words trailed off under Alqamar's relentless scrutiny. "I was busy," she finally blurted. "I do everything here, everything for you."

"And I always trusted you, Yarra," he said. "With my life, with all that's dear to me."

She hung her head. "Does that mean Honifa? Is she dear to you?"

"Yes," he answered simply. "She is."

"But here in camp you belong to me," she wailed. "That's always been the way. I depend on it."

"I belong to no one. You know that. None of us does. But Honifa—"

Yarra curled her small fists. "Don't say her name. I hate it. She's a witch who cast a spell and tricked you so she could escape with that English rotter. She prefers him to you. She told me so."

Alqamar's voice was murderously level. "Honifa would never desert Maliq."

"Don't despise me," she whimpered. "I can't bear it."

"Then tell me what you know and tell me now."

She reached up to him but he recoiled. He'd never been unkind to her; never. "It's you that's taken leave of your senses," she accused, wounded. "Can't you see it? From the moment you brought Honifa here, she's wanted to escape. She lied to gain your trust, pretended to care for you. Forget her. I'm the one who truly cares."

He covered his face with his hood and turned away. Yarra jumped up and dragged at his sleeve. "I love you," she cried miserably.

He shook her off. "And I you, as much as I loved Regin, the sister of my blood. She's lost to me forever," he said. "Now, so are you."

He left her then, his black cloak swirling behind him, his boots thundering on the rocks.

Chapter 15

Alqamar strode back to the central clearing. Several San stopped chattering over their game of *Awari* to stare in surprise as he pulled a flaming log from their fire and carried it to Davilow's cave.

The air inside was rank with sweat and filth but Alqamar also smelled vinegar and, entering with alarm, blood. The firepit was a cold pile of charred rubble and Davilow's restraints, a collar and leg braces, were bolted to the stone wall and hanging useless. Broken crockery and several of Honifa's carefully labeled medicine bottles littered the floor. Clearly, there had been a struggle here. When he shone the torch low, he discerned smeared footsteps, as if someone had slid on wet ashes. More footsteps led outside but the ground was dry and brown. Try as he might, he could find no traces of flight until caught in a low-hanging branch along the col, he spied three twined strands of long, reddish hair. Delicately, he plucked the strands, fragile as a cobweb, and twisted them around his finger. They were Honifa's. No one in camp had hair that length, and of that burnished color. He took a moment for his rage to cool. No good came of action dulled by emotion.

In the soft soil of the col, he saw a footprint, and then another a short distance away. His jaw set, Alqamar followed the prints down the narrow trail that led from camp, a trail that used to be secret but now, thanks to Yarra's hatred, no longer was. An escarpment formed a viewing ridge over the valley below. Traces of last night's frost lingered and two sets of tracks were sharply visible in the snow, the smaller ones close together and smudged as if the walker had dragged her feet. Alqamar's muscles twitched and his fists clenched. Davilow must have hobbled Honifa like a beast awaiting slaughter. What else had he done to her?

Seething but focused, Alqamar plowed back up the trail. The woman he loved had been stolen and the security of his camp was breached. He crossed to the group of San who were still moving pebbles around a painted board.

"You, sir," he addressed one of them, "run to the stables and bid the groom gather and saddle all the horses." And you two," he said to the others, "collect the livestock and prepare them for travel. Tell the people to douse their fires and pack whatever can be carried." He looked around. "Find the Kikuyu and bid him ride like the wind to halt the caravan. We break camp at sundown to join them."

The San hurried away. Alqamar took hold of Sultan's bridle and gently rubbed the stallion's velvety nose.

"We have a strenuous road ahead of us, friend. I know you won't fail me."

The horse snorted softly. Alqamar mounted and rode to Honifa's cave.

"Old woman!" he shouted, bending low. "Tie some food for you and the babe in a shawl and come quickly."

"What's happening?" Jeddah said, emerging with a frown. "Did you find Honifa?"

All around them people spilled into the clearing, talking, and gesturing. Tents were collapsed, fires hastily covered, children tied into slings.

"We abandon camp at once," he told Jeddah. "The Englishman has escaped. He knows our location and it's just a matter of time before the enemies of freedom come for us."

"But I don't understand," Jeddah replied, holding her ground. "Where's Honifa?"

Alqamar let out his breath in a rush of exasperation. "I'm taking you and Maliq to the Friars of the Holy Rood. You'll be safe there. The others will reconnoiter with Tamajaq until I can make another camp. I'll search for Honifa in every village from here to the sea."

"And if you don't find her?" Jeddah persisted maddeningly.

"Don't try my patience, woman," Alqamar barked. "I'll bring her to you, I swear, or die trying."

By sundown, goats had been herded, chickens caged, bundles hoisted and by morning, the entire camp arrived at Tamajaq's caravan. Alqamar deposited Jeddah and Maliq in the capable if surprised hands of Prior Florimond at Holy Rood and flew astride Sultan southeast toward the bay at Al Hoceima He stopped frequently and briefly along the way to ask after a tall half breed woman and a short Englishman. Nobody had seen the unlikely pair but after Alqamar rode off, they speculated about him, a foreigner dressed like them in dark robes, his golden hair streaming down his back and his face like fire.

****

Davilow, rum-soaked and staggering, dimly

recalled noticing Honifa's name printed on a sign somewhere along their route, but he couldn't remember exactly when or where. Nor, at this moment, did he much care. The little tavern in Al Hoceima had proved to be just his sort of watering hole, dark, discreet and unsocial. The patrons lolled about stupefied with the excellent local *khif* of which he partook, along with his share of syrupy rotgut even though, in his opinion, it was necessary to consume huge quantities of it to experience even slight inebriation.

The barkeep was blathering something at him in an ugly tongue that sounded like retching.

"Leave me alone," Davilow scowled.

But the dirtmouth heaved on and finally pushed roughly at Davilow.

"A pox on yer stones, varlet! I'm Captain Davilow." He scowled across the bar, pushing back.

A voice intervened. "Please, sir. Your language. The proprietor is merely wishing for you to be leaving, Admiral."

Davilow turned to the fat, oily Arab addressing him in English.

"And who the devil are you?" he demanded.

The man pushed a red fez further back on his hairless skull. "Thees taverna is close now, boss," he said, grinning inanely. "And most respectfully, you must to go."

"Well, I ain't ready, fezzhead," Davilow said, reaching for his glass. But the barkeep snatched it first and, glaring evilly, downed the remains himself.

"I paid for that!" Davilow cried and lunged at the barkeep.

He fell from his stool into a heap on the tavern

floor. The fat man picked him up and carried him outside. Davilow struggled but realized, as he hit the air, that he was too drunk to fight. He draped his arm around the fat man's shoulders and woozily flicked the tassel of the fez.

"Take me to my ship, there's a good lad."

"No ship here, Esteemed General. We are in the desert. Nothing but sand. How about I bring you to my niece? She have ten years old and plump like baby rabbit." He rubbed his hands. "She will bend like a snake in a tree for English penny, French centimes, even Roman lira, but"—he wiggled a finger—"no *dirhams,* no wallpaper cash, only good money."

"I don't want your scurvy whore," Davilow grunted. "I got one of me own tied to a tree yonder. Sweet Honifa. You know Honifa?"

The man tensed. "Honifa?" he said, suddenly deadly serious. "First wife to Ahmed ben Hassan?"

"Who?" Davilow said.

"Show to me thees woman, Venerable Colonel," the fat man said. "If she is who I am seeking, she is worth much money."

Davilow sobered instantly. "Money, you say?" He was supposed to leave Honifa in the desert, but this boozy little detour might have brought him luck.

"Such a woman ran from her esteemed husband months ago," the fat man went on. "She hides, some believe, in the outlaw camp of Dark of the Moon."

"That's the one!" Davilow crowed slapping his knee.

"Her mother-in-law offers a generous reward for her capture and much honor will be heaped upon the one who delivers her," the man whispered conspiratorially.

Davilow pushed him away. "Keep yer slimy hands off me, Ali Baba. The bitch and the money are mine!"

"No, no, Your Highness," the man assured Davilow. "You misunderstand. I want no money. I am the Prefect of Police of Al Hoceima. I will pay you the reward myself and deliver the woman into the hands of my dear compatriot, Madame Hassan."

Davilow eyed him slyly. "You'll give me the money? All of it?"

"Of course, Mighty Majesty. What is money compared to glory? With a kind word from Madame Hassan, I might be transferred north, away from this fly-ridden dung heap to a real city."

Davilow didn't hesitate. No need to remount the blasted camel. He'd trade it for a horse and be on his way.

"Give me the cash, man," he said, pointing out Honifa to the Prefect of Police. "She's over there."

****

Alqamar guided Sultan down steep slopes. The great stallion picked its way carefully but seemed to sense the restrained urgency in its master's hand. As soon as the terrain leveled, it picked up its hooves, poised to canter for the timberline.

"Easy, friend," Alqamar mouthed softly.

Night had descended and though the air in the foothills was warmer than at camp, the low ground was still hoary with frost and treacherous patches of ice hid under a carpet of frozen top leaf and brown pine needles. Alqamar knew it would have been better to wait until daylight or at least to stop now, make a small fire and listen for the owl's mournful call to cease, and the lark's to begin. But there was no time. Al Hoceima, a day distant, was the blackguard's most likely destination. Alqamar turned Sultan southeast along the road that ran between desert and plain.

The stallion trod through a slush-filled gully and snorted with distaste. Its breath rose in a clammy fog around ears stiffly pointed forward in concentration. Alqamar, too, was deep in concentration but his thoughts were focused not on the terrain nor the cold and wet, but on Yarra. The woman had become mired in wrongheaded jealousy. He could forgive that. In fact, he was partly to blame for it. He should have kept his distance, but he hated the hurt in her eyes when he sent her away. For so many years, she had been a child, a skinny, eager, intelligent child on the periphery of his vision. She'd dogged his footsteps whenever he was in camp, asking endless questions, begging to help. He made sure she was taught survival skills and reading and writing too and, little by little, as she matured almost unnoticed by him, she became indispensable.

Then one day, how well he remembered it, it was the first day of Yarra's nineteenth year, she played the *gimbri* and danced for him and he saw that she was a child no longer. But he'd never deluded her, never led her to hope he'd take her to his bed as he had so many women, although none had dug into his heart the way Honifa had. In some ways, Alqamar wished he'd never met Honifa, but that was a laughable wish. Great swells of ocean carved the shoreline and created the earth to their own design. No longing or might or witchcraft could change that. Honifa existed for him as irrevocably and inexorably as the sea and the land. She had become his firmament.

It was necessary to deal with Yarra, and harshly. He might forgive her jealousy but not its result, nor her reckless disregard of her duty. Once he had Honifa in his arms again, he would hunt down Yarra and exact punishment. She had probably concealed herself somewhere in camp or in one of the many small huts sprinkled like salt along the base of the Rif. He knew them all. He'd find her.

Alqamar reached the timberline as dawn was breaking. He traveled onward, gaining speed, stopping only to ask a question or two before galloping off. As the day grew molten and the sun gleamed on Sultan's flanks, he removed his turban; he had long since discarded his mask and hood. Fire lit his golden eyes and his flaxen hair streamed in the wind like a river of gold.

****

Honifa stared through the barred opening cut into the stone wall high above her cell. She had been waiting for Davilow to exit the little oasis tavern, wondering what he was going to do with her when a man who claimed to be the Chief of Police had carted her off to Al Hoceima Jail. Now, she stood tiptoe on the rough bench that served as her bed and peered at the fence where she had been tied two long nights ago, the tavern from which Davilow had staggered, and a slice of the dusty roundabout that led from the square in three directions, one to the coast, the other to the mountains, the last into the heart of the Sahara. She buried her face in her hands. Her breasts and arms ached for her son; her whole body cried out to him. What had become of Maliq? What had become of them all?

She crumpled onto the bench. Not ten feet away, the Prefect snored, his fez tilting slightly over one twitching eyelid. On the desk in front of him lay her wanted poster, carefully flattened and, beside it, the map Yarra had given Davilow, clearly defining the route from camp to the sea. Zalam Alqamar, the mighty scourge of slavers, had been exposed and his fortress laid bare.

A shaft of buttery sunlight fell on a small boy sitting beside the Prefect assiduously scratching on paper with a burnt stick. He had been there all night, working by an oil lamp. It was the time of prayer but Honifa felt no impulse to praise God. He had abandoned her.

The Prefect yawned, scratched his buttocks, and poked the boy. "Yussif!"

"Yes, Uncle."

"I'm going for breakfast. Keep an eye on our prisoner and your mouth shut."

"Yes, Uncle."

Honifa, freed from her iron collar and manacles, paced her cell in an agony of frustration. She'd been locked in for days without food or water, and nothing but a rough bench and the bones of desiccated creatures for company. She wrung her hands and tried to think. But thought, sensible thought, eluded her. Instead, she saw Maliq's dimpled face and knees as he crawled on his tiger skin rug and reached for his favorite toy, the rolling white horse Alqamar had given him, already trying to say its name, "Shanoo, Shanoo," after the mare, Shabanou. She saw Jeddah's toothless grin and Simon's blue eyes welling with pride when she handed his grandson to him. And she saw Alqamar, her lover, the man she had escaped and now longed for.

"Oh god!" she wept, shaking her fists at the thin swath of sky visible through the shutters.

"Don't cry, lady."

Honifa blinked through lashes clotted with tears. "What?"

"I said don't cry."

The boy, no more than twelve or thirteen, approached her cell. He had the pinched face of a rodent and his shirt was ragged and dirty. Honifa dried her cheeks.

"Who are you?" she asked.

The boy puffed up his chest. "I'm Yussif, the deputy prefect of police."

"Oh, I see," Honifa said, nodding with interest. "Such a big job for one so young."

"I'm nearly fifteen," he said.

Honifa smiled and clutched the bars. "Well, of course. I can see you're already a man."

"Yes. I have an important job." Yussif sucked his teeth dismissively. "But I'd rather draw pictures."

"No," Honifa exclaimed, gripping the bars. "You're an artist. How splendid!"

"My uncle doesn't think so. He says drawing isn't manly."

"That's nonsense," Honifa said. "Think of Michelangelo."

"Who?"

"A great painter from Tuscany. He drew the face of God."

Yussif's jaw dropped. "That's forbidden."

Honifa nodded gravely. "But surely not to true artists such as yourself."

Yussif accepted the compliment. "No. Not to true artists." He held up his drawing pad. "I drew a picture of a tree but your face is hidden in it. Would you like to see?"

Honifa clapped her hands. "Oh, yes, please!"

"I think I have your head right, but not the rest," he said. "You kept moving around."

He pressed the pad against the bars. Honifa squinted. "I can't see very well. The light in here is poor."

"I'll slide it through," Yussif offered.

Honifa protested. "No, don't do that. It's too big and you mustn't fold it. Why don't you come inside where I can examine it better?"

Yussif's face fell. "I don't have the key to the cell," he said.

Honifa bit her lower lip. *Damn.*

"I know!" Yussif suddenly cried. "I'll hold it up to the window."

Honifa clapped her hands again, this time in true, not feigned, delight. "A brilliant idea! Quickly, Yussif. Run."

He hurried out the door, the drawing pad flapping in his hand. Honifa mounted the bench and waited. Yussif began to slide the pad through the bars but she arranged her features in a desperate frown and stopped him.

"It's the same problem. But there's a latch. Can you unhook it?"

Yussif eagerly swung open the window bars and for the first time in two days, Honifa beheld the full, uninterrupted square of sky, white and sweet as a sugar cube.

"Here it is," Yussif said, gently easing the edge of the pad through the window.

Honifa deliberately let it drop. "Oops," she said as the pad fluttered to the scrub grass, scattering pages.

When he bent to gather them, she squeezed through the window and ran like a hunted roe.

Chapter 16

Throughout the night, Yarra sat in the copse, still as a statue. She'd committed a vile crime, abjured her honor, traduced those who depended on her, and betrayed a man who was everything. With feeble, despicable reasoning, she'd sought Alqamar's love through Honifa's death. She was truly a woman quit of her senses, not worthy of her honorable race; not worthy of Alqamar.

Night owls hooted in the dark, their call a condemnation. *You're evil*, they accused, *unworthy, less than a slug clinging to the underside of a rock. You don't deserve to hear the sweet, sunrise music of the parulas. You don't deserve to live another day.*

Near dawn, stiff with cold, she climbed to Alqamar's cave. She decided to welcome her death from there, the place where her beloved had lived, empty now but for the rushes on the floor sweet as the clean scent of his body, and his wood table smoothed by the pressure of his hands. For many moments, she absorbed his mighty spirit and then stood on the cliff face surveying his camp, empty too because of her, and expunged of all the promise it had once possessed. Calmly, she scanned the lightening sky and the violet hills and woodlands that rolled to the desert, the infinite magnificence of creation.

"I don't deserve mercy," she prayed softly to the

fullness and power of nature. "But when I fall, when my earthly self lies broken on the stones below, lift my spirit. Let it fly with the wind to wherever Alqamar is. Let it watch over him and protect him forever."

She stretched her arms to almighty Olorun and, with a smile on her face, stepped to the edge of the precipice and prepared to meet eternity.

But then, just as her foot was poised above the abyss, an eagle screeched and swooped down, so close upon her she could count the pearly tips of its talons. She staggered back and watched with awe as the eagle circled, squawking nervously, warningly. When it soared away, she inched forward slowly and saw, cupped like a feathered crown in a V of protruding branches, its nest. Two bald-pated eaglets chirruped noisily, their serpent's heads straining and their hooked beaks gaping open for life's sustenance. Yarra watched enrapt as their mother, her baleful eyes alert, spanned her great wings protectively.

Yarra picked up an eagle feather that had fallen at her feet. Her heart began to fill with self-recrimination, not for what she had done which was heinous enough, but for what she'd been about to do. Life was a miracle and she had compounded her sin of perfidy with sacrilege and profaned the holy force of God. Her death was nothing to give; her life, everything. Of all Alqamar had taught her, this was his most valuable lesson.

She stuck the white-tipped feather in her hair and walked from emptiness into light. She would dedicate herself to the redress of the wrong she had committed, live on as a humble penitent, and use the skills Almighty Olorun had given her to bring Alqamar and

Honifa together.

****

Honifa fled the jail, running as fast as she could, keeping clear of the road. As soon she could no longer make out the low, sandstone hovels behind her, she slackened her pace and began to creep along the inside of a natural trench, a long, waist-high gully that edged the plain. When the trench leveled, she dashed, head down, from the cover of scrubby bushes to the occasional outcrop, hoping to stay hidden. After many hours of these furtive, scurrying dashes, her back ached. She'd seen no one in pursuit, not even a lone traveler or goatherd. Cautiously, she began to walk normally and her pulse slowed.

The sun singed her skin, hunger gnawed, and thirst as sharp as a firebrand burned in her throat. Honifa had not eaten or drunk for many days, not since Davilow had tied her to the pull cart at the base of the butte. And where in blazes *was* the butte? Surely such an imposing rock should be visible in this flat landscape, and she needed it to get her bearings. But nothing looked familiar, no yellow pinnata flowers, no crunch of chitin beetles under her feet, and no broad expanse of savannah leading to the Rif.

How had she lost her way? She'd been moving steadily north, or so she had thought. It was difficult to tell. The land was featureless and the sky pressed down upon her like a white-hot burial cloth. She walked to her left, toward the road, but after many minutes of treading on unchanging pebbles of coarse sand, she realized with a sinking heart that there was no road. She had somehow veered into the arid climes of the desert.

The wind swirled, whipping grains of sand into her

face. Honifa hunkered down and covered her head with her arms, patiently suffering grit in her mouth and tiny, stinging darts pelting her skin. Sandstorms came and went in the Sahara like flocks of birds, swirling darkly, befouling the space around them, then moving on. She gripped Tor's pendant hanging from Alqamar's chain, treasured gifts from two very different men. Would she ever see them again?

When the storm abated, Honifa scooped up a handful of sand and could tell by its coarse consistency that she'd wandered only a little way into the desert and, thankfully was still at its rim. A few steps in the right direction, she was certain, would lead her back to the plain. But those same steps, wrongly taken, could also draw her deeper into the torrid, shriveled heart of desolation.

The air was heavy, granular, yellow-white, and smothering. She tried to think but her brain roiled uncooperatively with images of Maliq in peril, Maliq in pain, Maliq crying for her in terror. *I'm coming, my treasure*, her soul called to him. *Umma is coming.* But she couldn't move, only stand dazed, parched, and exhausted, her stomach cramping. If she could only sleep for just a few minutes.

No! She slapped the flat of her palm smartly against her head, rallied and walked on until it seemed to her that the sand beneath her exploring fingers had become finer, silkier. It was the wrong consistency, desert consistency. She turned and walked slowly in the opposite direction, and hopefully, to the plain. But that was wrong too. She tried many different directions, roaming haphazardly but the character of the sand never changed, and she understood with horror that she had wandered far from her goal and deep into the soul of the Sahara. Swallowing saliva thick as clotted cream, she felt the stabbings of panic.

Blindly, her reason shrunken to one goal, *Don't stop, don't sleep or you will die,* she kept moving until the straps of one sandal, then the other, broke. She left them where they fell, stumbling like a broken sprocket wheel, shuffling rhythmically for a few paces then hurtling forward. She collapsed, picked herself up, and collapsed again. The wind renewed its fury, and the sand churned. A fresh storm gathered and grew. Honifa dug into it, pushing with all her dwindling strength against its oppressive force. But her efforts were futile. For each step she lurched forward, the wind drove her many more steps back.

Despairing, she lifted her head to curse the heavens and saw, undulating on waves of heat, a tiny chapel, neat and narrow as a wayfarer's shrine. The white steeple shimmered like a beacon, and the bell swayed back and forth in silent welcome. Elated, Honifa surged toward the chapel and the little nun who was smiling warmly from beneath the fluttering wings of her cornette. *Dear Sister*, Honifa shouted. *Thank God.* Or maybe she only thought the words, for no sound reached her ears except the thunder of wind and sand.

She forced herself forward. But the chapel, so tantalizingly close, receded with her every step. The nun's happy face grew sad; her black sleeves wavered like wands of heat. *No,* Honifa cried bitterly as the mirage melted into the howling wind.

She walked on, walked until she crawled, pulling her agonized body through the wall of sand and fire until every muscle screamed. She tried to pray but her throat was dry as ash. Time slowed, minutes passed like hours and an insidious, debilitating lethargy softened her will. In a moment of cruel clarity, she understood she couldn't go on.

****

Alqamar stopped at a well to water and feed Sultan. He asked the women filling their jugs what he always asked: Had they seen a short Englishman with skinny legs and silver-buckled shoes traveling with a tall, titian-haired Maghrebi woman? They shook their heads. No, there had been sandstorms all morning, and they dared not venture from their homes. Desert storms were known to sweep up people, cattle, even houses and deposit them leagues away, under drifts of sand high as Mt. Tidiqin.

Alqamar continued toward Al Hoceima, his brow creased with worry, his eyes peeled right and left, scanning the plain and the desert. He saw nothing out of place, nothing that would cause him to investigate, only outcrops, scrub brush, and an occasional target-eyed buzzard pecking at carrion. A trench-like furrow had formed along the road and Alqamar reined Sultan to a slow walk while he examined every hollow and rut looking for signs that someone had hidden, or maybe was still hiding, there. His brain swarmed with a thousand suppositions, but he kept his focus, kept his gaze sweeping a broad arc from plain to desert and back.

Then something caught his attention, something small but strange, a dark brown smudge in the white immensity of sand. He dug his heels gently into Sultan's flanks and the horse flew to where it was bidden, a small, torn, half-buried sandal. Alqamar leapt from the saddle. The sandal was of a common design, but he knew by the delicate tooling, a sunburst flanked by a star and a crescent moon, that the shoe was Honifa's. He could still make out faint traces of blue dye in the points of the star. Ignoring the hope that threatened to burst in his chest, he put the sandal in his saddlebag and walked in ever-widening circles around the spot where it had lain. He found its mate some distance away, laid his head against Sultan's flank, and wept.

The sun had dipped below the horizon leaving a smear of flame in its wake. Night was descending, cold, Stygian night. Alqamar turned back to the road, his shoulders slumped, his face a mask of desolation. And then he saw it, a humped shape in the sand, a human shape with a crown of sand-encrusted hair.

****

The sun was sinking; night loomed. Honifa knew that soon the searing heat would give way to an eerie, chilling underworld where flesh-eating demons roamed. Done with torturous efforts, she rested quietly, stroking the moon pendant, commending her motherless son to the beneficent mercy of Heaven and herself to the languor of surrender. Her brief life had been pleasant enough; she had done some good with her healing, given and received love, and borne a son. Nestling her cheek on a pillow of sand, her heart at peace, she recalled the joys of a life that was ending: Maliq's soft skin, Simon's gentle hand upon her brow, the silkiness of cut aloe, and honey sucked from the comb. Honifa rocked her body to the sway of the *Witch's Moon* and opened her heart to Alqamar's magical embrace.

From out of the haze, the Archangel Gabriel, his

black wings billowing behind him like a cape, galloped toward her astride a stallion. *Dear Saint Gabriel*, Honifa mused dreamily. *How odd that a Christian saint has come to take me to a Christian heaven.* The angel dismounted and she tried to focus on its approaching figure. Gabriel was wearing Alqamar's boots and black trousers yet didn't look a bit like Dark of the Moon. His face was framed in a halo of heavenly gold and his eyes...*Bismillahi*! His eyes were pale as a river pearl and moist with tears.

****

With Honifa cradled in his arms, Alqamar lead Sultan along a circuitous path, avoiding well-traveled trade routes in favor of low-lying byways that afforded good cover. The great steed moved gingerly, understanding that it mustn't jostle its master's precious cargo. Honifa's head lolled and, from time to time, she moaned softly.

"You're safe now, my love," he said, his lips against her temple.

She burned with fever and though Alqamar continually wiped her face and neck with a wet cloth and dripped water from his fingers into her mouth, Honifa's skin remained dry and hot. She drifted in and out of delirium, mumbling garbled phrases, addressing Alqamar as Gabriel, and begging him to watch over Maliq.

When the moon was high and the stars glittered like shards of ice, Honifa's body began to shake. Alqamar reined in beside a small grotto, no more than a hollow at the base of a ridge of sandstone, wrapped her in his shirt and cape, and tenderly laid her on the ground. He made a fire and gathered the mate of his soul against his bare chest, whispering that he loved her and would avenge all the malignity she had suffered. Her tremors intensified and she raved throughout the night. As dawn broke, Alqamar lifted her high in his arms and waded into a deep pool of snowmelt.

"I'm sorry for this, Honi," he said soothingly as he lowered her slowly into the icy water. "But, unlike you, I have no skill with herbals. This is the only way I know to bring down a fever."

She did not react at first but, as he dipped and swirled her in gentle semicircles, Honifa's eyelids fluttered open.

"Where are we?" she said quite lucidly. "What is this?"

Smiling broadly, he hurried her out of the wet and set her on her feet. Her thin *kamis* and ragged trousers clung to the outlines of her body and, cursing himself for a rotter, he tore his eyes from the desire her sweet fullness aroused.

"You've come through an ordeal," he said. "I found you nearly dead in the desert. Do you remember?"

She touched the pendant at her throat. Her eyes searched inwardly then suddenly widened. "Maliq!" she cried with alarm.

"He's safe," he hastened to reassure her. "We're going to him."

"Merciful Allah," she said, shivering, hugging herself as Alqamar once again draped her in his cloak. "My brain is a muddle," she said. "I remember living for many months in your camp. But I don't remember much after that except I lost my way in the desert and you were the Archangel Gabriel."

He pulled her tightly against him. "Let's go back to the fire. You need to eat and drink something." He made to walk with her but she held him back and studied him intently, curiously, moving her hands across his bare chest and feathering the hard ridges of his stomach. She looked down at his heavy black boots and then into his eyes.

"Your—your eyes," she said. "And your hair." The bare-chested man standing before her was Alqamar…the raspy voice, the heavy black cloak he'd sheltered her with. But his face, a face he'd never let her see, it was…was…

"Who are you?" she cried out.

He took her arm. "Come. We have a tiring journey ahead."

"No. Stop." She lifted the heavy charm that hung from a strip of leather around his neck, a crude half-circle of stone. Three of the moon's phases were carved into it, full, half, and three-quarter. The gibbous and crescent phases were missing. Honifa ran the pad of her thumb along the charm's ragged, broken edge. Her eyes bore into Alqamar's. "Turn around," she demanded, her tone challenging. "Let me see your back."

He held her gaze. "My back is scarred," he said evenly. "You know that."

"I've never seen your back. I've seen Tor Kendrick's—" Her eyes were stark, shrewdly calculating. She lifted the amulet she wore around her neck. "The captain of the *Witch's Moon* gave me this token aboard his ship and Dark of the Moon gave me the chain." She held her half up to his and fit the pieces together. "Who are you? Tell me the truth."

"Which truth do you want to hear?"

173

"That you're not what you seem."

"I am exactly what I seem," he said. "Zalam Alqamar, scourge of slavers, liberator of the oppressed."

"Yes, but I've never seen your face, as well you know," she said, adding boldly, "When we lay together it was always in total darkness."

"Ah, yes," Alqamar nodded. "That magnificent darkness."

She stiffened and glared. "You mock me."

His mouth curved at one corner. "Never, not in the Rif and not on the *Witch's Moon*."

Her cheeks suffused with color and she put a fist to her mouth. "Oh, Tor, it's you. And-and—Alqamar."

He drew her against him. "I'm sorry I deceived you," he said holding her tightly. "I love you and I love our son."

At the mention of Maliq, they both grew pensive.

"Take me to him," Honifa said.

****

They rested until Honifa felt strong enough to forage for boxberry root and brew tea. Tor dug into his pouch for bread.

"What shall I call you?" she asked, enjoying her first meal in days.

"I was born Tor Kendrick. I only took the name of Zalam Alqamar when I began my work."

"I'm glad," she sighed happily.

"Glad that I'm not called Alqamar?"

"No," she said with mock exasperation. "Glad you're not a slaver."

He gulped his tea and stared out through the trees. "Slavery," he muttered, his voice tight. "When my mother died, I was just a boy. My older sister Regin cared for me. I loved her beyond reason. Then a party of raiders invaded our village looking for slaves. They beat me bloody; I bear the scars today and when my sister tried to intervene, they carried her off. I was a man when she returned, a shell of her former self, stooped and hag-ridden, her blonde hair gone white, her eyes empty even of suffering. They had yoked her to a plow and forced her to work sunup to sundown in broiling heat and numbing cold. They fed her rancid leavings and gave her brackish water to drink. She bore a child and watched it die. Then she bore another and begged her owners to take it from her so it would live. But it too died. My father hanged himself for the loss of her, but I came to view his death as a blessing. At least he didn't have to watch Regin shrivel like a flower ripped from its stem and crumble to dust."

Honifa touched his arm and he turned to her, his face hard. "I do what I can, what I must, for Regin's sake and for others like her who have no one to fight for them. Yes, there are slaves on the *Witch's Moon,* but they are on their way to sanctuary. Royce Davilow tells Tor Kendrick where to find them and Dark of the Moon runs them down."

"You play a dangerous game," Honifa said. "Who knows of your deception?"

"Other than Davilow who dares not expose me and lose his advantage, my First Mate, Tamajaq, ben Abbas, and Yarra." He accepted a handful of berries. "And now you."

"Why did you keep it from me?"

Tor threw the dregs of his tea into the fire and began to pack his saddle bag.

"Can you ride?" he asked. "We have the day ahead of us and will travel swiftly once we reach the timberline."

"Yes. I can ride," she answered but kept on eating.

Tor sighed and hunkered down beside her. "All right, woman. Hear it this once and trouble me no further. When ben Abbas asked me to take you from your husband's house, I refused at first, believing that your life was none of my affair." He shrugged his shoulders. "But I couldn't get you out of my mind and, even though I knew it was unwise, I was determined to see you again and dispatched the blue man to bring you to camp. I didn't know you were pregnant nor that the child was mine until I pulled Maliq from your womb." He held out his hands to Honifa, palms up, seeking accord. "Then Hassan's posters sprung up like mushrooms and I had both of you to protect. I couldn't risk revealing my identity. It was too dangerous, especially with Davilow in camp itching to capitalize on what he knew and you chafing to be free. I feared you'd be caught and forced to bargain for your life."

"Betray you? Never!" she gasped.

"Not to save yourself, or Simon, or Maliq?"

"No. I would have found another way."

Tor lifted her into his arms. "You're truly the mate of my soul," he said, pressing his lips to her forehead.

She trembled and melted into him until mindful of the day opening before them, he steeled himself against the pressure of his desire and whistled for Sultan.

Chapter 17

"What are you saying, you stupid boy. Speak up!"

Madame Hassan sat bolt upright on her divan and kicked away the servant who had been applying unguents to her feet.

"He's here, Mother, the Prefect of Police of Al Hoceima, but without Honifa," Ahmed mumbled. He kept his head bent to avoid his mother's anger and the scorn in his second wife's eyes.

"Do you hear that, Abiba?" Madame Hassan said to her daughter-in-law. "A year gone, and still his wife spits in his face."

"I'm his wife, too, Honored Mother-in-Law," Abiba simpered. She was small and plump and her pouched cheeks and tiny, glittering eyes gave her the look of a devious chipmunk, rather the same look as Madame Hassan.

"Yes, of course dear," Madame Hassan said, absently patting Abiba's hand. "Though I fear you're barren as a blighted swamp."

Abiba bridled. "I am not barren. If your son spent less time at his bubble pipe and more—"

"Enough!" Ahmed slashed a hand in the air. Abiba pouted but Madame Hassan regarded her son with disgust. He lowered his eyes. "Please."

"So, tell me, Four Kinds of a Jackass," she baited. "Where is Honifa?"

Ahmed addressed the floor. "The Prefect said she escaped while under the care of his deputy. She rattled the bones or used phylacteries or something. She put the deputy prefect in a trance and turned herself into a willow-wisp so she could fit through the bars of her cell window." Ahmed wiped sweat from under his nose and cleared his throat. "The Prefect believes she perished in the desert."

Madame Hassan snapped her fingers and stuck out a foot. The servant hurried to resume massaging.

"Now let me see if I hear you correctly," Madame Hassan said with deliberate emphasis on each word. "Honifa's astounding magical powers sometimes work and sometimes do not. She can make herself thin as smoke and slip through iron bars, but she cannot survive the Sahara. Is that right, my son? Is that what the Prefect told you?" She thrust her neck forward and shouted. "Is that what you believe!"

Abiba snickered, and Ahmed drew himself up to face his mother.

"Don't scream at me," he said. "It isn't my fault she escaped. She escaped from this house while you yourself had her under lock and key. Anyway, she's dead."

Madame Hassan studied her son silently for a moment. Then she clapped her hands. "Fetch me my shoes, my *kaftan* and *niqab*. I will see this Prefect now."

"No, you mustn't, mother," Ahmed said aghast. "This is men's business."

"Humph!" Madame Hassan snorted. "There are no men in this house. Nor any among the well-paid trackers I hired. Must I put on trousers and find the she-wolf myself?"

"No need, Mother," Ahmed replied eagerly. "The Prefect told me that Honifa was hiding in the mountains, at the camp of Zalam Alqamar. He has a map of the exact location. On the slim chance that she's alive, I've dispatched some men there to–"

"Be quiet!" Madame Hassan shook off the servant adjusting her gown. "Dark of the Moon is canny. I wager his camp is guarded by eight foot tall Watusis or that he's moved it by now." She adjusted her veil and only her eyes were visible, deadly as twin scorpions upon her son. "Answer me this, Dung Beneath My Shoes, was Honifa's bastard child with her in the jail?"

"No, Mother."

"Then we have her. Find the child and you'll find the woman."

She took Ahmed's arm and walked with him into the receiving room where the Prefect waited, fez in hand, upside down like a begging bowl. He bowed low at her approach.

"My dear Madame Hassan," he oozed. "You do me the great favor of an audience with your august self. May I say how well you're looking?"

She ignored the flattery. "What makes you think my daughter-in-law is dead?" she spat.

"The woman was alone, madame, with no food or water, in a threadbare *sulwarkamis*. And she headed straight for the desert on a day of violent sandstorms."

"Did you search for her?"

"As long as we could, madame, as the storms would allow. She walked north along the gully and then she was gone."

Madame Hassan nodded. "My daughter-in-law

gave birth, eight, maybe ten months ago."

"Yes, madame," the Prefect said excitedly. "She cried for her child all night. He's called Maliq."

"A son!" Madame Hassan aimed the accusing syllables directly at Ahmed. "She had a son."

"No son of mine," Ahmed said, muttering, "So, you tell me."

"Empty-headed cretin!" Madame Hassan hissed. "Unless I find you a third wife, that boy may be the only heir we'll ever have. Do you want your father's money to go to strangers when you die?"

"Allah will give me a son," Ahmed protested.

Madame Hassan observed her only child for a long moment, his gaunt cheeks, sunken, red-rimmed eyes, and skeletal form hung with a rumpled, dirty *djabador*. No sons would come from his loins and if he died childless, her husband's wealth would revert to his father's two brothers who despised her. Ifni and Sidiq would turn her out without even a pittance and send her to live in Tarfaya or El Aaiun with chickens and pigs. She needed that cursed child. True Hassan or not, she needed Maliq.

"Search for the babe in every hut and hovel in the foothills of the Rif," she ordered the Prefect. "Search the caravan that has been reported traveling south led by a giant blue man. Search all the towns between Meknes and Nador, Fez, Taza, and Oujda. Roust fishermen from their boats along the Moulouya and every other river you cross. Bring me the child or I'll flay you alive and throw you to the sharks."

"Yes, madame," the Chief said bowing out of the room. "Immediately. It shall be done as you say."

"And you, Ahmed," Madame Hassan charged her

son. "Wash your face, comb your hair and put on a clean shirt. Then go see what you can find out from Simon McLeod."

****

As soon as he reached the timberline, Sultan navigated the trail without guidance, moving smartly now that home was near. But at a break in the trees, Tor pulled sharply on the reins.

"Are we stopping?" Honifa asked.

Her back was pressed to Tor's chest and his massive arms held her firmly in the saddle.

"Tired?"

"No," she said, and then, cocking her head to smile up at him, "Well, maybe just a little."

He dismounted at the edge of a small bee meadow and lifted her down. The ground was covered with wild pansies and fragrant bee balm. Honifa rubbed her neck and took a cup of water from Tor.

"Thank you," she said, suddenly shy.

"You're welcome," he answered.

She drank and handed back the cup. "Thank you," she repeated stiffly.

"You already said," Tor replied with barely suppressed amusement.

"Oh. Sorry."

This was Alqamar, a man she cared for. But he was also Tor, a man she hadn't seen in a year. She marked the desire that flashed across his face like summer lightning and felt a kindred longing coupled with a kind of reticence. It was bewildering; but for that one night, Tor Kendrick was a stranger.

He tucked the water bottle into his saddle bag, withdrew a handful of pecans, and began to shell them with deliberate care. Honifa watched him.

"Hungry?" he asked.

She was, but her clothing was torn and dirty and her hair a nest of tangles. She'd rather a warm bath in water perfumed with hibiscus.

"Is the monastery far?"

"Not far, now," he said. "A few more hours. Prior Florimond is a good man. I'm sure he's watching over Maliq and Jeddah. But Holy Rood is a way station for pilgrims and the friars welcome anyone who knocks at their door. We'll stop only to thank them and be on our way."

He said no more but Honifa took his meaning. "On our way to where?" she asked, all animation drained from her face.

"To safety in England," he answered. "You and the boy, and Simon if there's time to arrange it."

Honifa digested the news. "On the *Witch's Moon*?"

"No. She's winched for the moment at the mercy of careeners. You'll sail on the *Mary Ellen.*"

Honifa's brow creased. "What about you?"

"I've work to do here. You know that. The *Mary Ellen*'s a fine ship and Captain Coffee keeps his lady wife on board with him. She'll look after you."

Honifa searched Tor's face. "When will I see you again?"

"I don't know. It depends on many things."

His eyes blazed like molten copper and his jaw muscle pulsed.

She pressed her hand to his beating heart. "Now you've found me, would you part from me so quickly?"

He grasped her hand and brought it to his lips, biting each of her fingers softly, drawing his tongue across her palm and the inside of her wrist. She moaned and he pulled her against him crushing his mouth onto hers. She felt the heat of his touch and his hunger as he untied the strings of her *sulwar*. In seconds he was inside of her.

Honifa's body leapt into flame, a flame that built until it flared into a thousand sparks and ignited her soul. Tor plunged deeply, his long, broad fingers caressing her flesh. With each thrust, she gasped at the ferocity of his passion and at the stark and overwhelming totality of her response. He was no stranger; he was the mate of her soul. There was no one in the universe more attuned to her, nothing at this moment but this exquisite torment, no beginning or end save the fulfillment of release. He spent himself with a low cry and Honifa clung to him, her body convulsed in wave after wave of pleasure so intense the essence of her being dissolved into his and was consumed by the force of his love.

She lay atop him, limp with delicious torpor, glorying in Tor's familiar bulk still heavy inside of her and the steady beat of his heart.

"I can't bear to be without you," she said.

"We've spent many nights together, Honifa, and will spend many more."

"When? How long must I wait?"

"Until all this business is over," he replied sadly. "Then I'll build you a house wherever you like, or we can live on the *Witch's Moon* and teach our son, all our sons, to sail and fish."

He nuzzled her cheek and swelling inside her again, rolled her onto her back. Fires blazed anew but mindful of the journey ahead, Tor banked his passion and they continued on to Holy Rood.

They passed several peasant huts, curiously vacant. This was the time for milking and evening meals and Tor remarked how strange it was that chimneys were cold and door yards empty of livestock and the bustle of busy folk. A few meters on, they found out why. A hoard of ruffians had stormed through, a weeping farmer told them, laying waste to everything in their path. The hoard spoke a city tongue not readily understood by the local inhabitants who were beaten for their stupidity. Some of them were slain, including the farmer's wife. He had just come from burying her and was going into the hills where his neighbors had fled in terror.

Tor listened thoughtfully his face impassive. But Honifa saw the muscles of his jaw clench. Without a word, he dug his heels into Sultan's flanks and they sped into the gathering twilight.

Only minutes had passed when Sultan reared up and whinnied. Tor spoke calmly but the stallion, eyes rolling in his head, was reluctant to proceed.

"What is it, Sultan?" Tor asked.

"Look!" Honifa pointed to the near distance where smoke was rising from a sandstone building whose façade appeared pitted and black.

"Holy Rood is burning!" Tor cried urging Sultan to a gallop.

The monastery was indeed on fire or had been. The massive wooden doors were crumbled to smoking rubble and the narthex walls, once the color of young mahogany, were gouged with striations that darkened from gray to deep, sooty pitch. The crenellated towers that flanked the domed entryway were intact but between them, half-burnt *prie-dieus*, rosary tables, a charred holy water font, and a wooden wine press lay like discarded children's toys. A young monk, his tonsured scalp gleaming in the half-light, sat dejectedly before a freshly dug mound of earth. When he saw Tor and Honifa, he pulled his hood over his head and ran screaming through the debris.

"Halt, lad!" Tor called, dismounting. "I mean you no harm!"

He cautioned Honifa to remain in the saddle, but she balked and together they hurried after the monk.

"Calm yourself," Tor told the trembling youth. "What transpired here?"

"They descended upon us like Horsemen of the Apocalypse," the monk sputtered. "Ten of them with knives in their teeth and hate in their eyes. They wanted the child but Père Florimond barred the way and, and"—the boy began to blubber— "they smote him down and killed him." He wiped his streaming eyes with the fringe of his cincture and looked toward the mound of earth that was the Prior's grave.

"Where's my son? Where's Maliq?" Honifa cried.

"They kidnapped him, madame. And his nurse too, the old woman, though she fought like St. Michael at the Battle of Light, God bless her."

"Which way did they ride?" Tor barked, casting a glance at Honifa who had begun to keen.

"North, sir, to Nador."

"How long?"

"I don't know. This morning, this afternoon. Oh, sir! The Prior is dead; Brother Etienne is cut and bleeding. The others scramble about trying to save our stores and holy relics. Oh, *dies irae, dies irae*!"

Tor gave the poor monk a single pat on the shoulder, put a supporting arm around Honifa and hoisted her onto the waiting Sultan.

"Courage, woman," he said, jumping into the saddle behind her.

"Wait!" the young monk shouted, running after them waving something above his head. It was the rolling white horse called Shanoo, Maliq's favorite toy, partially burnt and missing one leg. "The child was brave," the monk said. "He only cried when they took this from him."

Honifa pressed the toy to her cheek and put the horse's tiny ear, the one Maliq liked to chew, into her mouth.

"They'll not harm him," Tor said.

"How do you know?"

"Madame Hassan will use him to smoke you out."

"I don't care," Honifa cried. "Let's fly to Nador and kill anybody who tries to stop us."

His faced was hard. "This changes nothing. I'm not taking you to Nador. You're going to England aboard the *Mary Ellen.*"

She whirled to face him, her eyes wild. "You can't mean—are you mad?" She beat her fists against his chest and began to struggle, kicking her feet. "Let me down! Let me go to Maliq!"

He held her fast. "Use your wits, woman. It's you the cursed hag wants. She'll let Maliq live until she has you cowering before her begging for mercy. Then she'll kill you for sure, and perhaps even the child. Don't you see? With you gone, we beat her at her own game."

"Game? This is not a game. This is my son!"

"*Our* son, Honifa." Tor said tightly. "We do it my

way, with you out of danger in England"

Honifa fought and begged until she was so drained she could barely move. She slumped against Tor, against the steel of his imprisoning arms, and wept her misery into the folds of her cape. Sultan steamed toward Nador.

They reached Yom al A'had Street near midnight. Sultan's hooves clip-clopped on the cobblestones.

"Just a bit longer, old friend," Tor told the exhausted horse. "Then I promise you rest and a good feed."

Honifa, who'd been drooping with fatigue, suddenly snapped to life. She saw that they were at the waterfront and resumed writhing and kicking, but only feebly.

"Please, Tor," she begged. "I want my son."

Drained, exasperated, consumed by worry, he spoke harshly. "How do you want him, Honifa? Dead or alive? Your way or mine?"

She quieted in the face of his acrimony and implacable resolve, laid her head against his shoulder, and was still. When they reached the dock where the *Mary Ellen* was birthed, Tor helped her up the gangway. Her legs gave out in the middle and he carried her onto the deck. The scrubbed boards glowed whitely. It was the month of *Shubat,* the end of winter, when the moon is small and hard and lights the earth with pale phosphorescence.

"You must trust me, Honifa," he said, setting her down. "I'll make everything right."

Her eyes were bright with grief, but she spoke as though drugged. "How? You're not God."

He smoothed his thumb across her lips. "You

thought I was, once," he said lightly, though his voice broke.

Honifa pushed away his hand and walked unsteadily, holding onto the deck rail.

"What of my father?" she mumbled dully.

"I'll do my best to send him to you."

"Where am I to sleep?"

She swayed and, just before she fainted, Tor caught her in his arms and carried her below.

Chapter 18

Honifa's cabin was tiny but neat and clean. There were two bunk beds against the wall, the bottom one tidily made up with a rosemary quilt and counterpane, a small doily-covered table, a chair and a washstand. There was no window. She lay alone atop the counterpane praying for the oblivion of sleep but even this puny mercy was denied her. Instead, she listened to the *Mary Ellen* creak and groan and, as morning approached, to the shouts of the crew as they hauled in the gangway and prepared to cast off. Presently, Mrs. Coffee unlocked the cabin door and set a tea tray on the bedside table. After tisk-tisk'ing at the state of Honifa's clothes, she returned with a cabin boy who hauled in a tin hip bath just like the one Honifa had used in her father's house. While Honifa sipped tea and nibbled a seed cake without appetite, the cabin boy ran back and forth with endless kettles of boiling salt water until Mrs. Coffee dismissed him, pronouncing the bath ready.

"Now, I know you've been through a shock, dear," she said briskly. "But brooding is the eighth deadly sin. It says so in the Bible. So up you go into this nice, hot bath. Scrub away all the sorrow and when you're done, here's a nice frock and hair ribbon for you. They belonged to my daughter, Mary Ellen, may she rest in peace, and are a bit out of style, but only the frigate birds will know."

Honifa was grateful for the bath and eager to shed her soiled *sulwar* and *kamis*, still gritty with sand. Poor Mary Ellen's dress was of simple dark blue grosgrain with a draw collar and buttoned cuffs. Mrs. Coffee had brought a camisole and petticoat as well, but no shoes, so, after dressing and tying back her damp hair, Honifa sat on the bed, swinging her bare feet, and waiting for the sound of Mrs. Coffee's key in the lock.

Her plan was to overpower the woman; knock her down if she had to, then race for the gunwales and jump overboard. The ship was barely underway, still close enough, Honifa reasoned, for her to swim ashore. She'd have to shuck the dead girl's dress as soon as she hit the water of course, but thank God, the underwear would cover her well enough. She'd run fast as she could to Madame Hassan's house, barge in, snatch Maliq before anyone knew what was happening, and flee. Whether Maliq was even in Madame Hassan's house and where exactly she would take him, she wasn't sure. She hadn't progressed farther in her planning than the point where she held her son in her arms.

Honifa tapped her feet impatiently then paced her cabin from one wall to the other, six steps up, six back; the room was no bigger than her cell in the Al Hoceima jail. When she saw the doorknob turn, her heart pounded. She stood just behind the door, poised and trembling. As soon as it opened a crack, she must be ready to push with all the force and ferocity of a lioness defending her cub.

The door opened, but not a crack. It opened wide and swiftly, knocking Honifa down. Her mouth dropped in surprise at the sight of the man peering around the jamb, his dear face aghast.

"Honi! I'm sorry. I didn't know you were right there."

With a cry she threw herself headlong into Simon's arms.

"Oh, Da. He found you. Tor found you!" she cried, clutching him. "They have Maliq. I don't know where. I'm sick with worry. Help me. What shall I do?"

He re-tied the ribbon at her collar, smoothed her sleeves and guided her to the lone chair.

"There's not much we can do, lass, and there's no turning back. We've rounded the shoals already. Open water next."

Honifa's face fell. "Then you trust Tor? You know who he is?"

"Aye. A good man." Simon smiled. "Ahmed told me you were missing along with my grandson and said if I knew where you two were, I'd better tell him or else. He threatened me, can you imagine that? Sweet Ahmed?" Simon shook his head. "I fear opium and his mother have twisted his brain. I sent him packing but not two seconds later, out of the blue, literally out of the blue, Honi, this Kendrick fellow appears like an angel from heaven."

"I know what you mean," she said.

"Lowered himself from the roof smack dab into the kitchen again easy as peas pie." Simon mimicked Tor's deep baritone. "'Pack a bag, doctor,' he says. 'Your daughter is waiting for you on the *Mary Ellen* bound for England.' There was no arguing, especially when he promised to find Maliq and bring him to us there."

"So, you dropped everything," Honifa noted wryly.

"I did. Before I could say Jack Be Nimble, we were on our way here. The man's astonishing."

"You don't have to tell me."

The next morning, Simon and Honifa breakfasted with Captain and Mrs. Coffee on a dish of side bacon and biscuits in floury gravy that Honifa, who was usually hungry in the morning, could barely swallow. Afterwards, they strolled the foredeck of the *Mary Ellen* arm in arm. The sky was overcast and though she searched the horizon, the coast of North Africa had long since disappeared. Under a sprightly tail wind, the *Mary Ellen* had skated through the Pillars of Hercules, leaving the warm Mediterranean behind for the unpredictable Atlantic Ocean.

Honifa could hardly believe what she had forfeited; the only home she'd ever known, the man she loved, and her infant child. How was Tor going to make everything right as he had promised? How could he resume his work now that its base was destroyed and his men scattered; how could he avenge Davilow's transgressions, find their son, and love her again before she was old and feeble?

"Penny for your thoughts, daughter."

Honifa was seated on a hatch cover staring into the middle distance.

"What? Oh, I'm sorry. I was thinking."

"About slaying dragons? You looked right deadly."

"I don't want to be here," Honifa professed bitterly. "I should never have let Tor force me on board."

Simon sat beside her. "Seems to me the man has a powerful will and makes a deal of sense, too. What good could you do in Nador but be stalked like hounds to fox, making things worse for yourself and Maliq, not to mention for Tor?" He took her hand. "Don't you fret,

Honi. He'll never allow that poisonous toad of a woman to harm his son. If I thought that for one minute, I wouldn't have let Tor bring me here."

Honifa sighed. "Well, I'm glad he did."

Simon escorted her to the wheelhouse where one of the crew, who had been a cobbler, was going to measure her feet for a pair of shoes. From there she would visit Mrs. Coffee in her cabin to try on more of dear, departed Mary Ellen's dresses, which according to the brusque but kindly woman, she must wear with a proper corset. After that, there was to be an hour and a half of Bible reading in the lounge followed by supper, a game of quoits if the weather held, needlework or letter writing, something cold and gelatinous for supper, hymn singing in the mess, and bed. She would hate every minute of it.

Simon left to join the captain for a game of chess and Honifa watched him go. *He's happy enough here with me,* she thought. *He has confidence in Tor and so should I.* But she was gripped by a pernicious foreboding and a sense of unease beyond her distress over Maliq. She would need fortitude and tenacity, not to mention divine help, to face the next few months or years in a country as unlike the north of Africa as sand to syrup, and a future that promised nothing but loneliness and sorrow.

****

Madame Hassan chased Ahmed around her boudoir, beating him about the head and shoulders with her hairbrush.

"Stink beetle! Pea brain!" she harangued. "Can't you do anything right?"

"I did what you told me, Mother," Ahmed

193

professed, ducking and covering his head. "I went to see Dr. McLeod, but he didn't know anything; not even that Honifa had fled from Dark of the Moon nor escaped the Al Hoceima jail."

"Which, of course, you told him, you dolt! You numbskull!" She swatted his hands and arms viciously. "I said listen to him, not talk!"

"But the man had nothing to say," Ahmed insisted, trying to shield himself with a pillow.

"He's lying!" Madame Hassan screamed.

"Not to me," Ahmed muttered. "I've known Simon McLeod all my life and—"

"Nitwit! Bubblehead!" she screeched. "You're more of a fool than your father, soft-bellied newt that he was." She aimed the hairbrush at the small of Ahmed's back where it struck smartly and clattered to the floor. "Oh, why am I cursed with such a useless son?" she wailed. "I, a woman of substance and quality; a woman who deserves more than this offal, this pap, this thankless child I carried for long months of agony and birthed in hour after excruciating hour of scouring pain."

She raved on in this fashion for several more minutes while Ahmed waited. When her fury abated, she sank onto the bed and said, in a normal voice, "And now you say Simon is gone."

"Yes, Mother. He left most everything behind as if he meant to return but there's a sign on the door that says the clinic is closed until further notice."

"You found nothing?"

"We broke in and searched every room of the house and clinic. There was nothing that told us where he went or where Honifa might be."

Madame Hassan picked up her hairbrush and handed it to Ahmed who began to brush her long, thinning hair.

"They're together," she said reflectively. "Simon knows Honifa's whereabouts and he's gone to her. Those simpletons guarding the clinic are as useless as you are. Our best hope is the boy."

Ahmed brushed with rhythmic, soothing strokes. If his mother fell asleep, he'd be able to sneak out to the cafe before being roped into another night with her and Abiba, two harpies who made his life a misery. Honifa had never been cold to him, or shrewish or judgmental. He could talk to Honifa. She played passable chess and backgammon, didn't pester him for attention or badger him for money. True, she had left him but maybe she had a good reason. He'd dearly love to see her again and ask what it was that had driven her away.

"Ow!" Madame Hassan yelped. "Pay attention to what you're doing. You've scratched my scalp." She grabbed the brush. "Go dress yourself for dinner and no sneaking out when everyone's back is turned. I expect you at the head of the table, on time and cheerful." She smiled, showing all her teeth. "There's a good boy."

Supper was as deadly as he'd expected; his mother's greasy, highly spiced, heavily sugared cuisine, served in unctuous silence and consumed by her and Abiba with much lip-smacking and discreet belching. Ahmed ate sparingly, waiting for the moment to excuse himself and light his bubble pipe. That moment never came. He was drinking a thimble of the honeyed sludge his mother called Turkish coffee listening to her litany of his failings while Abiba gleefully counted them on her fingers and half expecting her to remove her shoes and start counting on her toes, when a servant whispered in his mother's ear. Her jaw dropped and her eyes popped open.

"God is good! God is great! God is merciful!" she whooped.

"What is it, Mother-in-Law?" Abiba asked. "Did your horse win the Fantasia?"

"Better than that, Daughter. Better than a hundred horses. Your son is here!"

"*My* son?" Abiba said appalled.

Ahmed dug his fingers into her wrist. "What are you saying, Mother?"

She shook him off and rolled her eyes. "What do you think I'm saying, fool? They've found Maliq."

****

For many weeks after Maliq was installed in the House of Hassan, the gossips in the medina buzzed. A baby, can you imagine, pale as the moon and a year old at least! It surely didn't belong to the young Mistress Abiba since the master spent his nights in the arms of an ephemeral lover who resided at the end of a hookah.

Every day, the old woman Jeddah raided the market stalls for sugar teats and lengths of batting and Madame Hassan had to dismiss her laundress for refusing to do nappies. The new laundress, who'd presented herself at the compound almost immediately, was round and jolly. She collected Maliq's soiled nappies in a large basket, washed them in the Moulouya and brought them back before evening, neatly folded and smelling of meadow grass. Jeddah liked her and so did Maliq. Whenever the laundress appeared, he squealed and ran to her, grabbing her skirts and digging into her capacious pockets for the little trinkets she brought him, a dyed pigeon feather, a string of colored beads, and once, a grasshopper in a cage that he watched solemnly for a moment then set free.

Maliq liked most people, though Jeddah believed he was quieter and more cautious than other children his age. At eighteen months old, his wheaten hair and fair skin had darkened slightly, but his eyes were like a lion cub's, large and yellow green. His father must be a handsome man, thought Jeddah, wondering, not for the first time, just who Maliq's father was.

Jeddah believed she owed her life to Maliq. When she was dragged into Madame Hassan's dining salon after being forcibly abducted from the Monastery of the Holy Rood, the insufferable old mistress had ordered her taken to the market at once and sold. The fat young mistress with the eyes of a roof rat tried to take Maliq from her, but he had kicked and screamed with ear-splitting ferocity and bit Abiba's finger so hard she threw him onto the floor where he vomited on Madame Hassan's pearl-encrusted sandals. The old mistress' face grew red as a pomegranate seed and Jeddah, fearing the witch was going to throttle Maliq, boldly picked him up. He quieted immediately and remained so until Master Ahmed reached for him and the whole scenario played anew. Finally, Madame Hassan bowed to the inevitable and allowed Jeddah to remain.

She and Maliq spent their days and nights locked in a room off the granary, with high sloping walls and a dome overhead where martens nested. It was cool and pleasant, but a prison, nonetheless. When Madame Hassan remembered their existence, she would send someone to unlock the door and, for a few hours, or until Abiba complained the boy was giving her a headache, Maliq splashed in the fountain and played among the fallen petals on the paths of the rose arbor.

Today Maliq was on his stomach, his arms folded beneath him, watching the goldfish circle the garden pool. At a movement in the doorway, Jeddah looked up expecting the laundress. Instead, it was the master. She knelt quickly and pressed her head to the tiles. The master's shoes were scuffed and the hem of his *djabador* frayed and dirty. He's trying to sneak away without his mother's knowledge, Jeddah thought as she watched Maliq's chubby legs toddle over to the master and disappear as he was swept into an embrace.

"Good evening, Jeddah," the master said. "Come sit beside me and tell me how well my boy does."

Jeddah rose and perched at the very end of the stone bench, no part of her touching Ahmed.

"*Masa alnoor*, Sidi ben Hassan," she said formally.

The master looked near death. His sunken cheeks were pale, his eyes and mouth ringed in blue. He smelled unwashed, unhealthy.

"So, is he well, our little king?" Ahmed asked, bouncing Maliq on his knee.

"As well as can be expected, master," Jeddah replied. "For a child who is locked in a storeroom most of the day."

"Ah, yes," Ahmed muttered. "I've been meaning to speak to my mother about that." He studied Maliq intently. "But the boy thrives, yes?"

Jeddah had resolved to say as little as possible in this house of thieves and kidnappers.

"He's alive, master, if that's what you mean."

Ahmed carried Maliq to the fig tree, plucked a ripe, purple fruit and fed it to the child.

"I'm going out, Maliq," he said. "Would you like me to bring you something?"

"Horse," Maliq replied without hesitation.

"But I've bought you a hundred horses. You never play with them."

"White horse," Maliq added.

"You have a white horse," Ahmed insisted. "I gave it to you just yesterday." He looked questioningly at Jeddah.

"That was a horse without wheels," Jeddah explained with ill-concealed impatience. "His horse has wheels."

"Shanoo!" Maliq exclaimed, kicking his legs.

Ahmed returned to the bench. "Can you draw me a picture of this horse, Jeddah? I'll have an exact replica made for the boy."

Jeddah supposed she had enough skill to sketch the toy horse that looked like Shabanou, but fury at her capture and confinement had rendered her more stubborn than usual.

"No, master," she said sullenly. "I cannot."

Ahmed sighed, kissed Maliq, and handed him back to her. "Then I shall have to return with every toy horse in the market."

He left the garden slowly, dragging his feet. Like an old man, Jeddah thought, and felt a brief pang at her rudeness.

"The master loves you," she murmured, kissing Maliq's tawny head. "But so does Alqamar and one day soon he'll come for us and we'll all be together again."

Just then, the laundress arrived. She sat where the master had and motioned Jeddah to scoot closer. They began to talk about their plot to liberate Maliq. Their voices threaded into the hall and Ahmed, returning to the garden on an impulse, overheard the astonishing conversation. He ran to his mother sobbing.

She listened to all he had overheard and clapped her hands for her body servant, a godless Sudanese with the gait of a wolverine. He accepted his task and leapt into action.

When it was all over, when the bodies of Jeddah and the laundress Fawzia Bareed, lay bleeding on the tiles, their heads severed from their necks, Ahmed scooped up Maliq, who had watched the carnage alone and forgotten under the fig tree.

"Lock him in the granary," Madame Hassan ordered.

But Ahmed gripped the bawling child and bolted from the garden. Eyes crazed, he shot like a burning comet through the house and into the stables, shouting at the cowering stable boy to harness the barouche, open the double doors and get out of his way or be mowed down.

Chapter 19

Directly after the *Mary Ellen* was safely on her
way to England, Tor's first instinct had been to storm
the Hassan compound, pistol in one hand, knife in the
other, seize his son, carry him to the *Witch's Moon* and
make for London, all in one, swift action. But the blue
man's voice of reason had prevailed. If the rescue
attempt failed, Tamajaq pointed out, Maliq might be
killed.

"Then what's your plan?" Tor asked. "I'm not a
tolerant man. My son and Jeddah are in that den of
villainy, and I want them out."

Tamajaq had nodded his understanding. "I know,
Captain, but certain risks are unwise especially when
caution and patience promise success. Now I happen to
know that Madame Hassan is without a laundress."

Tor scowled but waited to hear where his First
Mate's intriguing premise was leading.

It led to a plot wherein Malcolm Bareed's wife,
Fawzia, would hire on as the Hassan's new laundress,
befriend Jeddah and, when the time was right, smuggle
Maliq out under a pile of dirty laundry and deliver him
to the *Witch's Moon* for immediate departure.

Tor initially agreed and Fawzia quickly gained
Jeddah's confidence. She reported that Maliq was
unharmed and even growing fat. But after weeks had
passed and the moon waxed from scimitar to full, Tor

grew restive.

"I don't like it, Man," he told Tamajaq. "It's taking too long."

"A few more days, Captain," Tamajaq had begged. "Madame Hassan must never suspect Fawzia and Jeddah or their lives will become as expendable as Honifa's."

"Still, I don't like it," Tor repeated.

When at last Bareed advised that Fawzia was bringing the boy the next day, Tor asked Odin to bless this, his most important mission. But Odin spat in his face. Fawzia and Jeddah were slaughtered and his son carried off by Ahmed Hassan. In a fury, Tor rode out like one possessed to every corner of Nador and beyond, calling for the coward Hassan to show himself, challenging him to surrender or be hunted like a dog in this life and if need be, through the gates of Hell in the next. He suspended his searching only long enough to water and feed his flagging mount and even then, even during these hasty respites, he paced and fumed and raged at the indifferent skies.

Finally, with no other recourse, he sat down in his cabin on the *Witch's Moon* to write a letter to Honifa, his first since she'd landed in England. Tor had never been much of a correspondent. Words were expendable to him; deeds were important. But now, on this unfortunate day, he was constrained to send news that was sure to break a mother's heart.

He struggled with every word and when the letter was finished, he stared at the clean, firm script, cold marks on a cold page, and cursed his ineptitude. His pen had failed as miserably as he. Honifa must never know of his rage and frustration nor would she take reassurance in well-turned phrases that pledged his spirit, his life, his very soul to Maliq's liberation. He ripped up the paper, took another sheet, and wrote simply:

Ahmed has taken Maliq and hidden him. I will find our son and bring him back to you.

The pitiful sentences mocked him. Did he truly believe he'd find Maliq? He knew little about Ahmed ben Hassan apart from the fact that he was the scion of a well-connected family and there were hundreds of places where a man of influence could hide. He frowned at the letter and crumpled it just as Tamajaq entered the cabin. The Tuareg's eyes fell upon the ball of paper hitting the floor.

"Have you changed your mind about writing to my little sister?"

"I can't do it, Man," Tor replied. "Not until I've found Maliq."

Tamajaq nodded. "And the other one you seek, the Yoruba woman?"

Tor tightened his mouth into a hard line. "I haven't found Yarra either, but I will." He looked out into the blue expanse of water and sky. "First things first, Tamajaq. You remain on aboard until I recover Maliq. Keep my ship ready to sail at a moment's notice. Once the boy is on his way to England, I'll deal with the rest."

****

Yarra loosened the straps of her knapsack and let it slide to the sand. It was filled to bursting with dried meat and *injera*, a bag of tea, a small comb of honey, and her weapons, knife, bow, full quiver, and the small pistol with the silver stock Alqamar had given her.

Dear, wonderful Alqamar, who hid himself from all but a few trusted friends. She had been one of them and yet, in an irretrievable moment of madness, she had jettisoned his trust like trash. To add to her calumny, she had burned her *gimbri* and the Celtic harp.

A little more than a month ago, Yarra had been ready to dash her traitor's body against the stones without hope of mercy. Now, she stood foursquare above the bay at Al Hoceima, ready to complete her mission of atonement that had begun with an epiphany and would end with the murder of Royce Davilow.

It was twilight, a tricky time of evening when insubstantial shadows made one see more than, or not enough of, what was there. Yarra flattened herself on the crest of a dune and watched the *Dover Star* bob and sway in the gentle current of the bay. A few of the crew were loading bales of something into a beached dinghy while another larger boat, more like a tow boat, listed on its keel in shallow water. A dark, cylindrical shape, like a roll of silage, stood nearby. Captain Davilow, the silver buckles of his shoes gleaming dully, guarded the roll, a whip and musket in his hands.

Moving carefully, Yarra pulled an arrow from her quiver and strung it lightly, keeping the point down and away from her as she watched and waited. When the dinghy was full, a man hopped in, manned the oars, and pushed off. Other men moved over to Davilow, pistols drawn and at the ready. Suddenly, the captain cracked his whip. The bales in the dinghy and the roll of silage began to move and Yarra saw to her horror that they were slaves huddled and cringing at the strident lashings.

She stiffened with outrage, raised the bow and,

chin tucked, one eye squeezed, aimed directly at Davilow's black heart. But she had forgotten Alqamar's warning: strike true but without passion. Glorying in her hatred, she hesitated a millisecond and failed to notice a crucial fact: she was not alone. An arm thick as a cudgel grabbed her from behind and lifted her off her feet.

"What are you doing up here, *Negrita*?" a man grunted in her ear. "You belong in the boat with the rest of the cattle."

The skin of the sailor's arms was dark, dark as hers and he spoke a polyglot, like traders who worked the Bay of Hispaniola. Yarra twisted savagely, arching her spine, and kicking, but to no avail. The man was huge and stank like a rutting bull. When he threw her over his shoulder, she bit him on the neck, but he only laughed and bit her back, in the soft flesh above her waist. She felt warm blood ooze down her belly and fought dizziness. For all her practiced strength, she was no match for the behemoth.

"*Capitan*!" the bull shouted, laughing. "I got a wildcat up here. Send ten men to help me carry her down!"

He dumped Yarra on the sand at Davilow's feet and mashed his foot square in the small of her back.

"Ahh, the comely little aide-de-camp," Davilow taunted, toeing the eagle feather still threaded snugly in Yarra's curls. "I see you dressed for the occasion."

He grabbed a handful of her hair and yanked back her head. She glared at him, but her expression turned to revulsion when she realized what he was going to do. She jerked away too late and a gob of Davilow's foul-smelling spittle caught her full in the face.

"Bid her in," Davilow ordered, and Yarra was clamped in irons.

****

Tamajaq stood on the aft weather deck of the *Witch's Moon* staring out over the water, his dark face creased with worry. Some of the crew were perched on the master boom or bustling behind him, caulking, swabbing, coiling rope. The air reverberated with the rhythm of seamen at work, but not with the usual hearty shouts. Today, the lads were subdued, crestfallen. Tor had returned after an absence of many weeks only to order yet another delay. His ship was ready to sail but the captain wasn't.

Tamajaq was eaten with concern for his good friend, the man who, disguised as Dark of the Moon, had rescued him from a life of slavery. Indeed, most of the crew of the *Witch's Moon* owed their freedom to Tor Kendrick and though they'd been patient with the endless and unfamiliar procrastinations, the strain of being berthed when sea sirens called, of being condemned to idleness and uncertainty after action and decisiveness, was starting to show. Shipboard harmony had eroded; loyalty was next.

Like his captain, Tamajaq was a man of few words, but he'd made up his mind to speak of this loadstone between them: Tor's crushing inability to locate Maliq. In the beginning, Tor had returned to the ship after each foray disappointed but unbowed and, in a day or two, he'd set out again with renewed hope. But, as failures mounted, his sojourns on board became brief and troublesome. He stormed about, barked at the men, or brooded in his cabin. His unshaven face grew haggard, his eyes cold and manner distant. When Tamajaq once mentioned that the *Bainbridge* had been spotted breeching the Pillars just north of Cetua, likely with a cargo of slaves bound for Spain, Tor had barely looked up.

"We can intercept her, Captain, empty her hold and be back here in a day," Tamajaq had pressed.

"And then what?" Tor answered sharply. "I've no camp, no way station, no time."

So Tamajaq had found temporary headquarters for Tor's other self, the outlaw Zalam Alqamar, on a hidden plateau deep in the Atlas Mountains. The Atlas ran in three separate ranges from the Atlantic coast southwest to Algiers. The upper reaches were inhospitable, consisting of steep, saw-toothed peaks covered in snow, but the base lands might sustain for a time and in relative obscurity, a colony of freemen and their livestock. These lands were less than a day's ride from the inland city of Taza, a liability during flight and they possessed none of the comfortable caves and verdancy of the Rif. But there was passable access from the south and, once through the tree line, the region was dependably isolated.

Yet Tor had refused to act and an opportunity was lost whereupon the unmolested *Bainbridge* had delivered her cargo of slaves to Spain and, if Tamajaq's spies were right, joined the *Dover Star* at Al Hoceima. The blue man had challenged Tor with this information, but he'd disappeared again leaving the *Witch's Moon* to flounder, leaderless, pointless, and doomed.

Elbows on the deck rail, chin in hand, Tamajaq contemplated the infinity of the sea. If only Honifa were here. The captain spoke little of what was in his heart, but Tamajaq marked the light in his eyes when the beauteous half-breed was near and the catch in his voice when he said her name. With Honifa at his side, Tor might find the will to fight his demons; with Honifa's forgiveness, Tor might be able to forgive himself.

Tamajaq listened to gulls squawking contentiously overhead, to the boisterous rabble below him on Waterfront Street, and to the clamorous life that echoed from the decks of other ships in port. Only the *Witch's Moon* was hushed, her normal clatter subdued, her crew at the end of its tether, condemned to months of stagnancy with no reprieve in sight. With a leaden heart the Tuareg turned from the rail,

****

Sultan had thrown a shoe. Irritated at the waste of precious hours, Tor left him at a stable in Al Hoceima. Oblivious to his own exhaustion, he made for the nearest tavern, a squalid hovel above the bay filled with cutthroats and shabby women. He didn't care. These days, he hardly noticed where he slept or what he ate, if he slept and ate at all. Tor drove himself as ruthlessly as an overseer drove slaves, his whip an unshakable obsession to find Maliq.

He ordered rum, a drink he never used to fancy, and swallowed the first glass in two gulps. The rum was harsh, tasting of the keg and rusted barrel stays but he ordered another and then another, longing for insensibility. A woman detached herself from a cohort of men playing cards and sidled up to him.

"My but you're a big, handsome fellow," she crooned.

She could have been Berber or European or Chinee for all he noticed her.

"Buy me a drink and you won't be sorry," she promised.

He stared at her, his face closed. She wasn't young but her cheeks were plump and rosy, her eyes clear and without the world-weary glint of avarice. He hadn't had a woman in months, not since he'd taken Honifa in the bee meadow. Maybe a woman was what he needed, someone pliable and undemanding who knew nothing of the hate and despair in his heart.

Her hand was on his, her skin soft, her knuckles red and dimpled. Staring at it for a long moment, then trailing his eyes along the pale flesh of her arm to the tops of her breasts, round as two custard apples above her bodice, Tor studied her creamy neck and the tentative smile on her pink lips, imagining parting those lips with his tongue and tasting the warm wetness inside her mouth. He pictured her naked, splayed before him, the mound of her sex beckoning, glistening, drawing him in, and turned away unmoved.

"Are you ill, sir?" the woman asked, a queer expression on her face. "You look ill."

Without a word, Tor tossed a coin at the barkeep, slapped another in front of the woman, and left.

A breeze was blowing off the bay. Tor stepped from the quay onto the sandy shore. The marrow of his bones had turned to water and he thought he might throw himself down on one of the dunes and sleep for an hour. He'd searched every house and market stall for miles around, questioned beggars and magistrates alike, climbed embankments and crawled into ditches. All to no avail. Maliq and Ahmed had vanished like jinni in a bottle. Tor's defeat at the hands of the man who was still Honifa's husband, learning of the deaths of Jeddah and Fawzia Bareed, and the exile he had forced on Honifa, weighted him like waterlogged ballast. At the same time, it drove him on. He could not stop looking for his son and these broken wanderings from shoal to hilltop, his dogged, relentless questing, kept him from sinking into total despondency.

Tor dragged through plover grass and sea plum vines to the dune ridge that ringed the inlet. Wearily, he plowed up the leeward side of a large dune and lay prone, his head cushioned in his arms. But sleep eluded him. He opened one eye and morosely studied the shore. The beach appeared empty except for a tightly packed roll of debris and a dory listing heavily in the shallows, its dead rise submerged from keel to bilge. Tor sat up and looked more closely. The dory was overloaded, piled with what seemed to be wreckage. A ship waited close by, just beyond the reef line with a single lantern swaying from her rigging. Tor rose on one knee. Three men milled on the shore, one with a whip in his hand.

A whip? Tor's throat tightened. He peered fixedly through the dim light and saw that the wreckage in the dory moved; they were bodies, living beings, as was the mounded debris on the sand. Slaves! Soundlessly, he crept back through the grass to the far edge of the shoreline where it curved into the trees. He pressed his stomach against a boulder and stole quick glances at the slaves and the man who wielded the whip, a man in a frock coat and silver-buckled shoes. He'd heard the *Dover Star* was back in commission, heard but had relegated the information to the queue in his head: Honifa and Simon to safety; find Maliq and reunite him with his mother; hunt down Yarra and Davilow; then get back to work as Dark of the Moon. Yet, crouching on the dune, glaring at the stinking slaver, Tor rearranged his priorities.

Davilow laughed meanly and lifted a small woman into the boat. She was manacled, but her unfettered feet kicked wildly.

"Let me go, maggot!" she screamed. "Or I'll kick your sorry bollocks clear up your gullet."

Yarra.

"Heathen cunt," Davilow grunted.

He threw Yarra atop the other slaves and the boat cast off for the *Dover Star*. Tor rose to his full height. They were going to enslave Yarra, the girl who had begged him for sweets, and later for kisses. Yarra, his little sister, whom he'd loved above all other women until Honifa. It was true that she had betrayed those who depended on him and deserved punishment. But it was his to give, not Davilow's.

Tor marched down the dune to the shore. Clouds obscured the moon; the stars hid their light. He heard the slosh of oars and the terrified mewling of captives. The toe of his boot hit something in the sand. He picked up a quiver and a small bag of provisions. Yarra had packed for a mission, and he knew what it was.

He pulled off his boots and wrapped them and his pistol in his shirt. He stowed his knife, a slender *poignard*, in the waistband of his britches and after making certain the boats were well out to sea, he slipped into the water.

He swam like an otter, cleanly, barely breaking the surface, and reached the *Dover Star* minutes after the slaves. He waited to port, treading water while they were unloaded starboard and herded into the hold. He heard the slam of the hatch cover and the scrape of the dog bar that battened it shut. Davilow called for one of the men to take first watch, then all was silent. Tor waited for the crew to settle themselves then climbed a painter rope, slid over the rail and crouched against the bulwark.

The night was calm. Waves lapped gently against the ship's hull and fog, like a ghostly curtain, hung from mizzenmast to plank. Stealthily, he reached the quarterdeck. The watchman, his back to Tor, leaned against the railing, his rifle propped on its stock beside him. Tor grabbed the barrel and swung the stock at the watchman's head, knocking him senseless. Without breaking stride, he leapt to the cargo hold and used a marlinspike jammed into a coil of oakum to slip the lock. He thrust aside the dog bar and opened the hatch. The stink of fear and moldy dampness enveloped him. Slaves were packed to the bulkheads like cigars in a box, horizontally, one batch atop the other. All bore marks of the whip. Yarra slumped over the hatch ladder, her skin streaked with bloody gashes.

"Yarra," Tor whispered. "Can you move?"

She raised her head. Her mouth was swollen and caked with dried blood. A beam of light from the deck lantern fell across her eyes that widened at the sight of him.

"Alqamar! Is it you?"

"Yes. Are you chained?"

She lifted her manacled wrists. "My feet are free. I can climb out of here."

He pulled her from the unmoving body upon which she lay.

"I think he's dead," Yarra said. "Many of them

are." She sat with her back to the coaming. "I was going to kill myself for my perfidy but decided to kill Davilow instead." She swiped at her eyes with the back of one hand and her chain rattled. "I'm sorry. I did a terrible thing."

"Be still," he warned.

Working swiftly, he dug the marlinspike into the hasp of her padlock and snapped the pin. The chain hung from one cuff.

"Take my knife. When you hit the water, swim like a fish," he whispered. "Run to the blacksmith. Sultan is there. I'll be right behind you."

She righted the drooping eagle feather and together they crawled to the gunwales. Tor boosted Yarra onto the rail.

"Go!" he urged, but she gasped and crouched there, frozen.

Tor followed her terrified stare. The watchman had emerged from the shadows. He stood with his rifle shouldered and aimed directly at Tor's heart.

"Jump!" Tor hissed at Yarra.

"No!" she cried. "I won't leave you."

"Not a wise decision."

That was Davilow's voice. Tor looked up and saw him on the captain's flat, a small protrusion of the navigation deck. He held a pistol in each hand. "Your dusky princess can entertain you in the hold," Davilow sneered. "We left her ankles free."

Tor reached out behind him and grabbed Yarra's arm.

"No!" Yarra pleaded.

"Don't be a fool," he hissed, and threw her into the bay.

Davilow shouted an order and several men emerged from below, seized Tor and lead him to the hold. The last sound he heard before the hatch slammed over him was the gratifying thrash of Yarra's strokes diminishing in the distance.

PART TWO

Exile

Chapter 20

London 1855
It is the thirtieth day of Tammuz, Honifa wrote.
Then she crossed it out. *Today is June 30th. Happy*
Birthday, Dear Maliq. I can hardly believe your
grandfather and I have been in London for three
months. I wish you were here with us.

She stroked Shanoo who listed beside the inkwell,
and looked out her garret window at the line of rooftops
and chimneys that stretched in an unbroken line under
the slate gray sky. She had written forty-four letters to
her son since she'd left Nador in February, more than
two a week, forty-four promises that she held him
curled in a corner of her heart, that she hadn't
abandoned him and one day, they would be reunited.
The letters were all that kept Maliq and Tor alive in
Honifa's waking memories.

She raised her pen to continue.

London is an exciting city and we live in the most
exciting part. Minna Bundy, Captain Coffee's sister,
has given us a nice attic room on a street called Ivy
Lane.

True to its name, Ivy Lane crawled hectically
through the Parrish of St. Giles-in-the-Field, a former

215

haven for lepers and one of the most squalid and derelict sections of London. The lane was flanked by a warren of dank, sunless tenements and lead from the church of St Giles to the former "Hanging Tree" on Tyburn Hill. Its residents, the poor and lonely, the sick and corrupt, wolfish dogs and scraggly cats, rats the size of a grown man's foot, and birds with soot-stained feathers flapping madly in the hooked cages of mercenary bird-catchers, lived amidst a plague of noise that caused Honifa to grit her teeth. The maelstrom of sound began early in the morning with the clang of church bells and never let up. Street hawkers vied with braying animals, creaking wagon wheels, and hammering workmen. Bear baiters cheered, slatterns taunted, drunkards brawled. Skiffs and wherries on the Thames hooted shrilly and the whoosh and lap of ground conduits, meant to provide water as well as wash away sewage, underscored the cacophony.

Honifa and Simon lived directly under the steeply pitched roof of a narrow, white-washed boarding house situated on a plot of scrub between Ivy Lane and Dirt Alley. The floorboards slanted, tiny creatures skittered in the woodwork, and the garret window admitted scant light. There was an iron bedstead with a horsehair mattress that Honifa slept on and a second mattress on a trundle for Simon. The landlady, Minna Bundy, an orotund, middle-aged woman with bright cornflower blue eyes, had filled a pine chest with fresh linens, scoured the wooden table and chairs and laid in a supply of beeswax candles. Simon, initially at loose ends, had succumbed to Minna's bustling charm and made himself at home.

Honifa lit one of the candles against the early

evening gloom and bent to her letter.

Your Jad has settled in nicely and convinced your Umma that the city needn't be a frightening place. He has opened a clinic and works as hard as he ever did in Nador. We have put by a little and when I see you again, I will buy you a pony cart and a real pony, just like Shabanou.

At first, Honifa had spent her time huddled under blankets or downstairs with Minna in front of the parlor fire even on the mildest of days. But Simon, spurred on by Minna, had donned his plaid watch cap and walked the triangle from Shaftsbury Avenue to New Oxford Street to Charing Cross Road, uncovering in the process a Scots cheese monger, a clothier who sold on credit, and the *Bull and Bottle* where, before five, a full pint could be had for the price of a half. He'd crossed Blackfriar's Bridge and was dismayed and then elated to discover that, except for the muckety-mucks on Harley Street, there was not one physician's shingle in sight.

"These poor folks need doctoring and I'm going to give it to them," he'd informed Honifa and within days, he'd cleaned and bandaged the hand of a man who'd been bitten by his wife and accepted thruppence for his trouble.

"Didn't even ask for it, Honi," Simon boasted proudly, flipping the coin once before stowing it in his pocket. "I wager there's more 'n thruppence to be made hereabouts."

Within weeks, word of his skill with lancing, bloodletting, and bone setting spread throughout the parish. Honifa was roused from her lethargy to assist him and soon she'd attracted a cohort of her own patients partly due to fulsome endorsements on the part of Minna Bundy and Lizzie, the maid.

Lizzie was a frail, pale-faced girl of tender years who was responsible for all the housekeeping. She carried water, raked fires, and emptied chamber pots as well as swept the floors, dusted the furniture and polished the silver. The attic room was included in Lizzie's duties but she rarely needed to climb past the middle landing. Honifa cleaned her own room, carried her own slops, and washed her and Simon's clothes.

The poor, overworked girl confided one day that she'd been to the abortionist on Doyott Street not three days past but was still gripped in, "a bloody flux summat orful, like me insides be dragging chains." Honifa administered adderwort and black cohosh root and by morning, Lizzie's bleeding had stopped. A delighted Minna prevailed upon Honifa to concoct something for her rheumatism, the neighbor's skin rash, the butcher's chilblains, and a huge, debilitating wart on the mayor's toe. Honifa opened an account at the chemists and planned, come spring, to clean out the untidy backyard and put in an herb garden.

She completed her forty-fifth letter to Maliq, folded the pages carefully and stored them with all the others in a *Mother MacDoo's Banbury Biscuits* tin. She didn't bother to seal them in envelopes because she had no address for Maliq, and Tor had told her to commit nothing to paper. Letters could be intercepted and used to betray her, he'd cautioned; further contact between them was dangerous.

Honifa capped the inkwell, cleaned the nib of her pen and, though it was still early, prepared for bed.

****

Apart from longing for Maliq and wondering how many more days before Tor appeared on the front steps of Minna Bundy's lodging house holding their son in his arms, Honifa's resiliency and ability to adapt began to serve her well in London. The pervasive smell of mildew and damp stone, the vertiginous skies, the eerie glow of gaslight, pestilent fog and windows stuffed with rags slowly ceased to discomfit her. Mudlarks, chimney sweeps, and hawkers chanting hopefully, *goldfinches for a shilling to sing a brighter day,* no longer disturbed her sleep and she had made a second, nay, a third home for herself on Ivy Lane.

What she was trying hard to come to grips with, were the queasiness that woke her every morning, the tenderness in her breasts, and a kind of vagueness and inattention that plagued her brain. She'd thought for a while that her condition was a result of the long sea voyage on the *Mary Ellen.* But it wasn't. She was skilled enough to recognize the signs when she took the trouble to read them. Besides, she had felt this same way before Maliq was born. Honifa counted on her fingers, *Nisan, Ayyar, Huzirai;* four months gone and thirteen days into the fifth. By *Tishrinath Thani*, by November, the month of ghosts, she and Tor would have a second child.

****

In the hold of the *Dover Star,* Tor's eyes opened to blackness. He smelled the foulness of death and fear and when he swallowed, he tasted blood. Pain shot through his body.

He was bound; no, not bound, chained. His wrists and ankles were manacled and his neck clamped in a thick metal collar affixed by a short length to something above his head. If he so much as turned, he'd choke. He took a breath to calm himself but the air stabbed through his chest like a dagger. He must have broken a few ribs and shattered some other bones as well. He remembered being beaten for hours, maybe days, remembered swirling in and out of consciousness while scores of men had at him, taking turns, cheering one another on with Davilow the loudest of the lot. He remembered being cut from the whipping post and slammed into the hold and after that, he remembered nothing.

"Some water?" Tor felt rather than saw a large form moving at his side. "Drink, my friend. You've had nothing for days."

The rim of a cup touched his lips and he swallowed gratefully though his insides clenched. The man had spoken Setswana and Tor answered him in the same language.

"How many days?"

"Five, six," the man said. "Some of us were unloaded in Spain yesterday and now we're in open water again." He held up Tor's head. "Drink."

Tor forced down a few more sips. "You're not chained?" he croaked.

"Not the way you are," the man answered. "They must fear you a great deal."

Tor grunted a raw laugh then winced. He cast his eyes around. In the weak light leaching through the slats of the hatch cover, he discerned the huddled shapes of his fellow prisoners and saw that his collar chain was looped over a beam not more than an arm's length above his head. Did he have the strength to snap the wooden joist without decapitating himself? He pulled sharply. A bolt of fire shot from his neck to the base of his spine but he thought he heard the beam crack.

"Easy, friend," the man said. "You'll bring the roof crashing down on all of us."

Tor would have to wait until they were in port and the hold was empty. While the crew was distracted unloading the slaves, he'd break the beam, slip the loop of his neck chain, and make his escape. He'd move quickly, elude anyone still on deck and hurl himself overboard. He'd still be trapped in heavy manacles, but he'd do it. He'd do it and then return to kill Davilow.

The hatch cover was lifted and a beam of daylight shot into the hold.

"It's our bread," the man whispered to Tor. "I'll get some for you. You must eat if you want to stay alive."

Tor was beyond hunger but he very much wanted to stay alive. He would eat and drink and wait for his body to heal.

****

Londoners said it was the coldest fall in memory. By November, ice shards glinted on the surface of the Thames and the window in Honifa's garret room was laced with hoar frost. Every morning, she shivered in her bed until Lizzie knocked with the hot water jug. She washed and dressed hurriedly, pulling a capacious smock over her burgeoning belly, and made her way downstairs where she accepted a cup of cocoa and two Banbury biscuits from Minna Bundy. The nausea and malaise that had plagued her past few months had abated.

"I'm ready to work, Father," she told Simon, who was at the table beside Minna.

"Don't be daft, Honi," he scolded. "It's freezing in the clinic and you need to be off your feet."

Simon had divided a portion of the street floor of Minna Bundy's lodging house into two rooms. The smaller room was his examination room and dispensary, and the larger one, outfitted with chairs and a coal brazier, was the patients' waiting room. Honifa had worked happily there, but confinement was nearly upon her. This child would be born in England, most likely in a bed, and take its first breaths in the arms of a loving grandfather, a kindly landlady, and Lizzie, eager to be nursemaid.

Maliq had been born into an outlaw's hands, in a cave high in the Rif, attended by only his mother and father. How she loved Maliq! How happy she had been feeling the weight of him in her arms, his suckling mouth; how proud and excited and yet, how consumed with worry for his safety. Now, though a miracle was once again growing inside her, a commingling of her blood with Tor's, her mood was phlegmatic. When she was not sick or dizzy or bumping awkwardly into things, she tended to forget she was with child and its sudden quickening would stop her in her tracks.

She cradled her belly. *I'm sorry, little one,* she said in her heart. *Once you're here, I shall do my best.*

Dinner that evening was a festive affair. Lizzie and her young man, an apprentice to the blacksmith, had gotten engaged and Minna had baked a Lady Baltimore cake for pudding. Honifa felt well that night and after dinner, she doused the candle in her cozy attic bower and looked out into the foggy night. The moon was hidden but a spray of stars hung low above the backstreet called Dirty Alley. She watched them twinkle on and off and prayed, as she did every night, for Maliq.

The next morning, Honifa awoke from dreams swarming with sea monsters and other terrifying visions. In one, a broken ship rots on a barren shore. Tor, naked but for ragged britches, sprawls on the planks, back striated and bloody, yellow hair a matted tangle. Suddenly, Honifa appears before him dressed in dead Mary Ellen's clothes. Tor drags himself close to her with the raw-knuckled hands of a corpse, nails black and curling, eyes hollow sockets yet somehow also filled with anguish. He begs for help but she's not real, not there; she's only a useless vision. Perspiring, she swung over the side of the bed and pulled out the chamber pot ready to be sick, but the wretched heaves were dry and empty as a pirate's promise. Sick only at heart, she stood to begin another day and her bag of waters broke.

Honifa's daughter was born on the last day of November, swiftly, without trouble, nearly without pain. She held the delicate infant in her arms and smoothed her silken brow, dark and sweet as cinnabar, and stroked the ebony angel fluff feathering her scalp.

"She looks just like *Umma*," Simon said.

And it was true. The baby's turned-up nose and round, deep-set eyes were those of Honifa's Tuareg mother, as was her mouth, a lily bud nestled between dimples. But her chin, with just a hint of a cleft, was Tor's.

"Have you got a name for the nipper?" Lizzie asked, bustling about.

Honifa didn't need to ponder an answer. "Regin," she said, "for Tor's sister."

****

By his reckoning, Tor was four months in the hold before seizing his chance to escape. As the cabin boy knelt to close the hatch after the last coffle of slaves had been taken ashore, he steeled himself and grunting with pain, planting his feet firmly, he pulled with all his strength against the collar, first right, then left, then straight downward. The beam split into two sections. The cabin boy screamed and ran. Tor pulled his neck chain free and, though his wrists and ankles were fettered, he shoved aside the hatch cover and began to climb through the hatch. Behind him, the roof of the hold sagged and sections of planking splintered and toppled onto the floorboards. Tor rolled over the coaming but unable to run, he pressed his arms against his chest and pitched to the gunwales. Footsteps thumped behind him and Davilow's excited exhortations vibrated in the air.

"Look alive you scurvy lot! Kendrick's loose! Seize the prisoner before he jumps!"

Tor dragged himself over the top rail and, for a split second, he saw on the dock below, a dark line of slaves, their eyes white with amazement, their mouths hanging open.

"Look out!" many of them warned. "He's behind you!"

A searing blow smashed into the back of his head and he curled like a vector and crumpled. Blood spilled into his ears but he heard Davilow's snarling words.

"I should kill you now, Kendrick. But killing's too good for bilge like you."

Tor managed to open one eye. Above him, Davilow swung a bloody cudgel from hand to hand.

"Take him below," he commanded. "Wrap him in chains from head to foot like a pharaoh's mummy but mind he doesn't die. I have other plans for Dark of the Moon."

Chapter 21

"You're late getting back from the blacksmith's, Lizzie. Did you linger there to see your fellow?" Honifa teased.

Honifa was on her hands and knees in the garden, spreading compost. Two buckets of the rich, loamy mixtures rested beside her, one acidic, one alkaline, each carefully prepared and nurtured until it was the exact density and complexity required. Regin crawled after butterflies in the pansy bed.

"My Jacky was there," Lizzie replied. "But Colin kept him busy."

Jacky was apprentice to the smithy, Colin Slaney, a slender, soft-spoken man with black hair. Slaney's Forge served St. Giles Parish and its vicinity.

"Did you get the copper shavings?" Honifa asked. Lizzie had swept Regin up in her arms and was playing "nosy-rub" with the delighted girl. "Put her down," Honifa said laughing. "Between you and my father, she thinks she's Queen of Sheba."

"The poppet's barely four years old. Let her have her way. Soon enough she'll be at the beck and call of some silver-tongued scallywag."

Honifa stabbed her spade into a clump of spikenard, inadvertently shearing off several filaments of its root. "Maliq read books at nine months," she mumbled. "At least, I think he did."

Annie grew quiet. "Sure, and you're probably right. Whatever you say."

Honifa pushed a damp lock of hair from her forehead. "I'm sorry, Lizzie. This heat makes me cross, though it never bothered me back home."

"People change."

Honifa sighed. In some ways, her daily life hadn't changed at all. She ran a thriving dispensary from the front rooms of Ivy Lane just like she always had in Nador and the Rif. She lived in modest comfort and was raising a beautiful child who was the joy of her life. Yet Regin knew nothing of her father and brother, and Honifa despaired of ever seeing Tor and Maliq again. London was safe and busy, but although Simon and her daughter were ever by her side and Lizzie and Minna were dear friends, she felt profoundly alone.

Honifa rose to give Regin a kiss. "Can you take Regin inside for her tea, Lizzie and see if she'll nap. I'll have the copper shavings, please."

Lizzie looked nonplused. "Oh, the shavings. Right."

"You did get them?"

"It's how I did, and didn't, ma'am."

Honifa folded her arms. "You always call me ma'am when you've collywobbled, Lizzie. Out with it."

"Well," Lizzie began. "It's as Colin had them all right but they was in the back, and he was sore busy and it's a shame to vex a bloke what's sore busy for a penny's worth of metal dust."

Honifa scowled impatiently and Lizzie giggled.

"Anywise, Colin will bring them round to you tonight."

Honifa shook her head. "You must stop this

matchmaking. I told you I'm not interested in Colin Slaney."

For the past two years, the little maid had been championing the blacksmith as a husband for Honifa and a father for Regin. Honifa had explained that she already had a husband in Nador, a Maghribi aristocrat who probably spent his days pampered by five or six new wives. And Regin had a father, too, though Honifa was still haunted by terrifying night visions of a haggard, emaciated Tor with eyes deep as tunnels into Hell. Frequently her dreams were messages of truth and these nightmares made her shudder. She shook off the dark forebodings and took her daughter from Lizzie.

"I'll look after my little whirlwind," she said fondly. "You go back to the forge and get the shavings. I need them to make a plaster for Minna's knee."

"Why don't you go?" Lizzie persisted. "You've been in London nearly four years with nary so much as a cuppa with a feller though I know you've been asked. Colin's sweet on you, and he's a widower what lost his wife and child in a fire. You two have much in common and you don't want to be alone now I have my Jacky and your father's marrying Mrs. Bundy Sunday week."

But that's exactly what Honifa wanted, to be left to her daughter, her work, and her hopes of seeing Maliq. Though Lizzie believed five years an eternity, to Honifa they were but an interruption. She would hold her son in her arms again. Every nerve in her mother's body tingled with the surety that he lived, that he was fed and clothed and unaware of his loss. She was less certain about Tor. She had obeyed his warning not to contact him but she resolved to send him a message through Captain Coffee when he came to London for his sister's wedding to Simon.

****

The following Sunday, Lizzie was ladling Brunswick stew into Captain Coffee's bowl.

"Ahh, the aroma," Coffee enthused. "Did you make it, Lizzie?"

"She most certainly did not," Minna informed him good-naturedly. "She peeled the potatoes and scraped the carrots, but I'm the cook around here."

Coffee picked up his spoon. "Then it's lucky you are, Simon McLeod, to have my sister to wife."

It was Simon and Minna's nuptial dinner, served as all the meals on Ivy Lane were, in the parlor. Honifa, who usually covered her braided hair with a cap and hid her simple frocks under an apron, had taken special care today. Minna had helped her turn a length of sprigged muslin into a full-skirted gown with ruched sleeves and a scooped neckline. She'd worn the dress with a jade green spencer and matching ribboned bonnet to the wedding ceremony this morning and caught a glimpse of herself as she'd passed the hall mirror. *I'll do. I'm a little thicker at the waist,* she had thought, *but my arms are slender and my skin is clear.* Regin, clad adorably in pink dimity had babbled, "Pwetty Mummy, pwetty Mummy," all the way to the Church of St. Giles-in-the Field.

Simon gazed proudly at his new wife. "Lucky's not the word for it. Blessed, honored, unbelievably favored are better words."

"Go on with you," Minna countered, coloring.

They're in love; how wonderful, Honifa thought, warning Regin not to spill mashed parsnip all over her new dress. She too was blessed by Tor's love and she

229

pictured him as he was before the monastery fire, tanned and bare-chested, his hair a shining nimbus around his handsome face. Did Minna and Da love each other like she and Tor? From the looks on their faces, she reckoned they did.

"What of the old Maghreb?" Simon asked Coffee.

"Much the same," Coffee answered. "Lawless for the most part. Ben Abbas uses your former clinic and rooms as a safe house. He's installed a fortune-teller there as a front, a Berber slave woman freed by Dark of the Moon."

Mrs. Coffee cleared her throat. "Royce Davilow's king of the seas now, the way Tor Kendrick used to be."

Honifa's spoon clattered into her bowl. All eyes turned in her direction.

"Have you seen Captain Kendrick?" she croaked.

"Ah, um, n–no, dear," Coffee stuttered. "He may be plying different waters, the Americas, perhaps. In any case, I haven't seen him." He stared into his stew. "He's around; or maybe not. Anybody's guess; anybody's guess."

Later, after the bride and groom had left for their new rooms in Finsbury Square, Honifa joined Mrs. Coffee by the fire.

"It's been quite a day," Mrs. Coffee said. "The child asleep?"

Honifa nodded. "Regin loves the dancing doll you brought her from Bombay. She's taken it to bed with her."

"Mr. Coffee used to bring our dear Mary Ellen something from every port of call. Once, he was in Kingston, or was it Turkistan, no, maybe Afghanistan–"

Her eyes sought the ceiling.

"Mrs. Coffee," Honifa blurted, "I believe your husband knows more than he's saying about Tor Kendrick." She knotted her hands in her lap, preparing for any answer.

Mrs. Coffee patted Honifa's knee. "Now, now," she said kindly but firmly. "You must face facts, dear. The *Witch's Moon* was once a common sight along the Barbary Coast, but no one has seen her for years, nor her captain. Mr. Coffee thinks the ship may have gone down in northern waters with all hands lost."

A tremor passed through Honifa's body and her eyes filled with tears. "Is he, is Mr. Coffee certain?"

"As certain as can be, dear. My husband knew Tor Kendrick's father and after the poor man took his life over that sad business with his daughter, Tor became like our adopted son. If there were any way he could be here with you, believe me, he would. Now blow your nose and carry on." She handed Honifa a handkerchief and added gently, "Regin's his daughter, isn't she?"

Honifa nodded numbly.

"Then all the more reason to sail into the wind. You have a child to raise. Find yourself a good, God-fearing man and raise her together. Have many more children. After our darling Mary Ellen passed on to the Elysian fields, Mr. Coffee and I prayed for more like her, but the Lord saw fit to bless us in other ways. Trust in the Lord and his light will shine upon you. The bible tells us—"

Honifa heard nothing of the woman's evangelical ramblings. Tor was dead, claimed by the sea he loved. As Dark of the Moon, he'd nevermore fight for freedom and she'd nevermore thrill to his power and gentleness, hear his laughter, or see the blaze of passion in his golden eyes. Abruptly, she begged Mrs. Coffee to excuse her and as she passed the hall glass on her way to her room, she saw reflected there not the passable woman in a muslin dress anymore, but a sallow-faced scullion with hair the color of drying leaves. I'm truly alone now, she thought. Lizzie has her Jack, Da and Minna have each other, but I'll grow old and sharp-tongued and pass my nights in memories and regret. All I'll ever have of Tor will be Regin, not even Maliq, the son he swore to save.

****

Tor languished in the hold of the *Dover Star*, trussed to a bench like a buck on a barrow. There was a gaping wound in the back of his head that had festered for weeks. Illness, prolonged beating, and sporadic, meager rations had stolen what little strength remained to him. He tried at first to keep track of time, to gauge the feel of the air when the hatch was opened for the daily meal of water and mush. He called out to the captured men and women who were loaded and unloaded with regularity, asking what day, what month, what year it was but in time, he lost count and ceased to care, passing endless hours in oblivion, too weak to struggle, his anger dulled by suffering and deprivation. He dreamt of the sweet silkiness of a lovely woman, and of the tender spot on a baby's head that smelled like a morning meadow.

From time to time, he was shaken rudely awake and his bonds were tightened and doused with vinegar. He began to dread feedings when lumps of moldy bread were jammed between his cracked lips and sour water thrown at his face. What sustained his life also sickened him and he lay in his own foulness, his shrunken flesh digging cruelly into the slats of the bench, his skin branded to ridges by coils of imprisoning rope. He never saw the sun and turned away from the flash of light that filled the hold when the hatch was slid open.

****

"Look at me, Kendrick," Davilow ordered, kicking Tor awake from dreams of a woman with hazel eyes. "Let me see your miserable face."

Tor knew his captor wanted him to beg for death. "Cut me loose and face me like a man," he said with a snarl, injecting all the power of his will into the challenge.

Davilow laughed. "You've been on your back so long you can't even stand."

"Try me."

"Fool," Davilow hissed. "Your bravado bores me. You don't know who you are and whipping you is a waste of time. You swoon like a woman after the first blow." Nevertheless, Davilow aimed a few vicious blows and climbed from the hold. "That brute is like stinkweed," he joked to the cabin boy. "He refuses to die."

"Why don't you kill him, sir?" the cabin boy asked.

Davilow clapped the boy's back. "Death belongs to the spineless, lad. I have a better idea for Captain Kendrick of the *Witch's Moon*."

****

The sun rose and set; the moon changed shape; the tides rolled. In the blackness of the hold, Tor saw nothing but the images in his own head and even those faded until one day, the squeal of the dog bar against the hatch invaded his empty thoughts. He cringed as light flooded in.

"Over there," Davilow said. "On the bench."

"Is he alive?" a man asked doubtfully. "I won't pay for no dead bodies."

"He's alive all right," Davilow answered. "And there's plenty of work left in him."

The man pinched Tor's arm. "He ain't but skin and bones. How long you had him down here?"

"Who knows? He eats and shits. Do you want him or not?"

"Can he walk?"

"Let's see." Davilow took a knife to Tor's bindings.

As the ropes were cut from his body, Tor felt a moment of panic. His hands gripped the sides of the bench.

"Stand up!" Davilow commanded.

Tor willed his legs to move and was surprised when they obeyed. Using his arms as support, he stood, swayed, and fell to the floor. Someone doused him with a pail of seawater and the stinging shock enraged and enervated him. He rose to his feet and remained there, unsteady but determined.

"You must have been quite the Samson once," the man said. "From the north by the look of you."

Tor made no response.

"Can he talk?" the man asked Davilow.

"What do you care?" Davilow replied testily. "You want a white slave you can yoke to a grindstone. Well, here he is. He's stupid as an ox and doesn't know night from day."

Tor had to be helped on deck but once in the open air, his disorientation fled. The whiteness of the sky, the screeching gulls, the raw smell of paint, though these things assailed his senses in painful waves, they were nevertheless comforting. He knew the sea, knew it elementally, in his vitals. He must have been a mariner once, he thought, or worked around ships. On shore, people walked about, men in long robes and skullcaps, veiled women. He blinked. The image of a woman floated before him, a graceful, amber-skinned woman with the eyes of a cat. Who was she?

"Into the skiff with him," the man said.

He emptied a purse into Davilow's hands and Tor was clamped in irons and prodded onto the gangway. For the first time in more than a year, he stepped off the *Dover Star*.

Chapter 22

London 1860

Oranges and lemons say the bells of St. Clemens

You owe me five farthings say the bells of St. Martins

When will you pay me say the bells of Old Bailey

Here comes a candle to light you to bed

Here comes the chopper to chop off your head

On the last line, Regin glared with menace and slashed her arm through the air.

"Very good, luv," Minna said, applauding.

"You made me right shiver with the chopper bit," Lizzie added. "So dramatic."

It was Regin's fifth birthday and her family was gathered around the hearth in what used to be Minna's parlor, now converted into a bedroom and sitting room behind the dispensary for Lizzie and her husband, Jack. Honifa and Regin lived in three rooms overlooking the back garden. She and Lizzie shared the kitchen and scullery.

Honifa pulled her daughter to her. "You left out half the bells, sweeting."

"I'm sorry, Mummy, but I wanted to get to the ax part."

She looked downhearted and Jack quickly piped, "That's the best part."

"You had us all that scared, Poppet," Simon

soothed. "I'll say a pretty piece now, shall I, to calm my poor old nerves?"

Dutifully he rose, placed one arm on the mantle, winked at his granddaughter, and began to intone like a seasoned thespian:

At the corner of Wood Street when daylight appears

Hangs a thrush that sings loud; it has sung for three years

Poor Susan has passed by the spot and has heard

In the silence of morning the song of the bird

"Ooh, I do love that one," Lizzie gushed, resting her head on Jack's shoulder. "It's so sad."

Simon accompanied each verse of Wordsworth's *Ode to Cheapside* with sweeping gestures and bowed at the coda like Scaramouche, doffing an imaginary plumed hat. Honifa served cinnamon toast, bread and butter pickles, and hard-cooked eggs in curry sauce that Regin called "Hindoos." Lizzie carried in a large, iced cake topped with five candles and everybody sang *Green Grow the Rushes* starting with, *five for the symbols at your door,* and ending with, *one is one and all alone and never more shall be.* Regin blew out the candles one at a time.

When the party was over, Jack prepared to return to work at Slaney's Forge.

"Shall I take Regin with me, Miss Honi?" he asked. "Colin promised her a ride on Old Melinda for her birthday."

Old Melinda was Colin Slaney's antiquated Percheron, a gentle beast with a back broad enough for a dozen small children. Honifa hesitated. Regin's rose merino party frock would be ruined in the muck and dust of the forge.

"Another time, Jack," she told him.

"Mummy, please!" Regin wailed. "I promised Colin and there's new kittens in the barn. Pleeese."

"I'll look after her," Jack offered.

Honifa relented. It was the child's birthday after all. "All right. Just give me a moment to get her into Wellies and a smock."

"But, Mummy,"—Regin pouted—"I want to show Colin my party clothes. Mayn't I go like this?"

Honifa regarded her petite daughter, her brown curls gathered in a pink ribbon, her round, shining cheeks and determined chin. "Minx," she said. "You're fond of Colin Slaney, aren't you?"

"Oh, yes, Mummy. I'm going to marry him when I'm big and ride Old Melinda every day. You can marry him too if you like."

Honifa promised to collect her daughter after completing her work and waved as Regin and Jack bicycled down Ivy Lane, Regin on the handlebars happily clutching a slice of wrapped birthday cake for Colin. Honifa hadn't said more than four words to the blacksmith in as many years. They saw each other occasionally of course, once on Ludgate Hill, another time looking in shop windows on the Tottenham Court Road. He'd had a woman on his arm that day, a slender, pretty woman with yellow curls peeking from underneath her poke bonnet of chip straw trimmed in the same lace as her fashionable pelisse. Colin's face had brightened when he saw Honifa, but she bent her head and hurried by without a word. Now, as she attended to the routine scrapes and catarrhs her patients presented, she thought absently about the blacksmith.

Colin Slaney wasn't a large man, although his arms were well-muscled and his face was pleasing. He'd lost his wife and baby son when their house had burned to the ground and he'd never rebuilt, letting the blackened walls of the cottage stand as a grim memorial to his suffering. He slept in the loft above his forge winter and summer, a private man of simple tastes who ignored or didn't seem to notice the women who set their caps for him.

When her last patient had gone, Honifa tidied the dispensary and donned her woolen cape and gloves. As an afterthought, she took the manure sack from its hook above the compost pile. The trees along the Foundry Road leading to Slaney's Forge were nearly bare, and the air was aromatic with burning leaves. At the blacksmith's compound, she stood just outside the open doors of the forge. Colin, his back to her, was bent over the anvil pounding rhythmically with a mallet. He wore britches and his leather apron, nothing else. His back was sheened with sweat and the muscles of his arms and shoulders rippled like waves on a pale sea. Honifa watched him, her brain swirling with images of another man in a leather vest, a man with the arms and shoulders of an Atlas, a man who tied his hair in a queue like Mr. Slaney did, but a golden man with flaxen hair and the tawny eyes of a jungle cat. A pang gripped her. She turned to leave, nearly tripping over Regin returning from the orchard. Regin pulled her mother over to Colin.

"Mummy's here, Colin," she said excitedly. "I've picked up all the windfall apples and put them in the byre. May I feed Old Melinda now?"

Colin looked up. "Is that all right with you, Miss

McLeod?"

Honifa nodded and held up the gunny sack. "I'd like some honey chips, please. For the garden." To Regin she said, "You may go thank Melinda properly for the lovely rides she gives you."

Honifa sat under the chestnut tree as her tiny child scampered to a fenced paddock where the huge, sway-backed dray horse grazed placidly. Beyond the paddock, on the far edge of the meadow, the blackened husk of Colin's cottage loomed, and she imagined flaming timbers and the panicked screams of a small boy crying for his rolling horse. She trembled.

"You all right, Miss McLeod?" Colin stood above her, the filled chip sack in his hands.

"Yes, thank you. Shall I pay you now?"

"Jack settles your accounts at the end of the month."

"Well, then. Regin and I will be off," she said briskly.

"She seems to be having a last word with Melinda. Can you wait a bit?"

He sat beside her and in awkward silence, they stared at a little girl dancing around the giant horse.

"Have you seen the *Punch 'n Judy*?" Colin asked at last.

"The puppet show?"

"Aye, it's at the fair tomorrow, for Guy Fawkes Day. They have Harlequin and Pierrot and Columbine; rope walkers, acrobats, conjurers." He wiped his hands on his apron. "The little lass would enjoy herself. You too, Miss McLeod."

"We've been to see the dwarves at Drury Lane but never to the Guy Fawkes. Isn't it a bit rowdy?"

Colin faced her and smiled hopefully. "You needn't worry if I'm with you."

Honifa studied his hands. They were large with broad, calloused knuckles. Fleetingly, she wondered how they would feel against her skin.

"Please allow me to accompany you and the little miss to the fair tomorrow evening," Colin said eagerly. "It's at the foot of St. John's Street, almost to Old Bailey. I'll hire a landau."

Honifa thought about how nice it would be to ride in an open-air carriage with Regin on her lap, to walk the byways of the fair eating rock candy from a paper sack, and to arrive back home deliciously tired but with enough energy to brew a pot of sassafras tea and sit at the window counting shooting stars. In the years she'd been in London, a few men had asked her to step out, for a walk in Regent's Park or a pint at the *Bull and Bottle*, but she'd always declined. Her life was busy; her dreams were for Regin's happiness and the recovery of Maliq. Perhaps she was being foolish. Perhaps a partner was what she needed to provide Regin with a satisfying life and even to help her locate her son. The smithy was not unappealing. Regin liked him and, according to Lizzie, Colin was "right smitten".

"Thank you, Mr. Slaney," Honifa had said politely. "I accept your invitation."

But that night, Honifa dreamt of Tor. He was once again in frightening devastation and pain and she awoke with a start, lit the brazier and hunched before it, chilled and shaking. When Colin arrived the next day to take her to the fair, Honifa pleaded indisposition. He lingered in the doorway a moment, then nodded curtly and left.

****

Tor had been sold to an unscrupulous miller who harnessed him to a stone grinding wheel, chained his arms to the shaft, and set his feet in an ankle-deep groove worn into the ground by the hooves of the dray horse imprisoned there before him. Day and night, year after year, Tor trudged the groove, never stopping, his existence reduced to an unchanging circle. His body, clad in ragged pelts, was exposed to frigid weather, to ice and snow and hail that stung him like poisoned arrows. He slept in his bonds, his head on the wheel shaft. He ate the chaff that flew in the air and drank what fell from the heavens into his upturned mouth. Yet perversely, he grew stronger with every turn. Hatred surged through his veins, fed him, and made him powerful again. His muscles bulged; his chest rippled. He was like a wild animal, wary, instinctive, and blind to the past. His only memories were primordial, deep bone images that fueled his survival; and his only thoughts were of revenge.

Chapter 23

Lizzie barged into the attic fairly bursting with her news. "You'll never guess, Honi. You'll just never guess what I just learned."

Honifa looked up, mildly annoyed at the intrusion.

"The blacksmith, our Colin, has got himself engaged!" Lizzie crowed. "Can you fathom it? I thought he fancied you but he's gone and done a turn-around."

Honifa remembered the blonde woman she had seen with Colin on Ludgate Hill and felt a slight twinge in the pit of her stomach. "He never fancied me, Lizzie."

"Oh yes, he did. Jacky told me so, and you could see it plain in his face."

"That's nonsense," Honifa said. She vigorously applied the pestle to the dried corn berries in the mortar.

"Are you jealous, then?" Lizzie asked coyly.

"Don't be silly. I'm pleased for him." Honifa set the pestle aside. "And you know what? Just to prove it to you, I'm going to invite the blacksmith and his affianced to dinner."

"Coo, Honi. That's right decent."

"Not a bit of it, Lizzie." Honifa took off her apron and rolled down her sleeves. "He's not a lover who spurned me. He's Jack's boss and our friend. I'm off to the forge straight away. What do you think of that?"

She threw a warm coat over her brown dress, asked Lizzie to keep an eye on Regin, and, for the second time in a little over a month, walked to the forge.

The ground was covered with a light blanket of snow. The paddock was empty and Colin Slaney's ruined cottage hulked like an ugly blotch against the pewter sky. She stared at it, lost in unbidden memories.

"Miss McLeod?"

Honifa started. "Good day, Mr. Slaney. I was admiring your farm."

He smiled. "It's hardly a farm, though I'd meant it to be. Who knows, perhaps someday."

"Perhaps soon," she said cheerily. "Lizzie told me you're engaged to be married. I offer my congratulations." Their breath frosted the air between them and his gray eyes held hers. She cleared her throat. "So, when will it be?"

"When will what be?"

"The wedding, of course."

"Ah," he said neutrally. "The wedding." He began to walk toward the forge. "There's not going to be a wedding."

Honifa followed him. "There isn't?"

He slid the doors open. "Come inside, please." He took her cloak and his eyes held hers for a moment. "It's warm in here, isn't it?" he said. "A forge is the best place to be in winter. I'm afraid I haven't any tea. Will you take a glass of porter?"

"No, thank you. I-I'm sorry about—"

"No need," he said, pointing to his head and then to his chest. "Things that seem right up here are not always right in here."

"I see," she said. "Well, then, I'll run along and

save my felicitations for another day."

"But you've only just arrived." His disappointment was palpable.

She laughed. "That's true. Why don't you come to Ivy Lane for Christmas dinner? Minna and Lizzie are planning a slap-up. I'll have nothing to do, and we can get properly acquainted and call each other by our first names."

She walked home deep in contemplation, hardly taking in the pigeons cooing atop the frosted stone arches of Westminster Bridge, the stench of refuse on Pudding Lane, the brightly painted signs in every shop front along Hoop Alley. Colin was not engaged. He was not going to marry the skinny blonde in the ratty pelisse. He was free to marry someone else.

That night, Honifa stopped writing to Maliq. There were hundreds of letters neatly tied with twine and stacked in several *Mother MacDoo's Banbury Biscuits* tins, but she would add no more to their number. Not because she despaired of ever reuniting with her son but because she suddenly believed, suddenly knew with the shivering, soul-plumbing certainty of a seeress, that her life was about to change. She didn't love Colin but he was a good man. With him by her side, she could search for Maliq with renewed vigor and she might, with God's knowing mercy, finally be able to unlock her heart and accept the loss of Tor.

****

At Christmastime, London became a magical city. The trees in Regent's Park glittered like fairy wands, horse bells jingled, and impromptu carols echoed along the Thames. Buttery smoke from the potato hawkers' tin ovens coated the parish of St. Giles-in-the-Field like a fragrant caress. And, like the snowflakes that floated in the crisp air, romance flourished everywhere. Businessmen from the Royal Exchange promenaded with apple-cheeked ladies in furs, Covent Garden swains in Hessian boots bowed to blushing girls, and doxies blew kisses up to the windows of Newgate Prison. Lizzie and her Jack, even Minna and Da, acted like lovers.

Honifa had never celebrated Christian feasts, but she was no longer in her native land. Her brain still formed words in Arabic, but she spoke them in English, and though she made *Salat* every morning, she attended Sunday services whenever Simon and Minna invited her. She wore corsets, finger gloves and boots with hourglass heels and said *blimey* more than *bismillahi*. Her roots had sprung from the banks of the Moulouya River and would always cling to her like the scent of wild geranium, but England was home.

Honifa made pomander balls and paper lanterns. Lizzie pinned mistletoe above every doorway, and Jack dragged in a tree and promised Regin there'd be a kitten under it for her on Christmas Day.

On Christmas morning, Honifa awoke at dawn. She lit the brazier and fired up the stove. She would have liked to start a fire but Lizzie and Jack were asleep and she dared not disturb them on one of Jack's rare free days. Lizzie would be up shortly in any case, and so would Regin as soon as she smelled the chocolate bubbling on the hob. Honifa poured them both cups, set Regin's on her bedside table and took hers to sip by the garden window. The herb beds were covered with snow, the bushes bagged in a row like toy soldiers. But soon, in a very few months, the lush vibrancy of nature would reassert itself and life burst forth again, as it always did. Honifa sighed with pleasure, her hands warm around the chocolate cup, her body languorous. A new year loomed. She would face it as a new woman.

Colin arrived at noon, letting a blast of fresh, icy air into the front parlor. He complimented the table draped in red damask and garlanded with holly and told Minna and Lizzie they were the prettiest girls at the party and that Regin was the most beautiful. Regin proudly showed off Puss in his basket then pulled Colin into the scullery where Honifa was basting the goose.

"Tell Mummy she's pretty too," she said.

Honifa turned shyly. She wiped her hands on her apron and smoothed her hair. She was wearing her favorite green dress, the one that revealed the hollow of her throat and a smooth curve of skin below it.

"I must be a sight," she said apologetically.

"You are, Honifa," Colin said, his voice sober and his eyes bright.

Honifa said little at dinner and Colin, despite his energetic entrance, spoke sparingly, mostly to Simon and Jack, and winked occasionally at Regin. After jewel cake and Minna's plum pudding, Colin presented Regin with a gift, a carved Percheron horse with a red velvet saddle. Its reins were strung with tiny sleigh bells and each of its hooves ended in a shining silver wheel. Regin gasped with delight and ran to her mother.

"Look, Mummy! It's Old Melinda and she rolls like the white horse on your writing desk, only she's not broken and ever so much nicer. Oh, I love her, Colin! I love her forever!"

Honifa paled. She touched the toy horse, so like the one Tor had given Maliq and ran trembling into the hall. It was too soon; there could be no going forward with Colin and a new life while she still cherished the old one. She stared out at Dirty Alley thick with incandescent snowflakes. Two mud larks passed a bottle back and forth, lost souls hugging themselves in the frigid night. Far away, someone sang *God Rest Ye Merry Gentleman*. The cadences sounded mournful to Honifa, not merry.

"Have I offended you?"

She turned to see Colin's slim form backlit in the doorway.

"I'm sorry, Colin," she said, tears streaming down her cheeks. "I can't do this."

He was at her side. "Do what?"

She stepped back and opened her palms helplessly. "This," she said dismally. "I can't do any of it. I want to but I can't."

He took her hands. "I didn't think I could either after my wife and baby died," he said. "I'm still not sure I can, but you make me want to try."

Words welled from Honifa's heart. "I have a child in Morocco," she whispered. "A boy. His name's Maliq. Sometimes I look at Regin and compare her to him at a certain age and then I realize that I didn't know Maliq at that age. He was barely a year old when he was taken from me." A sob escaped her, a wrenching, hollow sound. "Maliq's father is dead. I loved him more than life. He possessed my heart and soul, my mind and body. I can never love another man that way again."

Colin drew her close and held her gently. "Maybe not, Honifa, but we can love each other a little. Don't turn me away. Give me a chance. Give us both a chance."

He pulled a cloth-wrapped package from his pocket and gave it to her. "I made this for you at the forge," he said. "It's a pendant. I know the one you always wear means a great deal to you. Perhaps mine will someday as well. "He kissed her softly and escorted her back to the table. When the evening was over Honifa retired to her room and unwrapped Colin's gift. It was a polished circle of metal inscribed with a delicate letter *H*. She held it for a moment, then pulled from between her breasts the two halves of the crude moon amulet now tied together just as she and Tor would forever be. She lay back against the pillows and touched her mouth where Colin's lips had been. They were cool and dry, not bruised, not aching for more.

****

Far away to the north, the seasons dragged on, dying, regenerating, each as glacial as the next. When spring arrived, Tor grew ever stronger and waited for the moment to seize his freedom. At first, the miller was pleased with his white slave. He boasted to folk from neighboring farms that the giant had cost him plenty but ground more grain than a team of plow horses and had no match in all the world for strength and tenacity. The neighbors gaped in awe as the miller proudly pointed out Tor's massive chest streaked with blood from the bite of the brace, his powerful thighs, and preternatural silence which the miller claimed was mindlessness.

One day, the miller unyoked Tor, jabbed the barrel of a musket at his chest, and ordered him to haul heavy sacks of flour to the millhouse. The miller's wife shyly offered Tor a pint of small beer. He drank, wiped his mouth, and grunted thanks. The miller's daughter took the empty glass from him, smiled, and fluttered her lashes. When the miller saw his women simpering over his slave, he ordered them to stay away. But they and many of the neighbor women continually ogled the robust, muscular man whose brooding scowl and ominous muteness began to haunt the miller's dreams. His envy blossomed into hatred and he decided to sell Tor. He visited a nearby farmer who had expressed interest in the behemoth and while he was gone, Tor called out to the miller's daughter that her father had neglected to unharness him and there were many more sacks to be carried into the millhouse. She removed his bonds and told him with a sly wink that she'd wait for him when his work was done. Tor fled and when the miller returned to an empty grinding wheel, he loaded his weapon and took off after the escaped slave. Spotting Tor in the woods, he shot him twice in the leg. Tor jerked and crumpled to the ground. The miller shot him twice more to make sure he was dead, dragged the body to a ditch and left it to rot.

****

"Why doesn't Colin come to see me anymore?" Regin whined stamping her foot.

"Keep still," Honifa scolded. "I don't know how you manage to get so dirty. Your brother never got so dirty."

Regin quieted instantly. Whenever her mother mentioned the boy called Maliq, she'd grow sad and distant and Regin needed full attention to plead her case.

"He has a surprise for me," Regin pouted. "Jack said so. Mayn't I see it?"

Honifa pulled a comb through her daughter's unruly curls so like her own. Regin had been going on for days about the surprise, begging to see Colin, but Honifa avoided him. She'd nod politely if they chanced to encounter one another in the square but always declined to stop somewhere for tea or a walk among the hedgerows.

"Mother, please," Regin whined. "Lizzie can take me."

"That I can't, luv," Lizzie said, entering Honifa's room with an armload of clean bedding. "Colin's made it quite clear that it's you and your mum he wants to see."

Honifa put down the brush. "What's this all about, Lizzie?"

The little maid looked flustered. "It's none of my affair and I don't have no idea why you and Colin aren't speaking when it's plain as char on a sweep that he's daft for you and—"

Honifa threw her hands in the air. "All right, all right. Let this be done with. Get your bonnet, Regin. We're off to the forge."

****

Colin was in the meadow. Regin ran to him, and he scooped her up.

"Jack has something for you in the foundry," he told her."

She ran off excitedly, her ribbons trailing behind her. Colin turned to Honifa. "You look well."

"You needn't have gotten anything for Regin," she said. "But I thank you all the same."

"It's a hobby horse like the one I gave her at Christmas. This one she can ride."

Honifa looked everywhere but at his face. "That's very kind of you, Colin. But I wish you hadn't."

"I made something for you, too," he continued. "Well, perhaps not solely for you."

"Please, Colin. The pendant was enough. I shouldn't have accepted it."

He took her hand. "Just let me show you."

He led her past the corral and across the field to the wasteland where his cottage had been. The shape of the building was no longer ragged. There were walls where crumbled stone used to be, the glint of windows, a shed in the cow byre, and a roof.

"You've built a house," she murmured.

"I have, and mostly alone, though Jack helped some."

He pushed open the door and ushered Honifa inside. She gasped. A wide, bare room vaulted above her like a church. Its floors, walls and ceiling were of polished ash, and the windows, so many of them, were peaked at the top like Moroccan arabesques. A stone fireplace was set at an angle, its hearth broad enough to heat the main room and the two additional rooms, one of them a kitchen already furnished with a table and four chairs.

"There's a loft above here," Colin said proudly. "And more rooms for—" He gave her a melting look. "For children. And see—" He drew her to the kitchen window. "There's a buttery and a cold cellar outside and I cleared a patch for an herb garden." He stood behind her and placed his hands on her shoulders. "You're a woman of the sun, Honifa and I wanted to make you a house you could bask in."

She turned to him. "Me? This house is for me?"

"For you, yes, and for Regin." His eyes darkened. "And for me, if you'll have me."

She could barely speak. This house, this beautiful, shining house built from the ashes of his old, ruined cottage was for her. There could be no clearer statement of the depth of Colin Slaney's devotion. Everything inside of her screamed acceptance. Her past life was fading with each new day. Tor was lost forever and vowing a wife's fealty and devotion to a kindly man who cared for Regin was easy enough. And yet, as his wife, she'd have to lie with him, give him children to replace those he'd lost and that was not easy, not without passion. What she'd felt for Tor, the shiver that gripped her spine at the very sight of him...no, that would never come again. And what of love? She'd loved Tor from the moment he'd rescued her in the Marhaba, loved him even before that, and would ever after, down through the generations. Colin, dear Colin, was no replacement for the bridegroom of her soul. Sharing herself with Colin was false when her heart beat for another. And she would never be able to bear the disappointment in his eyes when he discovered that though he claimed her, she was not his. He deserved better.

"I haven't the words, Colin," she began.

"There's trimming and caulking to be done," he said eagerly. "The banister and loft railing need bracing, but overall, I'm pleased with the outcome. Are you?"

Leaves scuppered on the roof of Colin's house, the magical roof that rose like a phoenix from the ashes of sorrow. Why couldn't she do the same? She clasped her hands to her waist and hesitated unable to find words.

Her face must have expressed it all.

He sighed. "So, it's not to be."

"No, Colin. I'm sorry."

Regin's squealed with delight as she dragged the hobby horse, almost as tall as she, across the meadow. Colin offered Honifa his arm. "Well, at least I've made the little one happy," he said softly.

"You're a fine man, Colin Slaney and I'm honored."

"But you don't care for me."

"I do, but love—"

"I understand," he said before she could explain further. "You have deep loyalties, deep passion. It's what drew me. But it's no good if I can't make you happy the way he did."

****

Summer arrived quickly along with a pall of ill humor Honifa couldn't shake off. Lizzie's questioning glances annoyed her, and she chafed to get out of the house. One sultry morning, she closed the empty clinic and went to visit her father. At the end of Chiswell Street, she entered the broad expanse of Finsbury Square and twisted the bell key of Simon and Minna's narrow half-timbered townhouse. Simon opened the door in his dressing gown.

"No patients today, Da?" Honifa asked.

"I'm forced to close on Fridays. It's fashionable around these parts, don't you know."

She looked askance at his uncombed hair and the stubble on his chin.

"Don't fuss at me," he said defensively. "My wife has run off to the shops and I've had no proper breakfast."

"Then let me fix one for you," she offered.

He led her to the back where a kettle steamed on the hob. "Biscuits and cheese will do me," he said. "What beastie is itching to get out from under your skin? I can always tell."

"My mind's uneasy and," she added softly, "my heart."

Simon folded his hands. "I see, lass. Start with the first."

"Well," she said. "Colin asked to marry me, and I should. I know I should, but I can't." She crumbled a bit of biscuit onto the tablecloth. "He's a sterling man. I'll want for nothing as his wife."

"But?"

"But he isn't Tor."

"Ah." Simon sliced cheddar and chewed thoughtfully. "Kendrick is dead, child."

"I know that."

"Tell his children about him, by all means, but get on with your life. You needn't marry Slaney but someday, there's bound to be another."

Honifa buried her face. "I know you found Minna, and I'm happy for you. But Tor is in my stars as well as my heart."

"It's not good to be alone, Honi."

"I know that too," she said sadly. "But I have Regin and someday, I'll go back home and find Maliq."

"This isn't your home, then?" Simon asked his daughter whose determined face was streaked with tears.

"No. Not without Tor."

Chapter 24

It was raining "pigs and chickens" as Lizzie liked to say and had been for the better part of the week. Honifa stared moodily at the rivulets streaming down her windowpane and worried her fingernails. Had she been wrong to refuse a decent man for the sake of destiny and lost love?

She sighed; maybe she should put on her apron and open the clinic, but who would come in this rain? The street was empty and quiet. Morosely, she moved from room to room. The grates had been swept and newly laid fires blazed. Something bubbled on the stove; a veal pie cooled; two manchet loaves sat under a cloth. There was nothing to do and nothing she wished to do. She went to the kitchen for a calming tisane.

"You're at sixes and sevens," Lizzie said. "Why don't you lie down and have a little kip?"

Honifa took to her bed. Her mind was empty, so empty she thought she might be in a trance or floating in the suspended place between wakefulness and sleep, when she saw a man in a sailor's cap and a striped jersey tapping at her window. She had to be imagining it; her mind was playing tricks; no one would dare brave this lashing downpour. But the tapping became pounding and she roused herself to open the sash.

"Who are you? What do you want?" she demanded of the bedraggled creature.

He was very tall, his skin brown and weathered, his face dark as the midnight sky.

"*Masa alkhair,* little sister,*"* he said.

Honifa went suddenly cold. The man's hands, hanging at his sides, were tinged with blue, the nails a deep cerulean.

"Oh, my god! Tamajaq!" she cried and ran to the garden door to pull her old friend inside. He dried his face and neck with the towel she gave him but refused to sit.

"Have you come with news of my son?" she asked.

"From what I have been able to learn," he said, "Maliq is with Ahmed ben Hassan. They move from place to place and are difficult to find."

Honifa breathed a silent prayer of thanks that her baby was alive. "I know that Tor is dead," she muttered.

"No, little sister," the blue man replied. "Tor is alive and he's here in London."

Lights blazed before her eyes. She fell to her knees and opened her lips to pray. But the lights pulsed and her head spun. When she awoke, she was lying on her bed, Tamajaq's worried face above her.

"How soon will Tor come to me?" she asked tremulously.

"He won't come," Tamajaq replied gravely. "He can't; not by himself."

The dread of her dreams hit like a bullet. "What's happened to him?"

"The captain put himself in his enemy's hands to save Yarra."

Honifa gasped. "Davilow!"

"Yes. We waited for our leader to return to us,

certain of his invincibility, but Captain Kendrick seemed to have disappeared. I prayed for his safety, prayed he was alive, hunted everywhere and did not find him." The Tuareg's voice caught. "Until he found me."

In the gloom of Honifa's bed chamber, Tamajaq narrated an account of the horror and suffering Tor had endured. She listened with a breaking heart and dried her tears. Tor was injured and ill but alive; that was enough. She would heal him.

The blue man's words droned on, heavy as the rainfall. "Captain Kendrick made his way south; how, I'll never know. He himself doesn't remember but he thinks he may have stowed on a whaling ketch and crawled on his hands and knees from Northumberland. He found me in Newcastle where the *Witch's Moon* had put to port. He was lean as a spar, his body reduced to raw sinew. His mighty spirit was intact but his mind –" Tamajaq swallowed and seemed unable to continue.

Honifa gripped his hand. "Please, Brother. Tell me everything."

"He wouldn't let me tend to his wounds. He wanted only one thing, to go to London."

Her breath caught. "He was coming to me."

"I don't know," Tamajaq replied gently. "His memories bloom and fade like the beacon on a lighthouse and he grows daily more detached from his senses. He has withstood much though his courage never faltered. I'm less certain of his sanity."

Distantly, Honifa heard the clock sound the hour. Footsteps started down the hallway. Tamajaq rose hurriedly. "I'll bring the captain to you tonight, but prepare yourself. The man you once knew no longer exists."

****

Thinking only of holding Tor in her arms again, Honifa turned away the anxious question in Lizzie's eyes and ignored Regin's request for a bedtime story. She dragged a pallet from the shed to her old room in the attic and lit the brazier. In the clinic dispensary, she pulled bandages from the shelves and prepared tinctures: feverfew, horsetail, ginseng, and cinquefoil. When Lizzie knocked on the attic door with a kettle of hot water to scrub the floors, she sent her down for several more.

"Keep them coming," she directed. "Fill the basin and this large jug. Then make up the pallet. Use all the quilts we have and plenty of pillows. Where's the brandy?"

Honifa marked nothing but the chiming hours so full was her brain with images of Tor, the passion in his eyes as he caressed her in his cabin under the orange sky, the dark heat of his body in the Rif cave, his tears in the desert, his gentle strength as he swirled her in the snowmelt, and the brilliance of his smile when she finally understood that he and Alqamar were one and the same. She tried not to think about his suffering. She would witness the results soon enough and would be strong as he'd want her to be. She would love him back to health and together with Regin and Maliq they would triumph.

"Your father's downstairs, Honi," Lizzie's voice rang up the stairs. "Honi? Can you hear me?" Her face poked around the attic door. "Crikey, but you look right mazed. Where have you gone?"

Honifa jumped when Lizzie touched her sleeve. It

259

was dark. Night had fallen.

"My da, you say?"

"Yes. Shall I send him up?"

"No; yes." Honifa wrung her hands. "Why has he come, Lizzie?"

"Well, I may have mentioned to my Jacky that you've been out of sorts. You hardly eat and your hair needs seeing to." Lizzie bunched her apron against her chest. "And, oh, the little one is that vexed. You lock your door at night so she crawls between me and Jacky, and bawls like to break my heart."

At the mention of her daughter's name, Honifa's head shot up.

"Regin? Is she ill?"

"Not so's I can tell. But she—well, she don't know what ails her ma. She thinks she's done you baby mischief and wants to make amends."

Remorse brought Honifa back to earth. She shot down the attic stairs to find Simon with his granddaughter. Honifa held out her arms.

Regin winced and recoiled. "I've been bad, Mummy."

"No, sweeting. It's Mummy who's been bad. I'm sorry I was mean to you this morning."

Regin dug a fist into her eyes. "I made you cry."

"I told her it's the rain makes you sad," Simon explained. "Didn't I, Regin? I told you all about the warm, sunny place your *Umma* comes from and how she must miss it?"

"Uh-huh." Regin sniffed. "Nador. The fruit on the trees is big as my head and it hardly never rains."

"Someday, I'll take you there, Regin," Honifa said. "We'll ride a camel and eat honey cake and splash in the Moulouya."

"What's a Mooya?"

Under Simon's studied gaze, Honifa told her child about Nador's peaceful river overhung with feather fern and brimming with fish in all the colors of the rainbow. When the child's head drooped, she laid her on the bed.

"I must go, Father," she said, one hand on the doorknob.

"Stay a moment," he said. "Minna asked me to come. She talks with Lizzie, you know and Lizzie's worried."

"I'm fine," Honifa said, cutting him off. "Please. I must go."

"Where?"

Honifa took a deep breath. "To the attic. I'm–I'm waiting for someone to—" Unable to contain herself, she cried, "Oh, Father. He's come back to me. Tor has come back!"

Simon's expression grew opaque. "That can't be. You're mistaken or someone's jesting. He's dead, lass. Captain Coffee told us so. It's been five years."

"He's alive, Father. He was captured and tortured; left for dead, but he's alive and he's come to me." She pushed past Simon. "He's gravely ill."

Simon knew the perils of longing, of wanting something so desperately, you conjure it up and think it's real. But Honi had always been level-headed. She was stubborn and sometimes reckless, but not the sort to become unhinged. Still, she had lost so much. He tucked the covers around his sleeping granddaughter and followed Honifa to the attic.

They waited together; Honifa rigid in front of the window, Simon alternately observing her with keen eyes and examining the medicines and bandages she had assembled.

"You'll need arnica and sutures," he said. "The poor man's sores probably haven't completely healed given what Tamajaq told you about his weakened condition." He peeked under the napkin that covered a dinner tray. "If that's for him, it's too rich. Broth is best if he'll even eat. Water with some barley sugar is what he needs; maybe ale with a dram or two of cinnabar to cleanse the blood." He sniffed the water and wood shavings warming in one of the basins. "Birch bark. Good. That's very good."

Ordinarily, her father's praise would have made Honifa swell with pride. But her pulse was pounding in her head, and she heard little but the clatter of wind and rain against the attic window. Ultimately, Simon stopped talking and held his child's icy hand.

It was after midnight when the wagon came into view, the horses' hooves thudding dully. Honifa tore downstairs with Simon close behind. He held open the front door as Honifa, ignoring the puddles and slapping rain, ran into the street. The blue man was helping Tor from the coach. Honifa's breath caught like a bone in her throat and she bit her lips to keep from crying out. Her masterful lover wore ragged britches tied with a rope and his feet were bare. His hair fell to his waist in a matted tangle that he raked back, nearly stumbling with the effort. It had gone completely white.

"Tor," Honifa said, the word escaping her lips like a whispered invocation.

He looked around blankly. His face was ashen and crosshatched with scars. His cheekbones jutted sharply and a stubble of beard the same dead white as his hair covered his jaw. Only his mouth was familiar to Honifa; the full, sensually curved lips made her want to weep.

"My love," she said gently.

Tor blinked and looked away.

Simon ducked into the rain and took hold of Tor's arm. "Stand aside, Honi," he ordered. "Tamajaq, let's get him upstairs."

The men laid Tor on the pallet and Honifa raised the lamp. Tor's chest, arms, and lower legs, every inch of skin visible, was a warren of welts and bruises. The mark of the grist harness cut deep around his neck and shoulders, scabbed in places, open and ulcerating in others. A sore on his thigh wept blackened pus. Honifa swayed; Simon took charge and examined his patient.

"He has a high fever," he explained, his voice professionally clinical. "His wounds need immediate attention, especially the thigh. It's gone septic."

Fighting panic, Honifa nodded. "Orpine, Father? And a burdock salve to draw the poison?"

"Yes. Wash him first then use a light dressing. Let the air circulate. Have you any foxglove?"

"Yes."

"Feverfew?"

She held up a vial. "Right here."

"Excellent." He rose. "Watch him carefully. I'll be downstairs. And you, my good man." He extended his arm to Tamajaq. "There's nothing more for us to do here. Your captain's in good hands."

****

All night and many nights thereafter until summer waned and the crisp air of early fall sweetened the sky, Honifa sat beside Tor's bed spooning honey water, later broth, and still later, thin porridge into his mouth. She cleaned his wounds and bathed his ravaged body, washed his silver-white hair, trimmed his beard, and dressed him in soft shirts and britches accompanying every tender ministration with words of love and soft kisses on his hands, his cheek, his mouth.

He lay inert, allowing himself to be tended. It was as if he felt nothing and heard nothing. On the rare occasions he looked at her, his eyes were fierce and bright as a hawk's, searching not communion but a distant, interior landscape of horror known only to him. He jerked spasmodically in his sleep and cried out, clinging to her. When he could walk unattended, he paced the attic like a caged beast, his heavy tread thunderous. He spent hours staring out the window, over the rooftops and chimneys of St. Giles Parish, occasionally turning his vacant gaze on the woman who never left his side. Honifa kept the door to the landing open, but Tor made no move to leave.

"I don't know what to do, Da," she beseeched Simon. "Tor doesn't know me. He takes no notice of anything around him but lives inside his head, in a shadow world filled with demons."

"Give him time, lass," Simon replied, as dispirited as Honifa. The poor devil was indeed quit of reason though his body had healed, surely by magic for no doctoring was adequate to such devastating injuries as Tor had suffered. It must be love, Simon deduced. His daughter's overwhelming, all-encompassing love had knit Tor's wounds and made him strong again. Would that it could rebuild his spirit. "He's been through an ordeal few men could have survived," he said to ease Honifa's constant worry.

Lovingly, she smoothed Tor's shining hair. "Has he survived? Sometimes I wonder."

Chapter 25

Though Honifa attempted to train Lizzie in the dispensary, the girl was hopeless. Some of the patients complained and she was forced to spend more time tending to them and away from Tor. Lately when she had a minute to dash upstairs, she often discovered Regin camped on the attic landing. The child was there today, sitting on the top step rolling her toy horse back and forth.

"You mustn't disturb the man, sweeting," Honifa said.

"But I want to go inside."

"You can't."

"Why can't I?" Regin asked stubbornly.

Honifa sighed. "The man's ill and he needs to be left alone so he can recover."

"But you and *Jad* go in to him all the time and Lizzie brings him trays."

"That's different. Your *Jad* and Lizzie and I are necessary."

Regin stuck out a miniature version of her father's cleft chin. "I'm necessary too."

****

Tor was at the attic window, his back to Honifa. The October sunlight gleamed on his platinum hair and rude animal strength emanated from his healed body.

"Tor?" she called softly.

He turned expectantly but his face instantly hardened. He looked her over, her cap and spilling tendrils of hair, her stained white apron, brown dress and shoes.

"I'm in need of nothing, thank you," he said impersonally. "You may go."

Not for the first time Honifa swallowed her dismay at his assumption she was a servant.

"It's a beautiful day," she said. "Would you like to sit in the garden?"

"No," he answered shortly.

Honifa turned to leave.

"Wait," he called suddenly. "There was a little girl here a while ago. Where is she?"

"She's been chastised," Honifa said. "She won't trouble you further."

"Is she yours?"

"Yes." *And yours*, Honifa wanted to add.

"She doesn't disturb me. She—she's—" He searched for words his face filled with anguish. "I think I'll sleep," he said, throwing himself onto the bed.

****

"Tell him everything, Honi," Simon advised Honifa. "Tell him who you are, who Regin is. He needs to hear it."

"I'm afraid it's too soon," she said.

She was sewing a cape for Regin and she ripped savagely at the row of stitches she had just put in.

"You're afraid it's too late," Simon replied evenly. "You're afraid he'll never remember."

She called to Regin who was supposed to be twisting spills. "Try on this cape a minute, Mummy wants to—" She looked toward the fireplace. The child wasn't there. Honifa hurried into the hall. Regin, with Puss over her shoulder, was climbing the steps and almost to the first landing. "Where do you think you're going?" Honifa asked warningly.

Regin hesitated but continued climbing. Honifa took the stairs two at a time and snatched up her daughter. Puss let out an affronted yowl.

"Now see what you've done, Mummy," Regin protested. "Puss and me are going to cheer up the poor man. He's ever so sad. Sometimes he marches about like a soldier, stomp, stomp, stomp, but then he smiles at me."

"He smiles?" Honifa said. Tor never smiled; not once since he'd immured himself in the attic room had he smiled. "What do you mean *smiles*?"

Regin pushed the corners of her lips apart with two fingers. "Like this," she replied, flashing all her teeth and gums."

"Are you sure? He looks right at you, right into your eyes and smiles?"

"Yes, Mummy. He even winked once. I think I like him."

Simon was listening from the bottom of the stairway. "He won't hurt her, you know, and she has a right to him."

No, Tor wouldn't hurt Regin, Honifa thought. Perhaps she should put them together. None of her gentle hints had had any effect on Tor's memory loss but blood sang out to blood. She set Regin down and took her hand.

"All right, sweeting. We'll say hello to the man."

"Let her go alone, Honi," Simon urged. "You can watch from the doorway."

Regin climbed to the attic and strode boldly across the top floor landing and into Tor's room where she announced without preamble, "My *Umma* and *Jad* said I could visit you. I wanted to bring Puss but Mummy scared him away."

Tor was in his customary spot by the window, straddling a chair and contemplating the world beyond his garret. He looked over his shoulder. Regin grinned at him.

"I live downstairs with my mum and Lizzie and Uncle Jack. *Jad* and Minna live in Finsbury, almost to Spitalfields. I haven't got a da."

"Hullo," Tor rasped then cleared his throat and said it again. "Hello."

Regin propped her elbows on the windowsill. "What're you looking at?"

He appraised her silently for a moment. The hard line of his jaw softened.

"The sky," he said. "Clouds."

Regin craned her neck. "You can't see too many trees from here but there's lots of them in the park, and the leaves are ever so lovely now, all orange and yellow."

Father and daughter stared at the shining blue dome of autumn sky pierced by the spires of the Church of St. Giles-in-the-Field.

"Why are you so sad all the time?" Regin asked. "Lizzie says you're not sick anymore."

"I was for a long time," Tor replied. "But I'm better now. You're a pretty, little girl. You remind me of someone. Are you African?"

"Mummy is. Well, half. She says I look just like her *Umma*."

Tor frowned and bent close. "I know you. What's your name?"

"Regin," she said proudly. "Regin Kendrick."

Tor leapt suddenly from his chair. It toppled to the floor. Honifa rushed into the room, her face awash with concern. She wanted to run to Tor's side but the look on his face, a forbidding scowl of confusion and anger, stopped her cold. His eyes swung from the surprised Regin to Honifa and back again. Finally, they rested on Honifa and swept from her flushed cheeks and parted lips to the vein pulsing at her throat.

Did he recognize her? Oh, Please God. Make it be so, Honifa prayed. His name escaped her lips like a supplication. "Tor?" she said wonderingly.

He dragged both hands through his hair. "Who are you? Who is this little girl?"

"I'm Honifa," she said. "That's Regin, my daughter." She took a breath. "*Our* daughter."

"Regin, Regin," Tor murmured.

"Yes. Do you know her?"

He blinked. "I had a sister named Regin."

Regin pulled his sleeve. "You scared me when you jumped like that."

Tor looked down at her. "I'm sorry."

"I forgive you." She settled on the window seat. "I don't have any sisters, but I have a brother who's called Maliq."

Tor's back stiffened. A flock of crows blackened the window as the bells of St. Giles began to peal.

"Maliq," Tor pronounced. And then, looking up at Honifa, "Maliq?"

She ran toward him, sobbing. Tor grabbed the back of the chair and held it against himself protectively.

Regin burst into startled, uncomprehending tears.

"What is this place? Where are my men?" Tor demanded. "I must get to my ship. My camp is unattended."

Honifa lifted Regin from the window seat. "Go downstairs to *Jad*."

"Why are you crying, Mummy? Why am I crying?"

"The man is ill and we feel sad for him. Now run to *Jad*. Go!"

Honifa waited until Regin was out of sight then shut the door and faced Tor. He was staring at her with malevolence in his eyes, the chair now clutched in one hand as if he would throw it at her.

"You can't keep me here," he said. "Stand aside."

"I will," she said evenly. "But first you will hear what I have to say."

His eyes narrowed. He set the chair down but held on to it.

"Your name is Tor Kendrick. You're captain of the *Witch's Moon* and as the outlaw Dark of the Moon, you rescued captured slaves and freed them. But you're also my," she took a breath. "My love."

He passed a hand before his eyes. The muscle in his jaw hammered. He stared coldly at her, calculating.

"You were captured by a slaver," she went on afraid to say more, apprehension building in her chest. "And sold into bondage."

Something flitted across his face. "The wheel," he said.

"Yes, the wheel. And there was more. But you escaped. Your friend Tamajaq brought you here to me."

Tor's knuckles gripping the chair were white. His

head moved from side to side. He was scanning the room but he saw, Honifa knew, not the walls and floor, but distant horrors. Finally, his gaze settled on her.

"And who are you?"

Her heart plummeted. "A healer," she replied simply.

He appraised her for a moment then moved toward her and touched her chin.

"You're comely," he said, adding when she backed away, "Do you fear me?"

"Do you mean to harm me?"

His grin was mirthless. "I mean to make love to you."

He seized her waist and pulled her tightly against him. She couldn't move. His hardness dug into her as his rough hands cupped her buttocks and tore the waistband of her skirt. She struggled but vainly, no match for his lust. For that's what it was; not love nor desire born of love, but raw need and the formidable will to satisfy it. He rent her skirt, petticoat and drawers, pulled them down, and lifting her, lay her roughly on the slatted floorboards. He straddled her, licked his fingers, and expertly probed and circled her cleft. She was helpless but dared not cry out lest Lizzie or Simon come running.

Tor unlaced his trousers and spread Honifa's thighs with his knee. She moaned as he made to enter her, the insidious wetness of her arousal glistening on his fingers. Her body craved him but not her soul.

"No, Tor," she cried out. "Not this way, please."

He drew back and ran his moist fingertips across her lips. "Don't be coy with me, woman. Taste your sweetness."

She kicked out, wrenched from side to side, but he would not be denied. Gripping her hips, he bore savagely into her and took her vehemently, plunging and rocking. She bit her lip; tears flooded her cheeks. She closed her eyes.

"Honifa," he groaned. "Ahhh, Honifa."

Her eyes sprung open. Tor's face was tender. He sat back on his heels taking her with him, holding her as he had so many times before. His shaft swelled and throbbed anew and he stroked her and sought her mouth with his.

"Tor?"

He kissed her deeply, exploring with his tongue, nibbling her lips and chin, trailing heat down her throat and the tops of her breasts. She tightened her legs around him as he teased her nipples, sucking gently, then avidly. She rocked her body and felt the pressure build inside her.

"Oh, my love," she groaned in his ear. "How I've missed you."

Seemingly without effort, he rose to his feet and holding her firmly, pressed her back against the door. Rearing and thrusting, he claimed her again, fiercely silent, harrowing deeply until surrender burst through her body like a rain of sparks.

He held her for a moment then released her. Panting, she slid her feet to the floor. He laced his britches and gazed down at her, smiling vacantly. The look in his eyes chilled her to the bone.

"Sorry for the roughness," he said. "It's been a while since I had a woman. Dress yourself and fetch me a flagon of ale. I'm parched."

Chapter 26

Tor's memory was unpredictable. One day he might ask Honifa, "Didn't we meet in another country across the ocean?" Another day he'd look right through her. He hadn't approached her again and, except for polite greetings, she kept her distance. He spent hours in the garden with Puss and Regin, spinning yarns about brave Viking mariners and a race of friendly, winged sea monsters who lived in an underwater city made of pearls and giant turtle shells. He played chess with Simon, tipped a few with Jack and teased Lizzie and Minna to giggles. He carried coal from the cellar, shored up the sagging porch and helped bag the bushes. One day, he asked Lizzie if there were any books in the house.

"A store of them, sir. Honi likes to read. My Jacky has a book of maps from his time at school. Shall I fetch it for you?"

Tor said please and, from that day on, he read incessantly. When he looked up from the page, Honifa saw a sad longing glazing his eyes, especially if some sailor whistled a chantey under the window. He was growing restless and, like a beast on a leash, strained for freedom. She could never hope to keep him in cramped rooms in St. Giles Parrish, force him to breathe miasmic city air, wear a cutaway and tip his hat. Tor Kendrick was a man of endless oceans, broad expanses of verdant wilderness and sparkling mountain peaks. His soul soared with hawks from crag to lowland, from desert to sea, against a sky as shimmering and faceted as a crown.

When winter approached, he took to wandering the streets and alleyways of London. Honifa tried to follow him, concerned that he'd lose his way.

"I can't keep up with him, Jack," she complained to Lizzie's husband after she'd lost Tor in the Mews. "He walks so fast. Do you think you can keep an eye out? I worry."

Worry she did, but not for his safety; Tor could well take care of himself. She worried he'd leave the house and not return.

"He causes quite a stir, Miss Honi," Jack reported after trailing Tor through the city. "But mostly, he ends up on the riverfront, staring at the boats and such."

Jack didn't add that Tor also looked in at the Tipsy Gull, a tavern frequented by sailors, where he was usually surrounded by a bevy of giggling females exclaiming over his silvery hair and rolling muscles.

****

"Where is the sea?" Tor asked one evening at dinner. "I can smell it but I can't see it."

"England is an island," Jack informed him. "The sea is all around us."

"Take me to it," Tor said.

Jack looked at Honifa. She looked at her soup.

"It's a good idea, Honi," Simon advised. He was dining at Ivy Street, Minna's curiosity having been piqued by a local Suffragette meeting in the Village Hall. "A whiff of sea air might jog your memory, Tor. We could ask Captain Coffee when next the *Witch's*

275

Moon puts to port or enquire at Seaman's Hall. They're bound to know."

Honifa paled but Simon didn't notice.

"I'll do that, sir," Jack offered. "And there's one or two other places that might know as well."

Honifa kept her counsel, but her worries increased.

****

On his way home from the blacksmith's, Jack stopped at the Tipsy Gull for a pint and a chat. He wasn't surprised to see Tor there, his long legs stretched before him, a tankard in his hand.

"You're usually gone by dark," Jack said, joining him. "What keeps you here tonight?"

"I'm meeting someone."

Jack surveyed the shadowy room. But for the septuagenarian barmaid, there were no women about at this hour, though he doubted Tor had an assignation with any of the pretty flitties that plied their trade in the Tipsy Gull. The man seemed somehow above tavern wenches. His heated gaze fixed on Honifa whenever she was in the room as if he was studying her, scrutinizing her every move, and slotting it away in some teeming mental catalog.

"Well," Jack said. "I'll have a pint with you until the, ah, gentleman comes along. If that's all right."

Tor drew in his legs and made room. "Not so much a gentleman as a sea rat," he explained. "Chandler on the *Witch's Moon* and a Scot like Simon McLeod; red hair, too."

The barmaid brought his ale. Jack quaffed and wiped his mouth.

"Saw him in here a few months ago and he looked familiar," Tor continued. "I bought him a pint and he called me Captain."

Jack put down his mug. "Captain? Is that so?"

"He told a tale much like Honifa's of oceans and deserts, and mountain valleys fragrant with mint." Tor's face hardened. "She doesn't speak to me anymore; keeps clear as if I wore a suit of leper's bells."

"And what else did the chandler say?" Jack asked casually.

"That my crew waits for me."

Jack drained his mug. "Crew you say?"

"Aye. On the *Witch's Moon*."

Jack slapped down his empty mug. "Be that as it may but the ice on the river will soon be thick as Old King George's head. Nothing's likely to sail these waters until spring."

"Then it's lucky she's here already," Tor countered with a grin. "Rounding the loop at Cornwall. In a fortnight, she'll berth at Land's End."

Jack declined a second pint. It was no secret that Tor was Regin's father, and father to their son back in North Africa. Lizzie had sussed it out and told him one night in their bed.

"Honifa loves him so," she'd sniffed tearily. "Imagine loving me the way you do and getting the cold shoulder, like I think you're some yob on the street. It's so sad."

And now Tor was planning to sail away, Jack thought, and poor Miss Honi had no idea.

****

When Jack told Honifa about the crewman from the *Witch's Moon*, she ran to Simon. "He'll take back his ship and leave us again. I know he will. What's to keep him here?"

277

"There's Regin for one, and you, Honi. You're his family."

"But he doesn't remember us the way he remembers the sea. He used to talk about the *Witch's Moon* like it was a dream. Now he knows it's real."

"Have you not considered that once he's on board, he'll resume his search for Maliq? The man's lost his memory, Honi, not his soul and certainly not his will. He's healthy and strong as ever he was."

"And what of Davilow? He'll remember him too and go after him." Honifa sighed. "Once he's back at sea, I've lost him."

Simon regarded his daughter. Her skin had paled somewhat under the overcast London skies. Her unruly curls were tamed with combs and the flowing *sulwarkamis* of her younger days had been traded for a homespun skirt and plain bertha. She wore petticoats, a corset, and laced shoes, restrictions no woman from Nador endured.

"Would you deny him his pleasure?" Simon challenged her.

"I used to be his pleasure, Da."

He regarded her fondly. "Then go with him."

Honifa's mouth dropped.

"You heard me. Pack up Regin and sail into the blue with the man you love. His child will be happy. She already dotes on him."

"I—I can't," she stammered. "I have responsibilities, the clinic, my patients. Regin knows no other life."

"You're blithering, child," Simon scolded. "You escaped from Madame Hassan, birthed a son in a cave at the back of beyond, survived the desert and are thriving in a land thousands of miles from where you were born. You can do anything you set your mind to."

"Can I make Tor love me again?" she asked almost in a whisper.

"I don't know," he answered truthfully. "But you've tried everything else. This might be your chance to find out."

****

Honifa maintained a close watch on Tor's comings and goings. When Jack took him to Slaney's Forge, she hired a brouette and followed them. She hid under a stanchion at Blackfriar's Bridge and reined in down the street from the Tipsy Gull, blowing on her freezing fingers and stamping her feet. Soon, it would be too cold to go about snooping. Soon, she'd have to face Tor directly.

Regin provided the opportunity. Her birthday dawned unseasonably warm and instead of iced cakes for tea and songs by the fire, Honifa buttoned her daughter's new redingote and sent her off with Simon and Minna to the Pantomime in Regent Square.

"I'll be along later, sweeting," she said. "As soon as I close the clinic."

"Can't Tor come, Mummy? I want him to come."

"I'll ask. But he's gone up to his room. He needs his rest."

"Pooh! Regin scoffed. "He hates rest. Why do you always tell him to rest? Make him come. He'll put me on his shoulders and I'll see everything."

In the dispensary, Honifa dressed cuts and rubbed camphorated oil on congested chests, but her mind was elsewhere. Tor enjoyed long conversations with Simon and Jack but rarely said more to her than Good Morning or Good Evening and she'd taken to steering clear of him as well, not wanting to risk a repeat of what had happened when he'd torn off her clothes in the attic. She deplored her shattering submission to him while all the while, he'd believed her nothing more than a passing tart. That he wanted her again was undeniable. She marked it in the hunger of his brooding gaze and damn her perversity, she wanted him too. She loved his gentleness with Regin and the sight of his muscled forearms and broad knuckled hands. The very look of him compelled her. Whether he was reading in the garden, moving through the rooms of the house, or striding the streets startling as a comet, he filled her surreptitious eyes with pleasure.

Honifa hung her smock on a hook and closed the clinic door. She smoothed her skirt and straightened her cap and, worried that Tor would once again blink at her with incomprehension, mounted to the attic and knocked. There was no answer.

"Tor?" she called. "It's Honifa. May I come in?"

She called again and Lizzie answered from the middle landing.

"He's out, gone while you was with the patients."

Honifa hastened down to her. "Where was he going? Did you see?"

"There was summat right peculiar about him. He shook my hand and told me Godspeed."

Honifa raced down the last flight of stairs and out the front door. Lizzie ran after her with her coat and gloves but it was as if Honifa had flown on angel's wings. The gloom of late autumn dusk had swiftly swallowed her and Lizzie trudged back to the house. Tor's room was just as she'd guessed, his things, such few of them as there were, were gone. The book he'd been reading to Regin lay on the table, open to a poem by Epes Sergeant:

A life on the ocean wave,
A home on the rolling deep,
Like an eagle caged, I pine
On this dull, unchanging shore:
Oh give me the flashing brine,
The spray and the tempest's roar

A sheet of paper rested beside the book. *I'll see you again, Regin. Never doubt it.* Beneath it, Tor had written: *Mind your mother. She is...* He hadn't finished his thought. The inkwell was open; the pen discarded on the floor. It looked as if he'd thrown it down and fled.

****

Darkness descended over the city. Honifa ran blindly down Dirt Alley and into Ivy Lane, stopping at every turning to call Tor's name. He was gone, concealed beneath the swirling mists of Whitechapel. She veered west and made for the river and the Tipsy Gull. The noisy tavern was filled with smoke. Honifa dared not enter. She beckoned to a serving woman, a hundred years old by the look of her, and described Tor. The woman spat a glob of tobacco and held out her palm. Honifa had no money, but she unpinned her collar and cuffs.

"Take these."

"Yer petticoat as well."

"I'll not," Honifa answered, affronted. "Here." She unpinned her cap. "You can have this. It's edged with lace."

The woman affixed the cap to her dirty hair and

stowed the collar and cuffs in her bodice. "The handsome giant's not here," she said. "He was earlier. Bought a round and left. Audrey was vexed," she added with a laugh. "Damned hussy never gives up."

Honifa knew no other place to go but the river. After soiling her shoes on the spongy banks, she spotted Tor walking Dock Side as if searching for something. She quickened her pace, determined not to lose sight of him. At Queen Street, he crossed the Southwark Bridge to the east end of London, less densely populated and not yet lighted with gas lamps. He stopped by a group of men huddled around a tun fire. She slid down the muddy embankment and eavesdropped.

"Whoa. Get a load of the brawny cuss," one of the men remarked as Tor neared.

Tor indicated an overturned poke. "This boat belong to any of you?"

"She's mine," the man answered. "You want to buy her?"

"How much?"

"Aw, take her," he said. "We was going to burn it for fuel, anyways."

Tor righted the boat and brushed off the oars. "She seaworthy?"

The man laughed. "Maybe. But the river's near froze and the North Sea's about ninety kilometers east. Not even the *Britannia* can make it afore spring."

From her post on the embankment, Honifa saw Tor's shoulders sink.

"You've the look of a sailor," the boat owner noted. "Old Gaffey here's a sailor too. If yer wanting ship's work, he can direct you to Seaman's Hall. There's plenty to be had for the able-bodied." He nudged his companion. "Which Old Gaffey ain't no more."

Tor threw the oars back into the boat and turned it over again. He accepted a drink from the bottle the men were passing around, thanked them, and headed for the embankment. Alarmed, Honifa turned to flee but the slippery verge impeded her progress. She stumbled and slid to her knees.

With a growl, Tor pulled her to her feet. "Enough, woman," he grunted. "You've been following me since The Tipsy Gull. What is it you want?"

"Let me go," she cried struggling.

He held her, his amused eyes on the neckline of her bodice.

"Are you mad?" she cried, trying to shrug him off, but he dragged her down the Gaol Stairs.

"This is not the first time I've caught you lurking around corners," he accused. "Jack, too, although I'm sure you put him up to it. You ignore me in the house but follow me through the streets like an albatross." He released her on the Promenade, leaned against the stone riser and folded his arms. His tone was playful but skirted menace. "You want me all to yourself; is that it?"

Honifa gathered the loose lapels of her blouse. Her hands were numb with cold, and her wet feet felt like blocks of ice. Her teeth chattered.

"I do—do not lurk," she fired back, ruing her stutter. "Your health is my responsibility. You were near dead when Tamajaq brought you to me."

"That I was," he said, suddenly serious. "You gave me my life."

A breeze stirred the water. Honifa shivered. "You

were so ill. You forgot everything that happened to you."

"You're wrong; I didn't forget. But it's over and I'm well now."

Honifa knew it wasn't over. There was still Davilow and Maliq. Tor shrugged off his jacket and draped it around her shoulders. He chafed her cold hands between his.

"I asked what you wanted of me, Honifa."

He had asked her the very same question on their first night together in his cabin on the *Witch's Moon*. Her answer had yielded much more than she'd expected: an enduring love, two children, and now, a loss so profound she would have given anything to redress it.

"Why don't you remember me, Tor?" she asked.

He slid his hands up her forearms warming her skin. "I remember the scent of your hair, and the feel of you in my arms."

Her body tingled everywhere his fingers stroked, and deep in the moist core of her.

She pushed him away. "I must get back. They'll be worried."

"Walk with me first," he urged caressingly. "It will warm you."

His arm tightly around her waist, he led her across the Watling Street bridge and into St. Paul's Churchyard. The headstones rose like sentries and fallen leaves crunched beneath their steps.

"What are we doing here?" Honifa whispered.

"Graveyards are sacred," Tor answered. "And there's no one to pry." He brushed his lips on hers. "I meant to leave you tonight," he murmured into her mouth. "But I can't. We belong together."

Her heart surged. She wanted to speak of their love, of Nador and Maliq and his daughter, Regin. But he lifted her hair and tilted back her head. Words died as he kissed the line of her jaw and the pulse at her throat. He laid her on a carpet of leaves and cupped her breast over the fabric of her chemise, caressing the nipple with his thumb. She writhed and powerless, clung to him. He unlaced her bodice encountering the stiff whalebone of her corset, but when he reached under her skirt, the prize he sought was buried under a full petticoat, a half-petticoat and drawstring pantalettes.

"Dammit, woman," he cursed. "You're a citadel."

She rolled away from him, hiked up her skirts and untied her drawers. Grinning, he pushed her back down. She opened her arms but he reached behind her to untie the strings of her corset.

"I want to feel all of you," he said.

She helped him remove her corset, blouse, and camisole, and shimmied her skirts over her ankles. With infinite slowness, he slipped off her shoes and unrolled her stockings, drawing them over her calves, ankles, and feet. He held each foot in his hands, massaging, circling his thumbs around the instep and up her legs to her throbbing core. Naked, she lay before him, her flesh prickling but with desire, not cold. Darkness enshrouded them, tree frogs sang, and the ghosts of St. Paul's watched as Tor's broad fingers probed, smoothed, and explored. And just when Honifa thought she'd die of longing, he raised her buttocks to nibble the tender insides of her thighs and darted his tongue into the center of her sex, sucking at the moist, engorged flesh, gently at first, then hungrily. She bucked and threw her arms over her head, abandoning herself to piercingly pleasurable torment as she convulsed against him. Only then did he say her name and enter her.

Tor's face was in shadow but her heart surged. Did he remember the woman or was she only a name he groaned? But she ceased to care as he plunged deeply, branding her with every possessive thrust, covering her mouth with his, emptying himself in wave after shuddering wave of release that devoured them both.

It seemed to Honifa, as she lay curled in Tor's arms, that something more than gratified lust had passed between them; something intrinsic. Not recognition for she sensed he still didn't remember her. But something beyond memory, an acknowledgment that she was a part of him more enduring than bone and blood.

She was his soul.

****

Pallid wisps of dawn streaked the sky as Honifa and Tor walked back to Ivy Lane and climbed the attic stairs, their arms entwined. The early light was vaporous and Honifa lit a taper. Slowly, Tor undressed her again, and filled his eyes with her, touching, caressing, the hard planes of his face now tender. He kissed her mouth and neck and sucked her crimson nipples, cupping each breast like a chalice.

"I can't seem to get enough of you," he said, tossing his shirt and boots aside and stepping from his britches. His hair in the candlelight was pearl white, his skin ruddy, the muscles beneath it long and smooth and forged by fire. He lifted her onto him.

"You've made me whole, Honifa," he murmured. "Everything I am or ever will be, good and bad, is yours."

He crushed his mouth onto hers, loving her against the hard edge of the table and again amidst the soft bed cushions until the first rays of morning sun slanted through the attic window.

****

Honifa slept as one drugged. When she awoke, Tor was standing by the window, one foot on the window seat, his chin in his hands. Something in his posture dismayed her. Wrapped in a blanket, she went to him.

"Tor?"

He didn't look at her.

"You don't remember," she stated bluntly. "How we were before. On the ship, the cave in the Rif. You know only who I am now."

His face filled with compassion. "Does it matter so much?"

She had no response. He was with her, loved her, made love to her and would, every night and day they were together. But although the *Witch's Moon* and slave raids were as fresh in his mind as morning dew, he had forgotten the woman as much a part of him as Eve was of Adam. Only his body remembered her.

"I'm Tor Kendrick," he said. "I hear my ship's moonraker luff and the cargo spar click in the boom rest. I smell cardamom and vanilla off the coast of Madagascar and fresh snow in the mountains. All this I remember and more. I know I have a son called Maliq, yet I can't see him or you on the day you tell me you climbed the hawser and fell into the sea, the day we first made love. I should remember but I don't." His face turned hard. "I'm sorry, Honifa. But I must go to Cornwall, reclaim the *Witch's Moon*, and be about my business."

Berbers believe hope never dies, but Tuaregs say that houses built too high invite lightning. Nevertheless, it was good to hope that someday Tor would remember even though Honifa decided to keep her feet on the ground.

"When will you leave?" she asked levelly.

He smiled. "I was on my way when something stopped me."

She smiled back. "And I would do it again."

"You would keep me prisoner in this room at your beck and call?"

She wrapped his arms around his waist and chose her words. "That's a fool's errand and I'm not a fool. I'm your soul and Regin is your blood. Take us with you back home to the Maghrib."

He pulled her close. "Leave behind your life here?"

"Without you, there is no life."

PART THREE

Freedom

Chapter 27

Morocco 1860
Home!

In a tent high in the Atlas Mountains, Honifa rolled off Tor. Her body, drenched with sweat, made sucking noises. Dark of the Moon's new camp was stifling.

"I can't breathe," she moaned, fanning herself.

"My charm takes your breath away," he teased.

"That it does. But it's bloody broiling in here."

"You'll get used to it again."

He planted a quick kiss on her forehead and rose from their nest of pillows. Honifa admired his tall, strapping form and the grace of his carriage as he pulled on britches, vest, and boots. All throughout their voyage to Nador on the *Witch's Moon* and their swift ascent up the Atlas Mountains, she had marveled that a healthy, passionate Tor was once again at her side. Even now, after weeks of sleeping and waking entwined in his arms, her heart overflowed with the wonder of it. Tor was real and substantive and once again hers. Well, hers when he was in camp at least, she thought ruefully. He spent many days and nights aboard the *Witch's Moon* rescuing slaves while she remained in the mountains applying her skills to ease their sufferings. Accordingly, she gathered her medicine bag and called out for Regin.

"She's in the corral," a diminutive woman answered. "Shall I fetch her for you?"

The woman's voice was familiar and Honifa ducked through the tent flap. A sturdy Ibo whose face bore a chevron of scars stood beside a tiny Yoruba woman, dwarfing her. They bowed respectfully. The woman was dressed in flowing white *kaba* and her long hair was intricately braided with beads. Honifa tried to place her.

"Have I not seen you before?" she asked.

The woman averted her eyes. Surprisingly, Tor barreled from the tent and embraced her, lifting her off her feet.

"Yarra! I hardly recognized you," he cried delightedly, holding her at arm's length. "You've changed."

"It's been a long time," she replied. "Welcome home, Captain."

Yarra. The name slithered in Honifa's head like a snake. The woman in Tor's arms haunted her dreams and her evil lie, the last words Honifa had heard her say, stuck like a burr. *He's chained. He can't hurt you.*

"No leathers," Tor said, appraising her fondly. "Does that mean you're not a warrior anymore?"

Yarra slid a glance toward Honifa. "I'm married now."

Honifa spun on her heel and stormed back into the tent.

"Husband, this is Tor Kendrick," she heard Yarra say.

"*Daalu,* Captain Kendrick," the Ibo greeted Tor. "I

see you reveal your true identity now."

"Aye, my friend," Tor replied. "When I lost my son, I gave up being Zalam Alqamar. It's this face you see on the wanted posters now."

"Your absence has only increased the hatred of your enemies, Captain," Yarra said.

"But not the struggle. The spirit of Dark of the Moon lives on."

"It's why I came back," Yarra declared. "My husband and I wish to fight by your side."

There was more talk, from Tor, from the Ibo, and from Yarra, but Honifa didn't listen. She had tried to banish from her mind the treacherous Yoruba who'd sold her to Davilow, afraid the corrosive hatred would shrivel her to bitterness. And after Regin was born, the daily concerns of life on Ivy Lane had squashed her enmity into a tight, dark corner of her soul. When Tor told her what Yarra had done, how she had contemplated suicide then trekked alone across the country, heedless of danger, with a quiver of poisoned arrows meant for Davilow, Honifa had not been moved. She found it hard to understand how he was able to welcome his former aide back to camp.

"Honi?" Tor's voice cut through her bitter recollections. "Are you all right?"

"Why is Yarra here?" she demanded hotly.

He put his hands on her shoulders. "I've made my peace with her. So should you."

She shook him off. "How can I? Because of her I was offered up to your sworn enemy like an apple on a stick. I lost my son; I nearly lost you."

"She has redeemed herself at great risk."

"There can be no pardon for traitors," Honifa cried

out. "No redemption for gambling with the life of a child." She beat a fist to her chest. "The life of *my* child. Tell her to go. I can't bear the sight of her."

Tor's jaw clenched. He glared at Honifa, and she glared back.

"Then I'll go!" she screamed. "I won't stay here with her."

His fingers dug into her arm. "She stays and so do you if I have to tie you to a tree."

Tears of frustration spilled from her eyes. "Why do you ask this of me?"

"Because we need her. She has news of Maliq."

****

Ahmed's second wife, Abiba, banged on Madame Hassan's bedroom door and barged in without an invitation. "He's here, Honorable Mother-in-Law! Sidi Ifni ben Hassan is here from the south, demanding to see you!"

Madame Hassan glared at the trembling girl. "Make your salaam," she ordered. "How dare you forget yourself in my presence!"

Abiba groveled hastily. "He's brought trunks and boxes, Esteemed Mistress. They are all over the reception room. The servants are filling them. He says we must pack for this is not our home." She raked her nails across her plump cheeks. "Oh Demons and Djinns, the Day of Judgment has arrived. We're doomed!"

Madame Hassan rose from her chaise and clapped for her robe. "Don't be ridiculous, Abiba. My senile brother-in-law has no power here. He can call himself the head of the family if he wants but everyone knows the position belongs to my son and his son after him."

She frowned. "If we can only find them." She clapped again. "Where is that stupid wretch with my clothes?"

Abiba helped Madame Hassan into her cloak and veil, and knelt to tie on her sandals.

"We search and search but still don't know where Ahmed and the child are," Abiba wailed. "They may very well be dead, in which case—"

"Silence!" Madame Hassan kicked Abiba aside and strode into the hall. It was strewn with boxes and the servants were busily filling them with household items.

Ifni ben Hassan, brother to her dead husband, sat imperiously amidst the assorted baggage sipping coffee and nibbling sweetmeats from the ornate brass tray reserved for dignitaries. Madame Hassan stepped into the room and coughed. Ifni drained his cup, ate a stuffed fig, and held out his fingers to be sprinkled with rose water. Madame Hassan coughed again. Ifni looked up and bowed a peremptory salaam.

"Greetings, dear relative by marriage," he said.

"What are you doing in my house?" Madame Hassan spat without returning Ifni's bow.

"Excuse me," he replied unctuously, "but this is my house now."

"What are you talking about, you buffoon?" She clapped her hands at the servants. "Empty those boxes and throw them into the street."

But it was as if their ears were blocked by a spell. They continued packing boxes and hauling priceless items of furniture out to a waiting cart. Abiba crept into the room, her forehead to the floor.

"*Asalamu alaykum,* Sidi Ifni ben Hassan," she recited.

"Ah," Ifni said. "The grieving widow." He rose and

lifted Abiba to her feet. "You must take heart, my child. I have a fine husband for you, my nephew the cloth merchant. He's almost rich. Feed him well, keep his nose hair trimmed, and you'll both be quite happy."

"What is this?" Madame Hassan hissed. "Abiba is wife to my son who will have you arrested and thrown in jail if you don't leave these premises immediately."

"My dear relative by marriage," Ifni drawled. "Your son and grandson are dead." He pulled a parchment from his pocket. "Here's the proof."

Madame Hassan snatched the document and read it. "This is a farce," she cried. "You cannot have them declared dead when they are still alive."

Ifni scoffed. "A piddling obstacle. As you can plainly see, I most definitely can and I have. As of now, Ahmed is officially deceased, null and void, off the records." He took another fig from the tray and bit into it. "The title of head of the family and all your husband's assets, including this compound, now pass legally to me. Some of my wives and children, my younger brother, Sidiq, and his family, and a few other relatives will be moving into this fine house shortly. You'll have to vacate."

Madame Hassan clutched her chest and sank onto a chair. "No. It can't be. I'm ruined."

"There, there, Madame Hassan. No, sorry, I can't call you that anymore. You have a first name. Wahdah is it? How appropriate as from now on, you shall be alone."

****

Night fell in the Atlas Mountains. Regin preferred to sleep under the stars, and Honifa usually allowed this. There was no danger. Fires were kept burning outside of every tent and guards manned the perimeter She searched the darkness for Tor's white mane of hair and was nearly asleep when he came through the woods, silent as a cat.

"I've spent the day with Yarra," he said, hunkering down. "What she says is true."

Honifa disliked hearing the Judas woman's name on Tor's lips, but she listened, hoping for news of Maliq.

"The Hassan uncles have evicted Madame Hassan," Tor began, "and had the court prepare a document declaring Ahmed and Maliq dead."

Honifa swallowed. "Can they do that?"

"It's a formality to give the uncles control over the Hassan holdings and all their money." He prodded the fire with a smoldering stick. "You'd feel it if our son was dead, wouldn't you?" he asked.

"As keenly as I'd feel that stick pressed to my skin."

The leaping flames starkly lit his face, his tight jaw and the deep creases on his brow. "No one has seen Ahmed for years," he continued. "He may very well be dead but if Maliq lives, he's the rightful heir and in greater danger than ever."

Honifa gripped the front of Tor's vest. "Then we must hasten to find him before the uncles do. Saddle the horses. I'll gather provisions." She made to rise but the look in Tor's face, loss, regret, and something she had never seen there before, failure, held her back.

"What is it, Tor?"

"There are Hassan family members in every city, town, and village in Morocco and I would gladly kill them all if I could," he said tightly. "But I couldn't find

Maliq on my own and then I fell ill and didn't even remember I had a son. Now when I would take up the hunt again, I risk being cut down before I begin."

"The posters," Honifa said grimly. "Your face is everywhere, as far as Algeciras and even Gibraltar." She thought a moment. "Then I'll go alone. This is my country. I know every inch of it."

"And you also know how dangerous the Hassans are. I won't deny you justice, Honifa, but hear me out. Yarra has a plan."

Honifa listened with growing anticipation and fear. Yarra's husband, a toolmaker who roamed the country looking for trade, had overheard two men talking in a tavern. They were searching for the underground ruins of the palace of Abu Inan where their wealthy nephew was rumored to be hiding. The Ibo further loosened their tongues with many glasses of arak and learned that the nephew in question was Ahmed ben Hassan whom they planned to murder along with his young son, Maliq."

"But the Palace of Abu Inan is a storybook legend," Honifa said. "It doesn't exist."

"According to the uncles, it does, and there's a tunnel under the dunes at Akhfenir that leads into it."

"Akhfenir is in the western dessert," Honifa said thoughtfully. "That's a journey of many days. But I can make it."

"I believe you can if you're careful and cover your face," Tor said. "But since I'm in everyone's crosshairs, you'll go with Yarra and travel south along the coast. I'll follow on *Witch's Moon*. When you reach Akhfenir, veer east into the desert, locate the tunnel to the palace, and signal me. I'll get Maliq."

"All right. But I don't need Yarra. Please, let me go alone."

"You'll go with Yarra," he responded sternly. "Or not at all."

****

Honifa knew it was useless to argue with Tor but thought she might convince Yarra. She found her sullenly slapping together the evening's meal. Yarra looked up at her approach then hastily averted her eyes.

"What is that?" Honifa asked in lieu of a greeting. "It smells awful."

Yarra grimaced. "I'm not sure. I followed my husband's directions, but it doesn't look right. I hope it's edible."

Honifa sat well away from the pungent aroma. "You don't need to come with me to Akhfenir. I can travel without you."

Yarra stirred the gray mass of fish and potatoes. "My husband had determined that your son is alive and for the moment safe." She took a taste and spat. "God, I hate cooking. This is swill. "She covered the pot and banked the ashes. "The dunes of the western dessert are vast and finding the ruins of an underground palace centuries old will be difficult. Tor says it's best I accompany you."

Honifa eyed her enemy warily. Gone were the nearly shorn hair, the short leather pants and the sturdy boots, twins to Alqamar's. Yarra wiped her hands on her soot-stained *kaba*. One of her braids was shedding tiny beads. She gathered a few more loose beads and threw them crossly into the fire.

"Too much hair. How do you stand it?" she groused.

"Have you any children?" Honifa asked.

A film clouded Yarra's eyes. "I lost a babe last year, barely born. I understand your suffering, and Tor's." She reached out her hand, but Honifa didn't take it. Yarra sighed. "Tor is my dearest friend and savior. I would do anything for him, and for you because he loves you."

"I can go to Akhfenir by myself," Honifa repeated. "Why must you come with me?"

"Because Tor says so," Yarra answered with a hint of her old animosity. "And I'm faster and lighter and not scared of the desert."

Honifa stiffened and felt the wind and heat of the Sahara that had nearly claimed her life.

"And Tor says you're Maliq's mother," Yarra went on. "It's been many years but your son might remember something of you and be less afraid."

"Tor says, Tor says," Honifa mimicked. "Why must we do everything his way?"

A small smile curved Yarra's mouth. "Here's what I say. The Hassan uncles are a barbarous bunch who'll cut your throat soon as look at you. They're also searching for the ruins and it's safer with two of us and Tor close by."

Honifa sighed and rose. "Very well. When do we leave?"

"Then you agree with the plan?" Yarra asked. "You trust me?"

"Yes," Honifa replied, lying to both questions.

Chapter 28

Tor neither insisted nor threatened. He merely reiterated the plan implacably and in less than a fortnight, Honifa and Yarra were on their way south. They rode tandem on Shabanou, down mountain passes, across the forests and fields of scrub, through villages and towns, and finally at Akhfenir, into the western desert where a shaft of lightening sharp as an arrow illuminated a path across the sand. Honifa took it as a sign, but Yarra dismounted.

"What are you doing?" Honifa said.

"It's getting dark. We should rest and eat, but I won't make a fire in case the Hassans are near."

"I haven't seen them anywhere."

Yarra looked around the rolling expanse of sabkha, a kind of mud flat typical of coastal deserts. "They're here and will show themselves when we find the ruins," she said. "Have some dried fruits and try to sleep."

Honifa gave the horse water and food but, maddened with impatience, ate nothing, nor could she sleep. Yarra tried to calm her with Yoruba folk tales and stories about growing up with Dark of the Moon.

"He brought me to camp alone and afraid. I was taught to hide my fears and so I struck out at everyone, made trouble, and fought without understanding that the enemy was me. But Tor was patient, and he became my father, my brother, my friend. He is like Aro the

Leopard Man come to life, beautiful, fierce, and complex as the markings on his pelt."

Hearing of the man who was the breath of life to her only increased Honifa's desire to bring his son home to him. For two more days, she and Yarra trudged and dragged through seas of sand and caking sabkha looking for some irregularity, some sign of a buried ruin, a bit of glass, a chip of marble or gilt from an ancient palace. But if anything remained of Sultan Abu Iman, it had been ground to dust by time and corrosive winds.

That night, however, as she scanned the starlit horizon, she noticed something odd, and woke Yarra.

"See that ridge of dunes?" Honifa pointed out. "The one in the center is different from the others. It's lower and sunken at the top."

"Yes, and the sand is lighter although that may just be a trick of the night. Shall we look closer under cover of darkness?"

Leading Shabanou, they climbed the middle dune. Honifa fell to her knees and began to sift handfuls of sand through her fingers.

"The texture of the sand here is drier." She lay flat on her stomach and listened. "Maliq is close," she whispered, barely containing her excitement. "I know it. I can feel it."

"If you're sure, ride swiftly to the sea. I'll keep watch," Yarra said.

But Honifa began to dig into the sand and hard dirt. "No. I'm getting my son."

Yarra held her tongue and ignored her doubts. They had found the boy and what better gift to offer Tor for all he'd done? Without hesitation, she bent to help Honifa, but the more sand they dug, the more of it there was. Her arms ached, and her skin was gritty. "We'll never finish," she said. "It's almost daylight. We need Tor."

But Honifa, red-faced and sweating, pulled at something.

"What is it?" Yarra asked. "What have you got?"

Honifa showed her the frayed end of a rope, thick and coarse as a tree trunk.

"The other end is hooked onto something," she panted. "Help me pull."

Yarra fitted her hands over Honifa's and braced her heels. Together, they pulled until something made a grating sound, like rock against rock.

"Can you see it?" Honifa asked.

Yarra reached down. "Feels like a flat stone probably meant to cover the mouth of the tunnel," she answered. "Let's move it." They slipped into the dune with difficulty, feet first. When Yarra's toes hit the stone, she crouched and tugged the rope while Honifa pushed the heavy obstruction. Eventually, it moved a few meters, opening a space wide enough for them to shimmy through. In single file, they crawled down a passage that led to another stone, this one a door set into a wall of earth and if anything, heavier and more massive than the first. Yarra pried the edges with her knife and after much grunting and heaving, got it open.

"We've done it!" Honifa cried. "We're in!"

****

Still and silent as the columns that once supported the palace of Abu Inan, Tor waited on the deck of the *Witch's Moon*. He had been docked at Akhfenir for three days, ordering the crew to peel eyes for Honifa's signal. But he knew her. If she had located Ahmed's sanctuary, nothing would stop her from throwing caution overboard and rescuing Maliq. Unfortunately, nothing would stop her pursuers either.

He called for Tamajaq. "I've waited long enough for your headstrong sister. Weigh anchor and catch the wind. I'll see you back at camp."

"Where are you going, Captain?"

"Into the desert."

"On foot?"

"Aye. It's the only way."

****

Honifa followed Yarra into a parged tunnel. It was dark as pitch and they crept blindly; the air was close but not fetid.

"I can breathe," Honifa said. "There must be ventilation."

A faint light, like a sputtering candle flame, flickered ahead. Honifa plowed forward to a mounded ridge and stood on her toes to peer over it into a kind of subterranean loggia, a gallery really, lit by torches and rimmed on three sides with limestone stalagmites. The room exuded an aura of ghostly taboo, like a burial ground. She hiked to the top of the ridge and pulled Yarra after her.

"Am I hallucinating?" Yarra said when they jumped down to the other side. "Or is this a bedroom in the palace?"

An emaciated man lay on an ornate bedstead, his head thrown back, his mouth open. A pipe stem dangled loosely from his splayed fingers, its tube coiling across the floor to a bubbling hookah. Filaments of smoke threaded through air that smelled at once acrid and buttery: opium.

"*Rahmatullah*," Honifa breathed. "It's Ahmed."

She picked her way around tufted footstools, a gilt table and chair, and an open chest spilling coins and jewels and bent over the man who used to be her husband. He was a shadow, thin as the pipe stem dangling from his fingers. She clawed the neck of his soiled *kamis.*

"Where's Maliq?" she cried. "What have you done with my son?" When he made no response, she shouted, "Speak, you hateful man!"

Yarra pulled her sleeve. "Stop that racket. He can't hear you anyway. He's dead."

Honifa's scream echoed in the cavernous room. She slapped Ahmed's sunken cheeks and tore the wrapping from his head, damning his name, cursing his wasted life. His turban unwound, the silken lengths floating to the floor. Seeing Ahmed's hair, that once luxuriant mane he'd been so proud of, reduced to oily wisps barely covering a scalp white as bone, she knew a pang of regret. There was nothing left of the man she'd been fond of a since childhood. She covered his face and stood.

"Maliq is nearby. We must find him."

"There are many rooms to search," Yarra said.

Skirting stalagmites, they ran from the room and through an archway into a cool, vaulted space smelling of pine and eucalyptus, overlaid with a sweet, almost cloying aroma.

"That's not opium," Honifa said, sniffing.

"Roses, I think," Yarra answered, mystified. "How can that be?"

Knives at the ready, they surveyed what appeared

to be a miniature forest glade hung with trailing vines and carpeted in a lush growth of emerald moss. Several kinds of dwarf trees from widely differing climates, evergreens, palms, ghost barks and creek willow, grew around a pond into which an elfin waterfall spilled jeweled droplets. Honifa rubbed her eyes and stared in awe at beds of colorful flowering plants. Chirping birds pecked seed from the ground or flew overhead; butterflies flitted from petal to branch.

"Are we in Paradise?" Yarra murmured softly.

"No, you're not," a young voice rang out, clear and fine as a mountain stream. "This is my garden."

The boy approaching them with a spade in one hand, a flower plug in the other, was about seven. He was dressed like a prince in silver and gold. Pointed slippers graced his feet.

"I'm Maliq ben Hassan," he said bowing a rudimentary salaam. "Who are you?"

Honifa's throat closed; her body shook. She tried to speak but couldn't. Maliq carefully removed his gardening gloves and brushed off his richly embroidered *camir.*

"Pardon my appearance," he apologized politely. "We never have visitors."

He was taller than Yarra and his features were strong, like Tor's. His eyes, the brilliant yellow green that haunted her, were unnaturally bright beneath a fringe of brown hair. Honifa took a step closer. His skin was light too, not dark like Regin's. She stared, and her appraisal seemed to disconcert him. He smoothed his hair and blinked. His lashes were long and thick and the pale color they had always been. She found her voice.

"Hello, Maliq," she said, making a salaam. "My

name is Honifa and this is my friend, Yarra. You have a lovely garden."

He proudly surveyed the colorful mosaic that appeared to be his domain; a neatly laid pathway of stones wove through beds of purple lavender, jade lettuces, buttercup tansy, and delicate, pink damask roses. Ambient light from dozens of oil lamps gave the illusion of a late summer afternoon.

"The roses are the hardest," Maliq said, indicating the spiky leaves of a wilting dog brier bush.

Honifa trembled, sensing distress in the child she longed to take in her arms and cover with kisses. Steeling her exuberance lest he run, she said, "Add a little chamomile to the soil. Roses need full morning sunlight."

"Oh, but they have it!" he crowed. "We aren't far from the surface here." He moved aside a curtain and tugged a rope pulley opening an enfilade of skylights in the ceiling. Natural light poured in. "My father used to worry about someone discovering us. But he's ill most of the time now so I do as I please."

Yarra poked Honifa and whispered. "Do you see that? Another opening to the surface. If we find a basket big enough to fit all three of us we can pull ourselves back up to the dune."

"Look," Maliq piped. "I have water, too." He pushed aside a screen of ivy to reveal a glistening wall of rock. "It drips day and night and I catch it in jugs. There must be a freshet somewhere, but I haven't found the source yet. When I do, I'll ask Father for tubing so I can pipe the water directly to my garden." He pointed to a pile of bricks. "I made those from sand, and I made the mortar too. I'd like to have a paved walkway, but mortar dries so quickly. Do you think I should add less straw?"

He rubbed his chin, a gesture so like Tor's, Honifa moaned and reached out. Yarra shot her a warning look.

"I have to make nearly everything myself," Maliq complained. "Father won't let me go out. If I were a man, I'd buy medicines to make him well and happy again." He was silent a moment but brightened quickly. "Come see my room."

Yarra shook her head and hissed through her teeth, "We have to get out of here."

But Honifa allowed Maliq to pull her into a small, untidy room. The floor and bed were piled with books and toys.

"This is my telescope," Maliq said, dragging a jumble of clothing from a long spyglass mounted on a tripod. "I used it every day when we lived in Essaouria. This is a bird I found. I think it's a cockatoo." He lifted a cage from its hook and wiggled his finger at a large, crested parrot. "See, its wing is broken but I splinted it. Soon it will be able to fly in and out of the ceiling with the other birds."

"How long have you lived here?" Honifa asked.

He shrugged, and then dug around in the debris. "I started a calendar when we left Essaouria," he said, showing her a book of days, each month illustrated with a drawing. The book had many pages.

"Today is *al Juma'ah*," he said, pulling her beside him on the bed. "I'm supposed to be praying, but look, I've made a picture of a lady in the margin here. I think she's someone I used to know."

Tears fell from Honifa's eyes blurring the sketch of herself in the orange *kamis* she'd worn nearly every day at Alqamar's camp. Maliq proudly pulled trinkets from every corner of his room. "Here's a book about ships and the ocean," Maliq said, handing Honifa *Norsemen, Vikings and Other Seafarers of the Ancient World.* "It has wonderful pictures of boats and men in horned helmets, but I can't read it."

"It's written in English, Maliq. I can teach you the language if you like," Honifa said.

"Oh yes, please," he said. "This is the Holy Qu'ran. I can read it, but I don't anymore because I know it by heart. This is a book of mathematics; this one is all maps and this—"

He chattered on and on. Honifa studied him, enraptured. He was thin but except for his pallor, he looked strong and healthy. She smoothed a lock of hair that had fallen over his eyes and he looked at her, his face suddenly shy.

"Do you have any friends, Maliq?" she asked softly.

"I have my father," he replied cautiously. "He's my friend."

"I know a little girl who'd love to meet you," Honifa said. "Would you like me to take you to visit her? Her name's Regin and she's very smart, just like you."

Maliq swallowed with apparent discomfiture. "Father says I'm the smartest, and it's dangerous to go outside."

"But you went out when you lived in Essaouria, didn't you?"

He pouted and shook his head. "I had to stay in my room and in my garden, just like here. The garden had a high wall around it and a dome, but–" He smiled in one of the quick reversals of mood that seemed characteristic. "There were windows, and I could see the hills and the sky. I made pictures of the clouds and the setting sun. Here, I'll show you." He rummaged under the bed. "Oh, wait. There's my bowl of blackberries and honey. I love honey. Next year Father says I can keep bees and make my own."

He stuffed a handful of berries into his mouth. With shaking fingers, Honifa wiped a dribble of blue from his chin. *My poor boy,* she thought. *My poor, lonely little boy.*

"I spill all the time," he mumbled, chewing. "Father says it's alright because I'm a prince and princes can do anything. I have lots of clothes, shirts, and pants and caps and jackets and vests. Father gives me whatever I want. He's the kindest man in the world."

Yarra was pacing nervously. "We must go, Honifa. I hear voices."

Honifa took the berries from Maliq. "Why don't we take these to Regin?" she said cheerfully. "We can bring the honey, too, if you like."

Maliq stiffened. "No, thank you."

"Your father can come," she coaxed.

"I told you no," he said as firmly as Tor.

"Hurry," Yarra said. "Someone's here."

Maliq twisted his hands. "I have to go now. Thank you for coming." He ran from his room.

Yarra uttered a curse. "We'll have to take him by force."

"Give him time," Honifa said. "He's frightened."

"Don't be a fool. We're not the only ones who want Maliq."

At that very moment, they heard a crash.

Chapter 29

Honifa ran after Maliq. The boy was fast, strong and agile as Tor. He skidded around corners and scrambled up steep, slippery grades at full speed. He was smart as well. But she was smarter. A small, frightened boy needed his father and she knew she'd find him in Ahmed's bedroom. But Maliq didn't go the way she and Yarra had come but headed straight into the wall of rock and disappeared through a crevice.

"It's too narrow; I can't fit," Honifa grumbled to Yarra. "But I smell opium. I'm sure Ahmed is on the other side of this wall."

Yarra contorted her wiry body and squeezed through the crevice. Just as Honifa had thought, it was a shortcut to Ahmed's room. "You'll never make it through," she called out to Honifa who was peering into the crevice. "Wait there. I'll grab Maliq and we'll make for the pulleys."

****

"God is great. God is good. Awwk, whawk," the bird cackled.

In Maliq's bedroom, Ifni ben Hassan poked the parrot's cage. The thing was common, not a gray black Palm Cockatoo worth a year's wages. And its wing was splinted. He raised his gun.

"Maliq," the bird said. "Maliq."

Ifni narrowed his eyes. "He's calling for the boy,

Sidiq," he said to his younger brother, lifting the bird out and letting it flap to the floor.

"What are you doing?" Sidiq asked.

"It's trying to go somewhere," Ifni said. "Let's follow it."

Sidiq eyed the treasures in the room; the telescope and other objects were sure to be valuable and, by rights, they were his. He and Ifni had followed the white mare and its female riders for days to this wasteland of dunes and sabkha and he was sweaty and thirsty and his back ached. His half of the Hassan inheritance wasn't enough reward for all he'd been through, but the riches in this room, even the few he could tie in his robe, amounted to a Pasha's fortune. If he hid them well, he didn't have to share. Sidiq picked up a slipper encrusted with diamonds.

"Leave it," his brother commanded. "We came here for one purpose only. To kill Ahmed and the boy."

Sidiq hastily scooped up a few onyx chessmen.

"We can come back, monkey brain," Ifni spat. "The bird is trying to fly."

He grabbed the parrot, removed its splint and it took off, dipping and swerving smoothly as a butterfly. The Hassan brothers hurried to keep up.

****

Yarra parted the curtain at the other side of the narrow crevice. Ahmed lay on the divan in his cluttered room just as she and Honifa had left him. Maliq stood beside him.

"Do you see Maliq?" Honifa called from behind her.

"Yes. He's here," she answered, adding, "I told you not to follow me."

"I know. It wasn't so bad, but my clothes are torn to shreds."

Maliq bent over Ahmed. Wake up, Father, please," he cried, shaking him. "There are ladies here and I don't know what to do."

Honifa pushed into the room and ran to him. "He's gone to *Jenn'ah*, my child," she said gently.

Maliq whipped around. "No. You are mistaken. My father sleeps soundly. It is what he does." He looked worriedly at Ahmed and back at Honifa, his brow creased the way no child's should be. "I mean no disrespect, but will you please go away? No one should be in this place."

"I can't leave you here alone, Maliq."

"It's alright," he replied staunchly although his golden eyes were uncertain.

"You must come with me," Honifa insisted

"I won't," he replied. "Father told me if anything happens to him, I must stay here. This is my kingdom." He pointed imperiously. "I command you to go."

Honifa quelled a sob. "Please, Maliq. Let me care for you."

"No, I –my bird, my telescope. I can't –I shouldn't." He sucked back tears. "I mustn't cry. Princes don't cry."

Honifa held his hand. "I'll take you to a meadow that's filled with flowers and bees. You can set your hives there and I'll show you how to scrape the honey."

He thrust out his small, cleft chin. "I already know how. I read it in a book."

Honifa wiped his nose with the hem of her sleeve. "We'll return here someday to give your father a proper burial. I promise." Gently, she pulled him away from

Ahmed's bed. "But now we really have to go."

Maliq glanced back at Ahmed. "Are you certain he's gone to Heaven and is not just sleeping?"

"Yes, I'm certain." She tried to lift Maliq in her arms, but he wrenched away when the cockatoo flew through the archway.

"It's my bird," he cried. "He's all better."

Honifa froze. *How did the bird get out of its cage?* She made a grab for Maliq but was too late. Ifni had him by the throat. She screamed and Sidiq swung his lighted torch at her. The hem of her robe ignited.

"Get the other one," Ifni yelled to Sidiq. "Burn her too. Burn them all."

With an ear-splitting screech, the bird attacked Ifni's face, pecking viciously, and sinking razor-sharp claws into his neck. Ifni screamed and flailed wildly. Maliq broke free of him, tore a quilt from Ahmed's bed, and beat at the flames. Yarra pointed her knife and squared off against Sidiq. He cowered.

"Kill her, you idiot," Ifni cried, blood streaming down his face.

Sidiq raised his torch. Yarra lunged forward, slashing. The tip of her knife caught Sidiq's chest, ripping it open. Sidiq collapsed. The torch rolled away.

"Imbecile," Ifni muttered. He threw Maliq over his shoulder.

Honifa tried to grab her son's ankle but Ifni planted a vicious kick to the side of her head, hopped over his fallen brother, and ran to the archway.

Holding his gaping wound, Siddiq gasped, "Don't leave me, brother. I'm dying."

Ifni ignored him. Yarra raised her knife to finish off Sidiq, but he scrambled for his flaming torch, threw it at her and missed. It landed at the base of the heavy curtains. Flames erupted and quickly spread through the room blocking all possible escape. In a hideous arc, Ahmed's blackened body lifted off the divan, bent backward on itself, and incinerated to char along with his pillows, blankets, and opium pipe.

****

Tor easily spotted Shabanou pawing the sand near an oddly shaped dune. He found the frayed rope, shimmied into the tunnel, and down the long corridors. He had no candle, only his knife and his wits, but he smelled the smoke. When the way widened, the smoke became thicker, and he thought he heard a mewling cry, like a cat or baby bird.

"Maliq!" he shouted, his lungs tight.

The bird that suddenly swooped down on him was no fledgling. It was yellowish pink and making a racket. It strafed Tor's head, zoomed back and forth, perched on a ledge for a second, then zoomed again. Tor raised an arm to shoo it off but when the bird said his son's name, his heart pounded, and his senses focused sharply as a rapier. He raised his arm, slowly this time. The bird perched.

"Maliq," it said again.

"Yes. Maliq," Tor repeated. "Where's Maliq?"

The parrot took off, banked low and flew below the worst of the smoke. Tor covered his mouth and followed. He entered a small alcove that resembled his childhood room; a mounted spyglass, an onyx chess set, and books everywhere. An open cage hung from the bedstead. Several drawings were scattered about, many of a woman resembling Honifa. Tor picked one up and crushed it to his chest.

"You remembered her, my son," he murmured brokenly. "You remembered your mother."

The bird darted out of the alcove and around a corner. Tor hastened to catch up. He passed a wall of ivy and stopped short. The leaves of the climbing plant were wet and behind them, water dripped down the face of a rock wall into a moat-like trench, narrow in places, then widening to the breadth of a man's arm. The top of the wall vaulted high as a cathedral and sunlight streamed from rectangular skylights. Frames covered in fabric, buckram or heavy linen, could be slid across the skylights as shields, and amazingly, stout ropes dangled from them in pairs, secured to winch blocks with copper pulleys. The setup was ingenious and looked as if it could haul an elephant to the surface.

The parrot landed on one of these pulleys as if calling Tor's attention to the magnificent apparatus. Then it spiraled downward and screamed. Tor dodged but the bird would not be deterred. It dug its talons into Tor's back and pecked at his hair. Tor offered it his sleeve, but the bird refused to light. It flew back to the wall of water, dipped its beak, and drank from the moat. It did this many times, each time more strenuously, fixing its beady eye on Tor as if in indignation.

Tor bent one knee and plunged his fist into the place where the parrot drank. The bird grew still as a decoy. Tor plunged deeper, up to his elbow and felt a protrusion, a kind of knob. He grasped and tugged. With a creaking groan, the water wall split in two filling the air with choking smoke. A fire raged behind it. Tor soaked his cloak in the pool and stormed forward, dodging falling rocks and flying embers, until he entered a burning room. Two figures lay huddled, clinging helplessly to one another. Tor dashed forward.

Yarra saw him and cried out. "I think she's dead, Tor. Honifa's dead."

His mind closed to anything but rescue. He gathered the women in his sodden cloak and carried them back through the wall of water to the pulleys. He laid them on a soft carpet of moss and took his first conscious breath. Trees and flowers; meandering walkways, an herb garden? What was this place? Ragnarok, the Doom of the Gods? Valhalla?

The hand that dug into his arm was raw, bleeding and very real. "Save her," Yarra rasped. "Save Honifa."

He snapped to action. "Can you walk?" he asked Yarra. She nodded. "Then sink your hand into the deepest pool at the bottom of the rock of water and pull the knob. Hurry before the fire reaches us."

He bent over Honifa. Her dress was in tatters; her lower arms were burned; her lashes singed. But she was alive. He ripped handfuls of moss from the ground to dab her scalded skin, breathed into her mouth and rocked her in his arms.

"Maliq," she mumbled.

He steeled himself against the anguish in her eyes. "Go back to camp with Yarra. I'll bring him home to you. I swear it."

The water wall boomed shut; thinning smoke drifted up through the skylights. Tor tied the rope securely to Honifa and Yarra, braced his legs and pulled, hand over hand, until the women were outside, high above him on the surface.

Yarra whistled for Shabanou and lingered a moment to peer down the pulleys. But Tor was gone.

****

Bent forward, hands on his knees, Tor measured his breaths. Emotions surged through his body, fury, torment, hope and despair. He rebuked them; they poisoned his judgement, dulled his reflexes, and compromised his will. If he stopped, even for a second to reflect on what had just occurred, on what might yet occur, his muscles would turn to jelly and he'd be useless.

He looked around for the bird, but it was gone, no doubt to its freedom. So be it. The creature had served its purpose. The rest was up to him. He couldn't go through the water wall again. What lay beyond it had to be nothing more than a heap of embers and rubble. But Maliq was near; Tor felt it the way he had felt the pull of Honifa's love when he was chained to the wheel. He didn't remember their past, but when he saw Maliq's drawing, he remembered her orange sulwar and her long hair, wild about a face so young and yet so wise. She was the wife of his soul, the woman who had stolen aboard his ship and begged for one night of love, who'd shared his cave in the Rif and delivered their newborn son into his hands. He would return that boy to her now.

He went into Maliq's room and stood amidst the books and games, his muscles flexed and his fists clenched in rage. Then he forced his body to quiet and his mind to open.

Send me word, he beseeched his son. *I searched for you until despair claimed my reason. But I'm here now. Speak to me.*

A fingertip breeze lifted Tor's hair. The back of his neck prickled. Alert for signs, he walked the brick paths and flower gardens back to the shimmering rock wall.

"Maliq?" he said softly.

A plaintive voice answered. "Who are you?"

Joy exploded in Tor's chest. He swallowed it. "I'm Tor. Say my name, Maliq. Say it over and over loud as you can."

"Tor."

The single syllable floated from somewhere above Tor's head.

"That's right. Say it again."

"Tor."

He looked up. The face peeking over a ledge in the rock wall was no bigger than a dust mote. Elation threatened again. Tor ground his teeth and chased it away. There were footholds in the wall, and he began to climb. Maliq's face disappeared and reappeared, growing larger and dearer each time until it was an arm's length away. Tor allowed his jubilation to burst forth and swung onto the ledge. Maliq cowered.

"Don't fear me, boy," he said. "I mean you no harm."

Maliq chewed his lip. "I ca –can't get down," he stammered. "Fire blocks one way and a man's body blocks the other. There was another man, too. I think they're both dead."

Tor spoke carefully. "If you get on my back, I can bring you down the same way I came up."

Maliq stared at the shining-haired giant. "Are you a Viking, sir? I know all about Vikings. I have studied them."

"I am," Tor answered. He held out his hand. "Come."

But Maliq hesitated. "My father is dead, and the ladies too." He began to sob.

"The ladies are safely on the surface," Tor reassured him.

"And my father?"

Tor lifted the boy in his arms. "He's in Valhalla. Since you know about Vikings, you know that's where warriors go to mingle with the gods."

Maliq nodded solemnly. "That's good. I think my father would like to be a warrior." He laid his head on Tor's chest. "I'm very tired."

Chapter 30

Maliq and Regin sat cross-legged on the sand outside their tent in the Atlas Mountains. She drew a cat and said the word in English. "Cat."

"Het," Maliq said.

"No, no, no. It's cat, caaat."

"Haaayt."

"I'll draw something else."

She erased the cat. Maliq watched puzzled as she boldly moved the chalk across the slate.

"That's not an animal," he protested. "You can't draw."

Regin threw the chalk at him. "Maybe not, but I'm smarter than you."

"No, you're not. You're a girl."

"So what? You can't speak English."

He hung his head. Regin handed him the slate. "*Jamal*," she ordered.

Maliq smiled. He picked up the chalk and drew a perfect camel complete with howdah and a cockaded harness.

"That's very good, Maliq," Regin complimented. "I guess we're both smart in different ways."

"*Shukraan*," he said.

"Say it in English. Say thank you."

"Henk hew."

She rolled her eyes.

****

Inside their tent, Tor dressed as Honifa watched from a nest of pillows. She never tired of looking at him, his height, smooth muscles, and leonine grace. She loved the way his golden skin and golden eyes shone. He was elemental, this man of hers, a creature of infinite seas and vaulting mountains. She loved him beyond reason.

"How long will you be gone this time?" she asked.

"There's no telling. My crew is aboard and with fair weather, the *Witch's Moon* sails tonight."

"And Davilow?" she asked.

Tor's jaw hardened. "He's shackled in the hold, his neck clamped to a beam so tightly he can barely swallow the gruel he's fed."

"Will he die?"

"Eventually." He smiled. "It will take a long time."

He gazed at the enticing curve of Honifa's hips, her long smooth legs and full breasts begging to be kissed.

"Must you go?" she teased.

"Would you have me shirk my duty?" He knelt beside her and pressed his palm to her rounded stomach with a quizzical look.

"Not yet," she chuckled. "In a month or two, he'll begin to move."

"Or she," Tor said, tossing aside the silken shawl that partially covered her nakedness. He clasped her wrists firmly and pressed them over her head and back against the pillows. Bending to her, he tasted each erect nipple and then her mouth.

"Did I not please you enough this morning, woman?" he teased, stroking the inside of her thigh. "Again this afternoon and again just now?"

"You always please me," she said and reached for the buckle of his belt.

He tightened his hold on her wrists and straddled her. She arched to him.

****

Throughout the Atlas camp, freed slaves and children called to one another. Lanterns began to flicker, dinner fires crackled, and tree frogs sang. Tor kissed his beloved's closed eyelids and left the tent.

"Regin," he called. "Maliq. Your mother sleeps. Don't trouble her."

They ran to him, and he lifted them both in his arms.

"When will you be home again, Da?" Regin asked.

"Yes, when will you be home?" Maliq parroted hesitating a moment before adding, "Da."

Yarra approached with Sultan.

"See to things while I'm gone," Tor said to her. "And see to Honifa. Don't let her—"

"Your wife pays me no heed," she interrupted, handing him Sultan's reins. "But together we keep your children and your camp safe. Godspeed, Captain."

****

In the tent, Honifa slept, dreamless and content, her hands folded protectively across her stomach.

A word about the author…

Maria Gil is a former academic Dean and writing instructor with the City University of New York. She has published numerous articles in professional journals and magazines and reviews Indian films for American audiences. She has worked as a personal chef, a United Nations tour guide, exhibits assistant at the American Museum of Natural History, and features writer for the award-winning independent newspaper The Island Current. An ardent animal lover, she rescues lost or abandoned animals, mostly dogs and cats, but once an injured seagull and a baby ocelot. She's lived all over the world and has intimate knowledge of the towns and desert locales of *Witch's Moon*. Currently she calls New York's Hudson Valley home.

Thank you for purchasing
this publication of The Wild Rose Press, Inc.

For questions or more information
contact us at
info@thewildrosepress.com.

The Wild Rose Press, Inc.
www.thewildrosepress.com